A WITCH BEFORE DYING

A WICKED WITCHES OF THE MIDWEST MYSTERY
BOOK ELEVEN

AMANDA M. LEE

WINCHESTERSHAW PUBLICATIONS

ONE

"*N*ow that we're roommates, I think we should talk about rules."

Landon Michaels, my new live-in boyfriend, rested on my bed – er, I mean *our* bed (it was going to take a bit of time to get used to thinking that) – and stared at the ceiling.

"Rules?" I cocked a dubious eyebrow as I folded my laundry so I could put it away in my dresser. "What kind of rules are we talking about here?"

"Well, for starters, I think you should do all the cooking and cleaning. I will handle all the manly jobs … like taking out the garbage and watching baseball."

I pursed my lips, trying not to return Landon's sly smile when he rolled to face me. He was testing me, trying to see if I would melt down. Now that we were officially living together he expected me to freak out. Well, he wasn't going to get his way on this one. I was done freaking out … at least about him. Ghosts, the fact that I would be taking over as owner of the newspaper I worked for in a few short weeks, and general family mayhem were another story. I reserve the right to freak out over them. As for Landon? I was comfortable and happy.

Yes, I, Bay Winchester, am a witch living with her boyfriend, and I'm fine with it. I never saw it coming, but it's made me downright giddy. Things are going extremely well, which means something bad is bound to happen. For once I'm not worried that bad thing will revolve around my relationship with Landon. It's … refreshing.

Landon snapped his fingers to get my attention. "Where did you just go?"

There was no way I could answer that without looking girly and ridiculous. "I was thinking about The Whistler." That wasn't a lie. Not exactly. "In a few weeks I'm going to be in charge."

"I know." Landon sobered. "That's a big deal. How do you feel about it?"

"Excited."

"Good."

"A little nervous."

"That's to be expected."

"What if I screw it up?"

Landon's lips curved as he ran his hand through his shoulder-length black hair. He looked happy and relaxed – something I couldn't stop marveling at – and he seemed to embrace the new living situation like a man constantly fed well and bordering on a food coma thanks to my family. Translation: He couldn't stop smiling. "You're not going to screw it up, Bay. You've been running the newspaper since William Kelly's death, no matter what his deadbeat grandson thinks. Nothing will really change … except you'll get the bigger office."

"I haven't been handling the advertising," I pointed out. "I've been handling the content and layout. The advertising end is vastly different."

"Is it?" Landon didn't look convinced. "You once told me that all of the business owners essentially run the same ads every week. So how will it be different?" He adopted an easy tone that managed to be pragmatic without being condescending.

I shrugged. "I don't know."

"I think you're just looking for some drama." Landon rolled to his back and stared at the ceiling. "This room feels kind of small with all of my work stuff in here, doesn't it?" Landon didn't obsess about much, but cramping my style seemed to be what worried him most. Neither of us had ever lived with a member of the opposite sex. I lived with my cousins Thistle and Clove for years. Now Clove lived with her fiance in a lighthouse, and Thistle would move into a converted barn with her boyfriend Marcus in about six weeks. Until then, we were all sharing the same roof.

"Once Thistle moves, we can turn her room into your office," I reminded him. "It really won't be that long ... and with the holidays coming up, I think Thistle and Marcus will be spending a lot of time in town even though the house isn't finished yet."

"You know they're technically moving into a barn, right?" Landon shot me a cockeyed look. "It's not a house. It's a barn."

"It's a very cool house," I corrected. I'd been watching the work since the beginning. Marcus knew exactly what he was doing when he designed the structure, giving Thistle a big space to work on her art projects and something that didn't look "normal" so she didn't feel penned in by expectations. Thistle wasn't much of a conformist, so the barn fit her personality perfectly. "Thistle will be happy there."

"I'm glad she'll be happy there," Landon said. "I simply wish she was happy there right now."

"Oh, I never noticed," I said dryly. "I thought all of that sniping between you and Thistle was our new form of dinner theater ... only you guys do it over breakfast, lunch, dinner, afternoon snacks, midnight snacks, drink nights ... ."

"Yeah, yeah, yeah." Landon waved off my sarcasm. "This place is too small for four big personalities."

"Marcus is easy to get along with."

"Fine. Three big personalities."

"I'm an absolute dream to live with, too," I supplied.

Landon narrowed his eyes as he glared. "Are you trying to say this is my fault, Bay?"

I immediately started shaking my head. "No. Thistle is to blame, too."

"Too? How has anything that has happened been my fault?"

That was a loaded question. Landon had spent every night here for the past two weeks – although he was still moving a few things from his Traverse City apartment – and it had been an exercise in my babysitting skills to keep him and Thistle from killing each other. They had many of the same traits, which was frightening, and they didn't always play well with one another. It would be a relief when Thistle moved in with Marcus.

"So, do you want to order in, go to The Overlook for dinner or head out on the town and do the whole schmaltzy romantic thing?" I asked, trying to change the subject.

Landon was having none of it. "How is any of this my fault?" he pressed. "Thistle is always picking fights."

He wasn't wrong. Thistle tends to dig in and torture people whenever the chance arises. She gets that trait from Aunt Tillie, although if you ever point that out to her be prepared for Armageddon. Thistle doesn't like being compared to Aunt Tillie, another trait she got from Aunt Tillie. Yes, it's a vicious circle.

"Thistle is a royal pain in the butt," I agreed, moving the stacked laundry I folded to the dresser. "You're a saint compared to Thistle."

"That's not really saying much," Landon pointed out. "Compared to Thistle, prison rioters look like saints. Gang members look like angels. Heck, serial killers look misunderstood next to Thistle."

That assertion was a bit overzealous. It was also kind of correct. "Well … ."

"I heard that." Thistle, her dark hair dyed a vibrant green color to celebrate the upcoming Christmas season, appeared in my open bedroom doorway. She wore an ankle-length skirt that jingled when she walked. Even her toenails were painted green. "I am much better than prison rioters."

"Of course you are." I forced a smile as I worked overtime to calm my cousin and head off a fight. She looked agitated. That's nothing new, mind you, but it's always cause for concern.

"I'm much more dangerous than serial killers, too," Thistle added.

"There's something to brag about," Landon said dryly. He didn't move from his spot in the middle of the bed, instead cocking his head so he could look my cousin up and down. "Did you use my electric razor to shave your legs this morning?"

Thistle adopted an innocent expression. "Why would you think anything like that?"

"Because the battery was dead when I got out of the shower, and I know I plugged it in to charge last night," Landon replied. "Also, there were little hairs stuck to it when I tested it. They were hairs I know I didn't put there, because I always properly clean my razor when I'm done shaving."

And here we go. This wouldn't end well. Of course, none of Landon and Thistle's spats ended well. They were not designed to share a roof. In Thistle's mind, Landon was the brother she never wanted, and she often wanted to kick him as hard as possible … or at least make him cry. In Landon's mind, Thistle was a big bully and needed to be taken down a notch or two … or ten. Now, Thistle was definitely a bully. I wasn't sure Landon had the power to take her down, though. She's too strong, like a kraken … or a professional wrestler without the spandex fetish.

"Why would I use your razor to shave my legs?" Thistle adopted a sweet expression. "An electric razor doesn't even get a close shave on legs."

"It's a closer shave than I got this morning." Landon gestured toward his stubble. "I had no juice to shave anything thanks to you."

"I happen to like your stubble," I offered helpfully, smiling in an attempt to draw Landon's attention. "It makes you look sexy and handsome."

"Thank you, sweetie." Landon never moved his eyes from Thistle's face. "You're always my biggest fan. That's why I love you."

The fact that he glared at Thistle while simultaneously flirting with me didn't do much for my nerves. "Landon … ."

Thistle cut me off before I could suggest … um … whatever I was about to suggest. I didn't have a clear plan.

"I didn't use your razor."

"It's fine," Landon said after a beat, his mind clearly busy. "I moved it in here so it won't be a concern again."

"I said that I didn't touch your razor," Thistle hissed, her eyes narrowing to dangerous slits. "Are you calling me a liar?"

"That sounds like something Aunt Tillie would say," Landon noted, making a big show of studying his fingernails. "Is there a right answer to that question, Bay?"

There was no way he was yanking me into this argument. Marcus and I did our best to be official representatives of the Neutral Zone where Landon and Thistle were concerned these days. It didn't always work, but there was no need to be lured into a fight that wasn't about me.

"What did I tell you about dragging me into your fights?" I challenged.

"That you're the Neutral Zone and should be treated as such," Thistle automatically answered. "Just for the record, are you Kirk or Picard when zipping around the Neutral Zone?"

"What do you think?"

Thistle spared me a withering glance. "You're Wesley Crusher."

Now it was my turn to be offended. "I hate Wesley Crusher!"

"If the annoying character fits … ." Thistle was haughty as she flicked her eyes back to Landon. "Now, about your razor … ."

"It's finished," Landon said, swinging his legs over the side of the bed and pulling himself to a sitting position. "I will keep my razor in the bedroom until you move out."

"I believe that's what I suggested from the beginning," Thistle pointed out sweetly.

"Yes, and I said that was a pain because I prefer my razor being close to the sink," Landon said. "Then we had a big fight – which I won – and I thought the matter was settled. Obviously not."

Thistle snorted. "You didn't win. I won. I always win."

"Another saying you get from Aunt Tillie," Landon muttered. "You're practically her clone."

Thistle extended a warning finger. "You take that back."

"I don't believe I will."

My stomach twisted at the strife. It wasn't that I worried either of them would kill each other – that would almost be a blessing at this point – but the constant fighting wore me down. I knew Marcus felt the same way. Occasionally we slipped outside to share a bottle of wine when Landon and Thistle really got going, because it was simply too loud to remain in the guesthouse. The final weeks of our forced cohabitation – a foursome desperate to become two twosomes – would be downright unpleasant. There was no doubt about that.

"Decide what you want to do for dinner, Landon, and text me," I suggested, getting to my feet. "I'm up for anything … including peanut butter sandwiches next to the fire if that's what you want."

Landon finally dragged his eyes from Thistle and focused on me. "We're not having peanut butter sandwiches. I'll take you out."

We eat out a lot. We also order in a lot. That was on top of the free meals we scored at The Overlook, the inn my mother and aunts operate, which is on the same parcel of family property as the guesthouse. The only thing we don't do is cook for ourselves. Wait … brewing coffee isn't cooking, right? By that measure, neither is mixing chocolate martinis. So, no, we really don't cook.

"That sounds nice." I slid past Thistle and moved to the living room, ignoring the way my cousin puffed out her chest as Landon approached. She was baiting him. Actually, she was constantly baiting him. It was another irritation under what felt like a shrinking roof. The problem was, Landon always rose to the bait.

"Where are you going?" Landon followed, using his hip to move Thistle out of the way.

"Hey," Thistle barked. "I'm pretty sure that was assault."

"And I'm pretty sure you're trying to drive me insane," Landon shot back. He was one snarky comment away from losing it. That's why I had to get out of the guesthouse. When he lost his temper – and it was inevitable – it was only a matter of time before Thistle lost her head. Then, when they both went crazy, I had no choice but to follow. I never want to follow, just for the record, but I always do. I think it's biological or something.

"I don't have to try to drive you insane," Thistle countered. "You're crazy all on your own."

"You're crazy," Landon snapped. "You used my razor to shave your legs and completely ran down the battery. You're short, by the way. Your legs aren't long enough to run down that entire battery."

"Who says I shaved only my legs?" Thistle challenged.

Landon's expression twisted. "You're sick."

Thistle balked. "Not that. I was talking about my armpits."

"So was I," Landon said. "Wait ... what did you think I was talking about?"

I heaved out a sigh as I grabbed my coat from the closet by the front door. "Landon, text me in a few hours and you can meet me downtown for dinner. I don't think I'll be long."

Landon recovered his faculties, at least temporarily. "Where are you going?"

"They're adding a new festival to the rotation," I explained. I was fairly certain we'd already had this discussion, but Landon was easily distracted when Thistle decided to push his buttons. "They're trying to stretch out the fall season. I have to attend the planning meeting to coordinate coverage and offer any ideas for the Thanksgiving-to-Christmas stretch."

"Oh, well ... another festival?" Landon was dumbfounded.

Thistle chuckled, genuinely amused. "Pretty soon Hemlock Cove will be one big festival. At this rate, they'll take over every weekend on the calendar before 2020."

"I know, right?" Suddenly Landon and Thistle were on the same side. This, also, was not new. Their allegiances swung wildly. It was almost worse when they were on the same side because then they ganged up on everyone else.

"I don't decide when they schedule the festivals," I reminded them. "I simply have to coordinate coverage. With Brian being around another few weeks it's difficult being in the office, so I figured I'd go to the meeting instead of asking Mrs. Little to come to the office."

Brian Kelly was my former boss. A few weeks ago he tried to stage a takeover that ended badly – for him. Landon helped me arrange a buyout, and after the first of the year I'd officially be the sole owner of The Whistler, Hemlock Cove's lone weekly newspaper. It was a daunting task. Until then, though, Brian was still hanging around the office, making things tense.

Landon's expression turned somber. "Do you want me to talk to him? If he's being mean to you I'll … ." He broke off, leaving the rest of the statement hanging.

"He's not being mean to me," I replied. "He's simply being … standoffish."

"What is that supposed to mean?"

"He's purposely freezing her out and acting like a martyr," Thistle supplied. "It's a man thing."

"I warned him that I wouldn't put up with any crap," Landon said. "I'll talk to him."

"That's really not necessary." I grabbed my purse. "I'm a big girl. You've done enough. I can take care of Brian Kelly."

Landon didn't look convinced. "Well … ."

"If she needs help, she'll ask," Thistle said. "You don't always have to swoop in and save her."

"I don't swoop in," Landon snapped.

And they were back to being snark machines.

"I'll text you with a timeframe, Landon," I called out as I opened the door. He was seemingly so lost in his argument with Thistle he didn't notice me leaving. "The meeting shouldn't take too long."

I paused as I stared at them. They stood toe-to-toe, as if they might actually throw down. I knew that wouldn't happen, but it was still a freaky picture.

"Try not to kill each other," I said finally.

"No promises." Landon broke away from Thistle and grabbed a knit hat from the closet, tugging it on my head before I could escape. "It's freezing out. I don't want you catching a cold over the holidays."

It was a sweet gesture. "Thank you. I promise I won't be too long."

"Don't worry about us," Thistle said. "I plan to teach Landon to eat dirt while you're gone. Now that he's an official member of the family, I think it's time he learns how we treat family."

I cocked an eyebrow. "Like dirt?"

Thistle bobbed her head. "Exactly."

"Great. Have fun." I tugged the door shut without a glance over my shoulder. I was massively excited about living with Landon. Living with Landon and Thistle together was a different story. Right now, it felt like my pain and suffering would never end. I mean ... I looked forward to a festival planning meeting.

How sick is that? Wait ... don't answer that. I don't think I want to know.

TWO

"*H*ello, sweetheart."

Hemlock Cove's police chief, Terry Davenport, loitered near the refreshment table when I let myself into the meeting room at City Hall. We'd always been close – he'd taken over a lot of fatherly duties for Thistle, Clove and me when we were younger and our biological fathers left town – and I was always happy to see him.

"What are you doing here?" I sidled up and looked at the paper cup in his hands. "Is that bourbon because you know Mrs. Little will be running the meeting?"

Chief Terry shrugged. "If I thought I could get away with bourbon in here I'd already be drunk."

"Really? I'm kind of looking forward to a little bit of order," I supplied. "Mrs. Little is a pain in the butt – I know, that goes without saying – but she always keeps things on point."

Chief Terry's gaze was curious. "What's up?"

I averted my eyes, mortified that I was turning into an overt whiner, and grabbed a cookie. It looked to have come from a box, but you can never go wrong with chocolate chip. "What do you mean?" I bit into the cookie and made a face. Apparently I was mistaken about never going wrong with chocolate chip. "Blech." I spit the cookie into a napkin and glanced around for a trash receptacle.

"What's wrong with the cookie?" Mrs. Little asked as she moved past us to pour a cup of coffee.

"It tastes like feet." I saw no reason to lie. The cookie was horrible. "It's stale and gross. I think whoever brought them was trying to unload outdated cookies on us."

"I brought the cookies."

Of course she did. "Oh, well, they're … not good." What? I'm not going to lie to make her feel better. Two weeks ago she was trying to force people to do her bidding thanks to a cursed wishing well, something she fought getting rid of because she enjoyed having power over everyone. "Next time you should bake your own."

"Not all of us have time to bake." Mrs. Little's expression was withering. "Some of us have actual jobs."

"Whatever." I tossed the offending cookie into the trash and focused on Chief Terry. "You didn't tell me what you're doing here."

"Chief Terry is here to handle security questions," Mrs. Little volunteered. "That's his job."

My temper flared. "I don't believe I asked you."

"You asked the question in front of me and I answered."

"Whatever." I rolled my neck until it cracked. I was sick to death of annoying people … and that included the ones I lived with. "Now I really want that bourbon we were talking about."

Chief Terry snickered as Mrs. Little murdered me with a dark glare.

"Drinking at town meetings is strictly forbidden," she said. "It's in the bylaws."

"Is that really in the bylaws?"

Chief Terry nodded. "Margaret had it added about two years ago because everyone was getting drunk whenever she called a meeting. The level of drunkenness went up and down given how often she talked."

Oh, well, that made sense. "Fun."

Chief Terry beamed. "I'll say."

"Just take your seats," Mrs. Little ordered. "We'll be starting in five minutes."

I mock saluted, snickering when Mrs. Little glared. Chief Terry tugged on my arm to separate us, pointing toward a pair of chairs at the edge of the circle so we could sit. He waited until Mrs. Little was distracted to speak again.

"You seem in an odd mood," he noted. "What's going on? Why are you so ... cranky?"

"I don't believe I am cranky."

"Then you clearly can't see the expression on your face." Chief Terry pulled back so he could give me a long and weighted look. "What's wrong?"

"Nothing is wrong," I replied hurriedly. The last thing I wanted was Chief Terry worrying about my domestic struggles. "It's not a big deal."

"Talk."

"It's just ... Thistle and Landon are driving me crazy. They're fighting like snakes and porcupines."

Chief Terry arched a questioning eyebrow. "Snakes and porcupines?"

"It's a thing. I saw it on YouTube."

"Ah, well, okay." Chief Terry shifted on the metal chair. It was a struggle for him to comfortably fit his large frame on one. "Why are Landon and Thistle fighting?"

"Today?"

"Sure."

"Today they're fighting because Thistle used his razor to shave her legs and purposely ran down the battery," I explained. "He couldn't shave – although I think his stubble is sexy, so I don't mind – and she's happy because she didn't want the razor taking up plugs in the bathroom."

"First, don't ever say 'sexy' when talking about Landon in front of me," Chief Terry chided, wagging a finger. "You know I don't like that."

"Duly noted."

13

"Second, have you considered that guesthouse is too small for four people?"

"Of course I've considered it. We don't have a lot of options. The new barn house isn't quite ready yet and it's too cold to force Thistle to sleep outside, although I have considered it."

"Maybe one couple should rent a room at the inn," Chief Terry suggested. "That would get you guys out from being on top of each other."

"Yes, and into a position where Mom and the aunts are on top of us," I pointed out. "That's actually worse than listening to Thistle and Landon argue."

"I guess I didn't consider that." Chief Terry rubbed his hand over his chin. "Have you considered telling them to stop?"

"Only about a hundred times."

"It didn't work, huh?"

"It puts me in an awkward position," I clarified. "If I take Landon's side, Thistle accuses me of putting bros before ... well, cousins."

"I know the saying," Chief Terry said dryly. "Why not take Thistle's side to head off a fight?"

"Because then Landon whines."

"Whines?"

"Like a little girl," I confirmed. "He doesn't like it when I take Thistle's side."

"And meanwhile you're caught in the crossfire," Chief Terry mused. "That doesn't seem fair."

"The good news is that Marcus and I have really bonded," I supplied. "We go out to the side patio and drink wine together even though it's freezing. He's quite knowledgeable on a variety of issues, including horse feed and the proper texture of paint for a barn wall."

Chief Terry snickered. "I see. That sounds ... great."

"I don't know if 'great' is the right word, but I haven't killed Thistle or Landon yet, so it seems to be working."

Chief Terry licked his lips. "Have you considered that maybe Marcus is a better fit for you?"

The question caught me off guard. "No."

"Just think about it," Chief Terry prodded. "He never finds trouble and he's not addicted to bacon. Plus, well, he's afraid of me. I can bully Marcus into doing what I want."

Realization dawned. "And you can't bully Landon because he's no longer afraid of you," I surmised. "I see the way your mind works. Alas, while I like Marcus, I think he's better suited for Thistle. I happen to love Landon."

"Why?"

"Because he makes me laugh."

"He's a pain," Chief Terry said. "Still, I'd be lying if I said I wasn't happy he'll be living here. That means he'll be available with federal help on a lot of cases."

Hemlock Cove was a tourist town, and its funds were limited. "And that will help you," I mused. "That's good. I was a little worried he'd be bored living here at first, but he doesn't seem to be. Other than Thistle, he's … happy."

"Of course he's happy," Chief Terry scoffed. "He has you. What's not to be happy with?"

I poked his side, genuinely amused. "You're good for my ego."

"You'll get through this, Bay," Chief Terry said. "Once Thistle has her own place and she's not jockeying for superiority with Landon, things will get back to normal."

I could only hope he was right. I opened my mouth to say just that, but Mrs. Little picked that moment to stride to the front of the room. She cleared her throat to get everyone's attention, clapped her hands together once, and then began her spiel.

"As everyone knows, we've been looking for an early-December festival idea," she started. "Hemlock Cove makes a lot of money on festivals, and we want to have at least one every month. There are some months we need two, including December. Early December has always been difficult, but we've finally found something special, and we'll be launching the new festival right away."

"Right away?" I spoke without raising my hand – a big no-no in Mrs. Little's rule book – but I couldn't help myself. "How can you possibly be ready to launch a festival without any planning? I thought this would be something for next year."

"That's what you get for thinking, Bay." Mrs. Little let loose with a condescending smile. "I believe you know the rules, by the way. When you want to speak you ... what do you do, Bay?"

I exhaled heavily through my nose to keep my temper in check. "Generally I open my mouth and form words."

Mrs. Little narrowed her eyes. "The correct answer is that you raise your hand."

"This isn't elementary school."

"Do I have to put you in the corner with a dunce cap on your head?" Mrs. Little challenged. "You seem to be keen on making a scene."

That was rich coming from her. I considered furthering the argument but Chief Terry rested a warning hand on my arm. His message was clear. "I'm sorry. Please continue, Mrs. Little."

Mrs. Little preened. "Thank you, Bay. I'm so happy to have your permission to do my job."

"I'm totally going to curse her green," I muttered under my breath, earning a stern look from Chief Terry. He didn't like talk of curses. "Not just green. Puke green."

"Okay. Calm down." Chief Terry's voice was low. "She likes being in charge. We all know that. She can't help herself."

I chewed my bottom lip as I watched Mrs. Little put on a show for the group members. "This festival is going to be a little different. We'll have our regular booths, of course, but we're adding two new elements.

"The first is a traveling theater troupe," she continued. "They'll perform special shows – including a historical witch program sure to thrill our residents and guests alike. They'll also interact with visitors on an individual level."

I couldn't stop myself from interjecting another question. "How? What kind of performers are we talking about? They're not mimes, are they? Mimes are totally creepy."

"Did you raise your hand, Bay?"

Oh, she was asking for it now. I raised my hand and immediately launched into the question without waiting for Mrs. Little to call on me. "How are they going to interact with the guests? Is it like interactive theater? Improv?"

"They're more of a renaissance festival troupe," Mrs. Little supplied. "There will be singing, fake jousting under the big tent, troubadours and the like, and they'll have horses."

That didn't sound terrible. In fact, it almost sounded like a good idea. The look Mrs. Little flicked in my direction told me I was missing something, though. She seemed far too pleased with herself.

"The other addition is something I think our town really needs," Mrs. Little said, something evil flashing in her eyes as she pinned me with a haughty gaze. "I want you all to meet Scarlet Darksbane. She's a real witch ... like ... a real one. And she's opening a new store in the old Cauldron Company space on the corner."

I stilled as Chief Terry shifted. "A real witch, huh?"

Mrs. Little's smirk was evil. "Yes. I think we need a real witch to balance all the fake witches. Don't you, Bay?"

It was a pointed jab. Mrs. Little, despite her protestations to the contrary, knew very well that my family was all witches. She'd been cursed enough times by Aunt Tillie that arguing against that fact would be ridiculous.

"I think that new people in town is always a good idea," I gritted out.

Chief Terry patted my knee, as if understanding my annoyance. "Are the individuals here?" he asked. "Can we meet them? It's always better to meet new people before deciding on matters like this."

"The matter has already been decided," Mrs. Little argued. "You guys put me in charge of festival preparation, so I made the decision."

"Yeah, but we did that to keep you busy and out of trouble," I pointed out. "We didn't do it to give you unlimited control over the town."

"Bay, please don't make me remind you to raise your hand again," Mrs. Little ordered. "You're starting to get annoying."

"I'm starting to get annoying?" I moved to hop to my feet but Chief Terry dragged me down before I could get a full head of steam.

"She's playing you," Chief Terry hissed. "Don't give her the satisfaction of melting down."

That was easy for him to say.

"I have two representatives here from the new additions to the upcoming festival," Mrs. Little said. "The first is Adele Twigg. She runs the theater troupe. Scarlet is also here to answer questions." Mrs. Little swept her hand toward a striking redhead in the corner. I wasn't sure how I missed her upon first scanning the room, but now that I was aware of her presence I couldn't look anywhere else.

"Now, I believe those are the main issues we have to go over," Mrs. Little said. "I have instructions for everyone – and they're already printed – so pick up your folder and meet our new additions." Mrs. Little's eyes locked with mine, something dark and hateful passing between us. "I think, with everyone's help, this will be the best festival ever. Our new additions are just the shot of adrenalin Hemlock Cove needs to stay fresh and exciting."

I swallowed hard as I worked to contain my temper. Chief Terry grabbed my elbow and helped me stand.

"Do you want to tell me what's going on here?" Chief Terry kept his voice low. "Why are you so upset?"

That was a very good question. "Because Mrs. Little is clearly up to something," I replied. "What do you know about this Scarlet Darksbane woman?" I wasn't particularly worried about Mrs. Twigg. She would be here for a week and then go on her merry way. I could tolerate that. But the new witch was something that set my teeth on edge.

"Not much," Chief Terry replied. "I can pretty much guarantee her real name isn't Darksbane."

I flicked my eyes to him. "What is it?"

He shrugged. "I only know Darksbane is something made up."

I kept my gaze fixed on Scarlet as she conversed with other members of the festival group. She seemed to be easygoing and gregarious, genuinely interested in what they had to say. Her eyes kept drifting to me, though, and the smile she sent me was friendly but chilling at the same time.

"I don't like this," I muttered, scratching my cheek. "If Mrs. Little brought her here it has to be for a reason."

Chief Terry arched an eyebrow. "My understanding is that she's been eyeing a spot in Hemlock Cove for the past few months. We didn't have any openings until they decided to close The Cauldron Company. It seems there wasn't big money in selling cauldrons and nothing else."

"Have you met her?" I finally yanked my gaze from Scarlet and focused on him. "What is she like?"

"I met her very briefly when she was looking at the space," Chief Terry replied, worry licking his features. "Bay, what's wrong?"

He clearly didn't get it. "Haven't you asked yourself why Mrs. Little would tout the fact that Scarlet Darksbane is a *real* witch?"

"I figured it was a dig at you guys."

"Exactly. What if she is a real witch, though?"

"I don't understand the question." Chief Terry moved a bit closer. "Why is that an issue?"

"Because all witches aren't nice and sweet like my mother and aunts," I replied. "There is such a thing as a dark witch."

Chief Terry risked a glance at our new resident. "And you think she's a dark witch? You don't even know her. You haven't exchanged so much as a greeting."

That was true. I had a feeling, though. How do you describe a feeling? "I know, but ... ."

"But give her a chance." Chief Terry cut me off with a firm shake of his head. "She's new in town and she seems genuinely excited to open another magic shop. This town can always use a new shop. The guests love it."

"So she's starting a shop that will be in direct competition with Thistle and Clove?"

"I guess, in theory, that's true," Chief Terry conceded. "I doubt it will cut into their business. They're very well established."

"That doesn't mean anything." My emotions were charged and I couldn't seem to rein myself in. "If Mrs. Little is playing nice with her, that means she's probably evil."

Chief Terry was dumbfounded. "And you have the queen of evil witches living on your property."

"Aunt Tillie isn't evil. She's ... misunderstood."

"Since when? She tells people she's evil."

Sadly, my great-aunt was known to do that. She wasn't big on conversing or making nice. "I'm suspicious," I said after a beat. "It's as if Mrs. Little brought in a ringer. After what happened with the wishing well ... you can't possibly think this will run smoothly."

"Bay, none of these festivals ever run smoothly," Chief Terry said. "They're always a mess. This will be no different. That doesn't mean it'll be an evil mess."

I wasn't convinced. "What if they're up to something?"

Chief Terry held his palms out and shrugged. "Your family is always up to something, but we manage to survive."

"But ... ."

"No." Chief Terry gave me a firm headshake. "You're being ridiculous. Why don't you try meeting the woman before you burn her at the stake?"

Oh, well, that was a cheap shot. "That's not what I'm doing."

"Do you want to know what I think?"

"No."

"I'll tell you anyway," Chief Terry pressed. "I think you're worked up because of the situation at home and you want something external to focus on. Sweetheart, I don't know her very well, but I very much doubt Scarlet Darksbane is that thing. She seems sweet. She's friendly and engaging. She listens and doesn't order people around. She won't be an issue."

I considered arguing further, but it seemed pointless. He wouldn't understand and I was incapable of explaining. "Okay. Well ... if you say so."

I could only hope Chief Terry was right. My inner danger alarm told me otherwise. Something very odd was going on here. Given Hemlock Cove's standards, that couldn't possibly be a good.

THREE

*L*andon waited for me outside of the meeting. He looked strong and handsome leaning against his truck, his attention fixed on his phone screen. He didn't glance up until he heard my shoes scuffing against the pavement.

"Hey, sweetie." He pocketed his phone and gave me a quick kiss. "How was the meeting?"

"Oh, don't get her started on the meeting," Chief Terry warned. I didn't know he was following me until I heard his voice.

"That good, huh?" Landon brushed a strand of hair from my face. "What happened?"

"Well, for starters, Mrs. Little made me raise my hand every time I tried to talk," I started.

Landon snorted. "That sounds just like her. It doesn't, however, sound like a reason to get worked up."

"Oh, that's not the reason."

"Here we go," Chief Terry muttered.

"She brought in a ringer," I volunteered.

Landon furrowed his brow. "Is that some weird person who makes rings in Hemlock Cove?"

"No. It's a supposedly new and improved real witch."

"Huh." Landon kept his face impassive but I didn't miss the way his eyes flicked to Chief Terry. "I'm going to need more information."

I opened my mouth to let loose with a righteous diatribe, but Chief Terry stopped me with a hand on my arm.

"I've got this." Chief Terry launched into the tale, telling it in forty-five seconds flat. I was mildly annoyed at his brevity. He missed a lot of dramatic and potentially damning stuff.

"And that's it?" Landon's gaze drifted back to me. "That doesn't sound like a reason to freak out."

"He didn't tell the story right," I protested.

"I told the story exactly right," Chief Terry corrected. "You're getting yourself worked up for no good reason, Bay."

"That sounds nothing at all like me." I folded my arms over my chest. "You can't tell me that Mrs. Little doesn't have something up those ugly sleeves of hers."

"She's always got something up her sleeve," Chief Terry pointed out. "So does Tillie. That's why they're such a fine pair."

"If Aunt Tillie were here she'd be massively insulted by that."

"If Tillie were here we'd all be worried about something else," Chief Terry shot back. "I don't understand why you're so worked up about this. Scarlet Darksbane seems like a perfectly nice woman."

"Scarlet Darksbane?" Landon snorted. "That can't be her real name."

"Of course it's not her real name," I scoffed. "That's a made-up name. She's trying to make sure everyone knows she's a witch. Scarlet Darksbane is the dumbest name I've ever heard."

"You have a cousin named Thistle," Landon reminded me.

"And what's wrong with that?"

"Oh, such a good question," Chief Terry lamented. "I don't have time to answer it, though. And you don't have time to do any more complaining, Bay. Let it go."

I had no intention of following his demand, but he slapped his hand over my mouth to let me know he meant business. I was understandably affronted. "Hey!" The sound came out muffled as I tried to pull away, but Chief Terry ignored my outrage.

22

"Wonderful meeting, Margaret," he called out. "I'm really looking forward to seeing what you have planned for the new festival. I'm sure it will be lovely."

"Yes, because another festival is exactly what this whackadoodle town needs," Landon drawled.

I slapped at Chief Terry's hand, but he refused to move it. I tried to argue my point, but all that came out was a series of muffled noises.

"And it was lovely meeting you, too, Ms. Darksbane," Chief Terry added, causing me to stiffen. I slowly turned in that direction, disgust rolling through me at Scarlet's amused expression. "I think you'll make a lovely addition to the town."

"Oh." Landon smiled at the fiery redhead. "You're the new witch on the block, huh? It's nice to meet you." He extended his hand and I made a mental note to smack him upside the head with it when I was free of Chief Terry's iron grip.

"It's nice to meet you, too." Scarlet's voice was like honey as she flashed a wide smile in Landon's direction. She wore a corseted top that pushed up her breasts to unbelievable heights and I briefly wished for a pin so I could pop them. They had to be fake. There was no other explanation. "I don't believe I saw you at the meeting Mr. ... ?"

"Michaels," Landon supplied, his smile friendly. "Landon Michaels."

"Mr. Michaels is an FBI agent," Mrs. Little supplied, her grin so evil movie villains everywhere lined up to take notes. "He often works with Chief Terry to keep our beautiful town safe."

"Oh, that's nice." Scarlet shifted her gaze to me. "Is something wrong?"

"Why would you ask that?" Chief Terry queried, straightening.

"Why do you have your hand over Ms. Winchester's mouth?" Scarlet asked.

"Oh, right." Chief Terry jerked his hand away. "We were ... playing a game."

"What game?"

Chief Terry shifted from one foot to the other, uncomfortable. "It's a private game. It's not important."

I narrowed my eyes at the color flooding Chief Terry's cheeks. The new witch made him nervous, and I was fairly certain it was because she was so freaking hot. Good grief. "You're old enough to be her father," I hissed.

Chief Terry snapped his eyes to me. "Don't be rude."

"Did you say something, Bay?" Scarlet asked, her smile never so much as threatening to drift. "Oh, can I call you that? Bay, I mean. Or would you prefer I call you Ms. Winchester?"

"You can call her Bay," Landon supplied, frowning when I scorched him with a dark glare. "What? Everyone calls you Bay."

"You'll be calling me something else when you sleep on the couch tonight," I warned, working overtime to collect myself. The new witch probably thought I was altogether batty. That might be a good thing, of course, but I didn't want to make an enemy of her before I knew her true motivations.

"Oh, are you two together?" Scarlet asked, her attention back on Landon. She looked a bit disappointed. And, no, I didn't imagine it simply because I was determined to dislike her. "I thought Chief Terry and Bay were a couple."

I screwed up my face in an expression of complete disgust. "Excuse me?"

Even Chief Terry was offended. "Bay is like a daughter to me," he clarified. "She's not actually my daughter but ... well ... she's close enough that this fool makes me want to punch him occasionally." Chief Terry playfully cuffed the back of Landon's head.

"I see." Scarlet focused on me. "You're dating an FBI agent? That's ... interesting." The way she said the word "interesting" stirred my suspicious nature.

"Why is that interesting?" Landon asked, genuinely curious.

"You two simply don't look like a couple," Scarlet replied. "I thought Bay was either single or involved with Chief Terry. Now that I give it further thought, it's clear that you two are together and ... happy."

"We're definitely happy," I said. "We're so happy we gather around the fireplace and sing every night. Oh, and we get naked and stuff, too."

Landon slid me a sidelong look, his expression quizzical. "We don't often sing while naked by the fire, Bay."

I knew that was a stupid thing to say when it escaped my mouth, but he didn't need to point it out. "Oh, whatever." I expected Scarlet to leave, but instead she merely let her expectant gaze bounce between us. "So … um … you're opening a new store, huh?"

"I am," Scarlet confirmed. "I'm really looking forward to it."

"Well, I'll stop by one day and conduct an interview for The Whistler." My heart wasn't in the offer, but scrounging up stories this time of year was always difficult. This was an easy fix. "I can't wait to see what you've done with the space."

"I would love that." Scarlet sounded sincere, but I couldn't make myself relax and take her at her word. "I think Hemlock Cove is a wonderful place. I can't wait to get to know you guys."

"That sounds like fun. Doesn't that sound like fun, Bay?" Landon's eyes were unnaturally wide. I knew he was trying to mess with me.

"It sounds lovely," I lied, forcing a smile. "We'll definitely have to get to know one another." I turned to face Landon, essentially dismissing Scarlet. "You're taking me to dinner, right?"

"I am."

"Let's do it. I'm starving."

Perhaps sensing that I was done with her, Scarlet didn't let her manners lapse as she offered up a cheery wave. "I'm so glad to have met you all. I can't wait to spend more time with you." Her gaze lingered on Landon longest. "Okay, well, bye."

And just like that she turned on her heel and walked across the parking lot with Mrs. Little, their heads bent together as they plotted the end of the world.

"Oh, she's clearly up to something," I said.

Landon merely sighed. "Well, at least you have something to focus on besides Thistle and me. Frankly, I'm relieved."

He wasn't the only one.

"**DO YOU WANT** to tell me what that was all about?"

Landon waited until we were seated in a corner booth at the diner – Hemlock Cove's most romantic (although that's not saying much) dinner option – to ask me the obvious question. I expected it, yet I didn't have a proper answer.

"Mrs. Little is evil."

"That's hardly news, Bay," Landon pointed out. "I was talking about your reaction to Scarlet."

"Oh, Scarlet." I made a disgusted face as I gritted out her name, which made Landon smile. "Don't give me that look."

"If you tell me you're jealous I'll be flattered. Then I'll never let you forget about it. You might want to think long and hard about admitting something like that."

"I'm not jealous," I argued.

"Then what are you?" Landon asked. "As far as I can tell, you're angry for no good reason. You were in a perfectly good mood when you left home."

"I wasn't in that good of a mood," I clarified. "That being said ... I like that we now call the same place home. That's kind of neat, huh?"

Landon's expression softened. "That's very neat. Why weren't you in a good mood when you left home?"

"Really?" I rolled my eyes. "You and Thistle are being complete and total jerks."

"That's how we're venting our frustrations over the situation. Do you think it's easy given the fact that we both like to take control? Snarking at one another is keeping us sane."

"Huh. I hadn't thought of that."

"It will only be a few weeks, Bay. Soon it'll be just us and you'll be complaining that you miss her."

"I think that's a gross exaggeration."

"And I think you're fooling yourself, but it's something we'll deal with when it comes around," Landon countered. "You're going to miss her. It's okay to admit it."

"I don't really see how that's the point of this conversation."

"It's not," Landon conceded. "I want to know why you don't like the new witch. I thought at first it was because she was flirting with me, but now I think it's more than that."

"I knew I didn't imagine the flirting," I groused.

Landon chuckled. "You're not jealous, though. I consider that progress."

I cocked an eyebrow. "Should I be jealous?"

"Never. Should I be jealous of Chief Terry? Apparently you guys are sending out a certain vibe when in public together."

"She's making that up," I countered. "She said it because she wanted to get a reaction. She acts all sweet and nice ... all wonderful with her fake boobs and overstuffed lips ... but I know she's up to something."

"I would comment on the fake boobs, but I don't think my target audience would like that." Landon grabbed a breadstick from the basket and broke it in half. "Do you want to share?"

"Not really."

Landon took a big bite and swallowed before continuing. "I've seen you around women who flirt with me. You generally don't like it, but you don't react like this. Tell me what's bothering you. I can't help fix the problem when I don't know what it is."

"It's just ... ." I was back to having to explain a feeling. I exhaled heavily to center myself. If I couldn't confide in Landon after all we'd been through, then there was something seriously wrong with our relationship. "If I tell you something, do you promise not to laugh?"

Landon shook his head. "No. You say funny things quite often. If you're serious, though, I promise to help even if I laugh."

I couldn't ask for more than that, right? "The thing is ... I get a vibe off her."

Instead of laughing, Landon leaned closer. "What kind of vibe? Do you think she's ... evil?"

"I said I thought she was evil."

"Yes, but you spend an inordinate amount of time with Aunt Tillie and maintain she's not evil," Landon pointed out. "Sometimes I think your judgment is skewed."

Ugh. I hate it when he has a point. "I don't know how to explain it," I offered. "I didn't see her right away, which is weird. It's a small room."

"I'm not sure what that means," Landon said. "Are you saying she was invisible?"

"No, but she could've masked herself. I know it doesn't sound likely, but ... she wasn't there and then suddenly she was there. She's running around with Mrs. Little – as if they're suddenly best friends or something – and Mrs. Little acts as if she's about to pull one over on us. I don't know how to explain it."

Landon leaned back in his seat and gave me a long look. "If you don't like her and think something is up then I believe you. I'll run a background check on her."

He capitulated so easily I couldn't help being a bit sheepish. "You don't have to do that."

"If it will make you feel better, I'll gladly do it."

I rubbed my cheek as I regarded him. "No. That doesn't seem fair. She hasn't technically done anything except assume I was dating Chief Terry and flirt with my boyfriend."

"You obviously don't like her," Landon pointed out. "I'm guessing it's because you don't trust Mrs. Little – and rightfully so – but if you want me to check on her, I'll do it."

It was a nice offer, but now, after melting down and admitting my worries, I felt a bit foolish. "No. She hasn't done anything. Let's wait until something unexplained happens and then you can do it."

Landon cracked a smile as he patted my hand. "That sounds like a plan."

"If she flirts with you again, though, I'm totally going to yank out her hair and make her eat dirt."

Landon barked out a laugh. "Now that sounds like a stimulating idea ... as long as I can watch."

"Men are so easy."

"We are indeed."

We lapsed into comfortable silence, happy simply to be together. Then a hint of movement from the other side of the restaurant window grabbed my attention and I caught sight of Mrs. Little and Scarlet Darksbane walking along the street. They seemed deep in thought, intent on one another, until Scarlet lifted her eyes at the exact right moment and pinned me with a lingering look. The exchange was brief – probably three seconds at most – but it was powerful and obvious. Then it was over and she was gone. I remained troubled by the exchange after they disappeared.

"That was a little weird," Landon said, taking me by surprise.

"So I didn't imagine it?"

Landon shook his head. "It was as if she sensed you."

If Landon noticed, at least I wasn't alone in my paranoia. "Maybe one little search wouldn't hurt."

Landon smirked. "I'll do it when I get to work in the morning. I'll make a note of it."

I was about to thank him when another furtive movement, this one much smaller, forced me to stare out the window a second time. It took me only a moment to recognize Aunt Tillie. She was dressed completely in black and hurrying down the sidewalk, her head bent to cut off the sharp wind. I had no doubt what she was doing.

"Of course, Aunt Tillie might terrorize her into leaving town before it's even necessary," Landon noted.

"I wonder how she found out about her," I mused. "I don't think the information has been made public yet."

"How does she find out about anything?"

"Good point." I pursed my lips and brushed my hand through my hair, determined to push outside forces out of the forefront of my brain for the remainder of the night. "So, after dinner, do you want to go home and sing in front of the fire? We can be naked and everything."

Landon's laughter was warm as it washed over me. "That's the best offer I've had all day."

FOUR

I was in a much better mood by the time we returned to the guesthouse. Landon thought it was the food – he was convinced eating delicious comfort meals fixed everything – but I believed seeing Aunt Tillie stalking the new witch brightened my spirits. I could hardly admit that to Landon, though. He didn't always understand the way the female brain worked.

Thistle and Marcus sat on the couch watching a movie when we entered, but other than a silent exchange promising mayhem at a later time Landon and Thistle didn't immediately start fighting. Landon kicked off his boots and settled in the chair at the edge of the living room while I joined Thistle and Marcus on the couch.

"How was the festival meeting?" Thistle asked, lifting the blanket so I could slide beneath it. The weather was turning quickly and winter was almost upon us. You could feel the bite in the air.

"Don't get her going," Landon warned, stretching out his legs as he focused on the television. "I just talked her down."

Thistle ignored the admonishment. "How was the festival meeting?" she repeated, her eyes gleaming as Landon made a growling noise in the back of his throat.

"There's a new witch in town," I replied. "Her name is Scarlet Darksbane."

Thistle snorted. "What a stupid name."

"Says a woman named Thistle," Landon muttered under his breath.

"I heard that." Thistle shifted, as if she meant to launch herself at Landon and rip out his hair, but Marcus shot her a quelling look and she remained seated.

"I happen to love your name, honey." Marcus absently patted her knee. "I think it's very cute."

"Cute?" Thistle wrinkled her nose. "I am not cute."

Landon pointedly caught my eye. "Notice I didn't say a thing."

"You just opened your big mouth," Thistle shot back.

I pressed the heel of my hand to my forehead as I tried to refrain from screaming at them. Landon noticed my reaction and his smirk slipped.

"I'm sorry," Landon offered, instantly contrite. "I shouldn't have started something the second I walked through the door. It's not fair to Bay."

Thistle was incensed. "Bay? What about me?"

"Oh, it's fair to you."

My stomach shifted as I rolled out from under the blanket and stood. "I think I need a drink."

"Me, too," Marcus said, standing. "If you two are going to fight ... ."

"We're not going to fight," Thistle said hurriedly. "This is simply how we communicate."

"I tried explaining that to Bay over dinner but she didn't listen," Landon complained. "I don't think she gets us."

"Oh, I get you." I shuffled to the kitchen and collected the ingredients for chocolate martinis from various cupboards. Marcus quietly joined in, seemingly happy to steer clear of the potential war zone. "I don't see why you guys can't ignore each other the next few weeks."

"Because this place feels small and it's too cold to spend a lot of time outside," Thistle said. "You shouldn't get worked up about it. It's not a big deal."

"I'm not worked up about it," I countered. "Do I sound worked up?"

Thistle glanced over her shoulder and arched an eyebrow. "You sound worked up about something. What gives?"

"She's turning her focus to the new witch," Landon supplied. "She's convinced that Scarlet Darksbane is up to something."

His tone irked me. "You said that thing she did at the window was weird."

"It was definitely weird," Landon agreed. "It was as if she sensed you watching her or something. I just think she might've reacted that way for a reason other than you think."

"And what reason would that be?"

"She might very well be a real witch, like you guys are the authentic deal," Landon replied. "You said there are a lot of witches out there. Wouldn't it make sense for another real witch to move to the area?

"I mean, think about it," he continued. "This town is made up of people pretending to be witches and warlocks for the public. That might be very appealing for a real witch because she would no longer have to hide who she is."

"I guess that's fair," I conceded.

"Thank you."

"I still don't like her."

Thistle chuckled as Landon rolled his eyes.

"What's she like?" Marcus asked. "I heard someone was coming in and taking over the old space from The Cauldron Company. That must be her, right?"

"That's her," I confirmed. "She's opening a magic store."

Thistle, who had been enjoying the conversation only moments before, narrowed her eyes. "She's opening a magic store?"

I knew that would irritate her, so I forced a smile. "Just like your magic store."

"Nothing is like Hypnotic," Thistle argued. "We have thirty kitschy stores in this town and Hypnotic still stands out."

"According to Mrs. Little – who is best friends with the new witch, by the way – Scarlet's new store will offer exactly the same things you do at Hypnotic."

"Well, she's clearly evil and has to go," Thistle pronounced, hopping to my side of the argument with little thought. "We need to find out who she really is. There's no way Scarlet Darksbane is her real name."

"Landon is going to look her up," I offered. "I bet he finds a bunch of dead husbands and decimated families in her wake."

"Oh, well, I'm so glad you're not taking this to a dramatic place," Landon drawled.

I ignored him. "That's not all. Mrs. Little plans to whip this new festival into shape and is launching it in a week. She's actually bringing in renaissance festival performers and everything. She said she's going to put a lot of focus on Scarlet and her new store because that's the neighborly thing to do. Those were her words, not mine, but she wouldn't stop blabbering about it when she was handing out assignments."

"I've always hated that old bat," Thistle complained, tossing the blanket onto the floor as she stood, fire in her eyes. "She's just doing this to get to us."

"I told you." I locked gazes with Landon. "You didn't believe me. You said I was making something out of nothing. I was right."

"I fail to see how Thistle jumping to the same conclusions you did is proof," Landon said dryly. "So far, from what I've seen of Scarlet Darksbane, she seems like a perfectly normal woman trying to get to know people in a new environment."

What a rube. "You're so naïve."

"What has she done that's so terrible?"

"You saw the way she looked at me."

"Yes, and I saw the way you acted with her," Landon pointed out. "You were aggressive from the start."

"I was not."

"You were, too."

"I was not."

"You were, too."

"She was not," Thistle snapped, tossing one of the throw pillows from the couch at Landon's head. He smoothly caught it in the air and glared at her.

"You weren't there," Landon argued. "You don't know whether or not she was aggressive."

"I know Bay," Thistle said. "If she says there's something wrong with this woman, then there's something wrong with her. I have faith in Bay's instincts. I'm loyal."

"Oh, geez." Landon pinched the bridge of his nose. "Are you saying I'm not loyal?"

"I'm saying that you're a butthead," Thistle said. "As for the loyalty thing ... perhaps it comes and goes with you."

"I can't deal with this," Landon muttered, leaning his head back and staring at the ceiling. "I have no problem running a search on that woman. She did give Bay an odd look, and I'm curious to see what I'll find in her past. As a law enforcement official, though, I need proof. What I saw tonight wasn't proof. It was Bay being ... weird."

"I'm not being weird," I protested. "I'm being ... proactive. Yeah, that's the right word. I'm being proactive."

"Against what?"

"You've complained on multiple occasions that I accidentally find trouble, and then you cry when I almost get hurt," I said.

"I don't cry," Landon groused, wrinkling his nose. "I hardly ever cry."

"You cried when she was almost shot," Thistle pointed out.

"You cried when she was attacked at the guesthouse when you were in that fight," Marcus added.

"You cried when you had to race out to the Dandridge to save her on that ship," Thistle said, warming to the game.

"Okay, that will be enough of that." Landon held up his hands to stall the argument. "I get what you're saying, but Scarlet Darksbane hasn't done anything yet."

"Aunt Tillie was following her," I said. "We both saw that. If Aunt Tillie believes she's up to something, she's definitely up to something."

"Aunt Tillie believes the minister at the church is up to something because he looks at her funny," Landon said.

"She hasn't been proven wrong on that," Thistle interjected. "He might very well be up to something ... or he could simply be suspicious because she likes to steal wine."

"I notice you only take Aunt Tillie's side on the rare occasions it coincides with your side," Landon said. "Don't you find that a bit ... convenient?"

"No. Aunt Tillie is amazingly ingenious." The fact that Thistle said it with a straight face was impressive. I couldn't help but purse my lips to keep from laughing at her defiant countenance. Landon's expression was something straight out of a sitcom. "Okay, she knows all and sees all," Thistle corrected, immediately realizing her mistake. "She's a diabolical old crone who likes to mess with people. That doesn't mean she's wrong about Scarlet Darksbane."

"Fine. I give up." Landon held up his hands in mock surrender. "I will run the new witch through the system, share all of the gruesome details, and hope that you guys don't get arrested for doing something terrible to her. How does that sound?"

I flashed him a warm smile. "That's all we ask."

"Great." Landon accepted the chocolate martini I carried to him with a smile, placing it on the end table before snagging me around the waist and dragging me into his lap. "Try not to get in trouble with the new witch." He smacked a kiss against my cheek. "I don't want to have to bail you out."

"Oh, Chief Terry would never arrest me."

Landon studied my face. "Probably not." He shifted so we were both comfortable sharing the chair. "Be careful, though. You don't know this woman. I would hate to find out you went after her for no reason."

He had a point, which was unfortunate. "I'll wait to see what you find out in her background check," I offered. "I have no intention of going after her just to go after her."

Landon didn't look convinced. "Do what you want to do. But if it means my fighting with Thistle bothers you less, I want you to focus on the new witch. I don't care if she is innocent and you're embarking on a witch hunt in the process."

Marcus chuckled as he handed Thistle a martini and reclaimed his seat. "So you're basically sacrificing the new witch to be more comfortable with the current living conditions. That's what you're saying, right?"

Landon shrugged. "I never pretended to be altruistic."

"I'm not going to go after her just to go after her," I promised. "There's just something off about her." Despite the fun and games, that was true. I couldn't shake the feeling that something was about to happen. The problem was, I had no idea what.

"Drink your martini," Landon prodded. "You'll feel better when you have a buzz."

"You're just saying that because you want to take advantage of me."

"Again, I never pretended to be altruistic."

I giggled as I rested my head on his shoulder. It was nice when it was just the four of us and no one was arguing. "I promise to be good." I lowered my voice. "I just want to know a little bit more about her. I have this ... feeling."

Landon shifted his eyes to me. "Then we'll do it together. If you really believe there's something wrong with her, then there probably is. I have faith in your instincts."

"Thank you."

"Just don't do anything crazy."

"When do I do crazy things?"

Landon shot me an exaggerated look. "When don't you do crazy things?"

"I'm a very pragmatic person."

"Yes, that's the word I often think in my head when my mind drifts to you fifty times a day."

Even though he said it with a sarcastic tone I couldn't help but focus on that particular statement. "You think about me fifty times a day?"

"How did I know you would latch onto that part?"

"You must be psychic."

"No, sweetie, I'm going to leave that little bit of magic to you. I think it's best for both of us."

"SO, I WAS THINKING ... ."

Landon squeezed the tube of toothpaste as he watched me in the bathroom mirror right before bed. He was clearly trying to prepare me for something.

"You were thinking about what?" I asked, shifting one of Thistle's bras hanging on the towel rack.

"First, I was thinking about grabbing all of these bras and tossing them on Thistle's head," Landon said, glaring at the offending lacy objects. "But that's what she wants, so instead I'll ignore them. She'll win if I mention them."

I tapped his chin. "Now you're thinking."

"Actually, I was thinking about something else," Landon hedged. "The bra thing just came to me and I got distracted."

"Okay. What were you thinking?"

"You know how we were going to turn Thistle's room into my office and Clove's old room into your office?"

I nodded.

"What if we switched that around?"

The question caught me off guard. "I thought you wanted the bigger room."

"I don't really care about the size of the room," Landon explained. "I'm fine with you getting the bigger office. It's just ... I would like some space of my own. It's not that I'm not happy with the living arrangements," he added hurriedly. "It's just ... ."

"The walls are closing in on you," I surmised, smiling. "You're just as antsy as me, aren't you?"

"I don't know that 'antsy' is the word, but I would like a room to retreat to that's just for me," Landon admitted. "I'm thrilled at the idea of living with you. I need you to know that."

"I know."

"Living with Thistle is a chore, though. She's always in my face. I would like a room where I can shut the door and not see her stupid face."

"I think that's more than doable," I said. "In fact, I was going to suggest it myself, but then I thought maybe you'd think I was trying to steal the bigger room from you."

"How much bigger is Thistle's room?"

"Like a foot in each direction."

"That's nothing."

"It was a big deal when Clove and Thistle were fighting to see who got that room," I said.

"And where did you land?"

"Oh, you know me." I beamed. "Size doesn't matter."

Landon poked my side. "You're lucky you're cute." He bent over and pressed a sweet kiss to my forehead. "Thank you for not making a big deal out of this."

"Did you think I would?"

"I honestly had no idea," Landon replied. "You're hard to read sometimes. All of the fighting Thistle and I are doing is driving you crazy. I see it on your face. I want to ease that burden."

"And your own burden," I added. "It's okay. I get it. Everyone needs alone time."

"You're used to living with Clove and Thistle," Landon supplied. "I've lived alone for a long time. I've spent every possible night with you during the last year, but I still spent a few nights alone every week."

"Do you think you'll miss it?"

"Sleeping alone? No. I think you and I will be perfectly fine," Landon replied. "It's getting to the time when we'll be alone that's the issue. I don't want to keep fighting with Thistle because I know it drives you crazy, but ... ."

"But you need to fight with Thistle or you'll go crazy," I finished. "I get it."

"You usually do." Landon rested his cheek against my forehead. "She's trying to drive me insane. Like 'I should be committed' insane. You know that, right? I'm not imagining it."

"She gets that trait from Aunt Tillie. She can't help herself."

"She's very good at it."

I smiled. "It'll be okay. We can survive a few weeks of this."

"Oh, sweetie, we can survive anything." Landon tipped up my chin. "Now, brush your teeth. There's something I want to show you in the bedroom."

"I already told you that size doesn't matter."

Landon's eyes flashed. "Keep it up."

"I plan to."

"And that's why I love you."

FIVE

*W*e woke in the middle of the night to a ringing phone. I knew right away it was Landon's because mine rang with Cat Stevens' "If You Want to Sing Out" and his was the boring tone the phone came with. Landon made a muffled groaning as he rolled away from me and reached for the phone, his voice slurry with sleep when he answered.

"Hello."

I shifted closer, curious. He got the occasional late-night call on important cases, but they were few and far between.

"Wait ... what are you saying?" Landon struggled to a sitting position, whatever the caller told him bad enough to help him shake off the doldrums of sleep almost instantaneously. Landon is a heavy sleeper, so it had to be big.

"Ritual? As in witch ritual?" Landon's eyes drifted to me and my stomach churned.

I sat up, narrowing my eyes and opening my ears. Landon switched hands with his phone so he could reassuringly rub my back as he listened.

"I'll be there in twenty minutes," Landon said after a beat. "Do you want me to bring Bay?"

Bring me? Since when was that an option?

"Okay. We'll see you in a few." Landon disconnected and met my gaze. "We have a problem."

"I figured that out myself." I worked overtime to tamp down my anxiety. "What's going on?"

"It seems there's a dead body downtown."

"Downtown? Here?"

Landon nodded. "A woman has been strung up in the town square," Landon explained. "She's been exsanguinated. Do you know what that means?"

"All of her blood was drained from her body."

"And it was used to create some sort of … symbols, for lack of a better word … on the ground," Landon said. "Terry says it looks ritual."

That wasn't good. It was one thing for Hemlock Cove to be a friendly paranormal vacation destination. It was quite another for tourists to start believing we had dark witches at work. "You want me to come with you, don't you?"

"Not if you're uncomfortable with it," Landon replied. "It's brutal, Bay. If you don't want to see … in fact, I shouldn't have suggested you come. I don't want you to see it."

We both knew it was too late for that. "Do you know who it is?"

"Terry didn't say."

I made up my mind on the spot. "I'll get dressed."

Landon grabbed my hand before I could escape the bed. "If you don't want to go, I understand. I should've thought things through before I volunteered your services."

"You need to know if those symbols mean anything," I pointed out. "You need a real witch for that. Hopefully I'll be able to recognize them."

"I can go wake up Aunt Tillie."

It was a lame offer. He didn't mean it.

"I'm going." I forced a smile. "I need to see what we're dealing with."

"Okay." Landon ran his fingers through my hair to smooth it. "You don't have to see the body, though. You can wait until it's gone and just look at the symbols if you want."

"I need to see the body," I argued. "I might see something you miss."

"Like a ghost?"

I hadn't even considered that. Seeing and talking to ghosts wasn't my most comfortable gift. It came in handy a time or two the previous year, though. "I guess we'll have to wait to see."

"I guess we will."

IT WAS COLD SO I bundled up, dragging out my winter coat and hat. Landon grabbed my gloves for me so I wouldn't forget and turned his truck heater on full blast, pointing the vents in my direction as he headed toward town.

We made the drive in silence, Landon's mind clearly busy with a variety of scenarios. He would be involved in the investigation from the beginning, which was different from what he was used to. Chief Terry trusted him, though, and he must feel he needed Landon right from the start. It seemed Landon's move to Hemlock Cove would put him in the thick of things going forward. There would be no departmental jockeying. Chief Terry and Landon would work together to solve this. They were often a team, but now it would happen regularly.

The town square blazed with police lights. Landon parked in front of the police station, making sure I pulled on my gloves before exiting the vehicle. He tried one more time as we approached to get me to wait until the body was cleared from the scene, but it was already too late for that.

"I can handle it." They were bold words given the scene. I sucked in a breath when I saw the body, my mind momentarily going blank. Landon took a step in my direction to steady me, perhaps thinking I would do the chick thing and faint or something, but I regrouped quickly. "This is unbelievable."

"Bay, you don't need to see this," Chief Terry said, hurrying in my direction. The look he shot Landon was pure venom. "I thought you were only bringing her to look at the symbols."

"She wanted to come," Landon said. "I couldn't very well stop her."

"Of course you could stop her. You could've locked her out of your truck."

"And then she would've simply driven down here alone," Landon argued. "Do you really want her out on the roads in the middle of the night when we know someone did … this … in town?" Landon gestured toward the body, his eyes lighting with fury.

"I guess I didn't think of that." Chief Terry rubbed his chin. "Still, sweetheart, you don't need to see this."

I leveled my gaze on him. "I've seen dead bodies before."

"I know, but … ."

"Go ahead and look," Landon said. "You won't be able to stop your-self, so you might as well look."

I sucked in a breath and flicked my eyes to the left, widening them when I saw the garish tableau. I recognized the dead woman right away. I'd met her only once, and very briefly, at the festival meeting a few hours before. Adele Twigg. She ran the renaissance group. I hadn't taken the time to talk to her other than offering a polite "hello" – figuring I could interview her later – and now she was dead in the middle of town.

The woman's face was unnaturally pale. The fact that someone had shoved a tube in her arm to withdraw blood, and then used that blood to paint symbols on the pavement probably accounted for her ashen features. I swallowed hard as I stared, the woman's sightless eyes seemingly boring into me.

"How did she die?"

"We don't know yet," Chief Terry replied, his voice soft. "The medical examiner is on the way. He should be here any second."

"Hmm." I wasn't sure what to say. I insisted on seeing the body, and now that I had I wanted to forget everything about the terrible scene. "Where are the renaissance people staying? I forgot to ask earlier."

"They're spread out among a few inns," Chief Terry replied. "I think you even have a few at The Overlook. There's some at The Dragonfly, too. I'm not sure where Mrs. Twigg was staying."

My father and uncles owned The Dragonfly. They moved back to town several months ago. Reconnecting with them was an ongoing process for Thistle, Clove and me. It was hard work, but we were slowly getting through it.

"What was she doing down here in the middle of the night?" I asked.

"We're not sure, Bay," Chief Terry never moved his gaze from my face. "We don't know that she chose to come down here. You know Hemlock Cove. Town was deserted by nine. It's cold, so there's no reason for people to hang out."

"Right." I managed to drag my eyes away from the body when I heard a vehicle park at the edge of the square. I recognized the county medical examiner's van right away. "I guess the first thing is finding out how she died and where she was right before it happened."

"That's our job," Chief Terry said. "Your job is to look at the other stuff."

The other stuff. Right.

"Look at the symbols, Bay," Landon prodded, forcing my attention away from the medical examiner as he let out a low whistle and stopped in front of the body. "Call out what you see. Don't look at her. Don't look at the medical examiner. Look at the symbols and tell me what they mean."

That was easier said than done, but I was determined to make it work. "Okay." I rubbed my gloved hands over my face as I stepped to the nearest symbol.

"This is the labyrinth."

"And what does that mean?" Landon asked, warily keeping his eyes on me.

"It's generally meant to signify twists and turns, but there's only one way through the maze. One right way."

"Okay. What else?"

I exhaled heavily as I moved to the next symbol, forcing myself to be strong. It was a simple X with a circle at the top. "This is the deadly symbol."

"I think we can guess why they used that," Landon muttered.

I nodded. "This box here." I pointed. "It has an X through it, as you can see. This is the pagan witch symbol."

"So someone is either trying to come out as a witch or point the finger at witches," Chief Terry noted. "Can you tell which?"

I shook my head. "I have no idea. The way these symbols are used, they don't seem to have any rhyme or reason. Like … those triangles." I pointed again. "Those are the four symbols for earth, air, fire and water."

Landon glanced around to make sure no one was listening. "Those are the elements you use when you do your big spells, right?"

"Yeah, but the four elements are common in all pagan circles," I replied. "It's not just a witch thing."

"It still looks ritual," Chief Terry pointed out.

"Yes, but is it really part of a ritual or did someone come to a witch town and try to cover up a murder by painting pagan symbols everywhere?" I challenged.

"That's a very good question," Chief Terry noted. "What else have you got?"

"See this here?" I pointed to what looked to be a fancy cross. "This is a witch's knot. It's a protective charm that was sometimes used to protect people from witches centuries ago. It was initially meant to protect witches from bad spells and then stolen by people who didn't grasp the power of the symbol and co-opted it for something else. They didn't understand what it was really for."

"Okay. What else?" Landon followed my progression around the circle. "That's a pentagram next, right?"

I shook my head. "Pentacle. A pentacle is a pentagram enclosed in a circle."

"And what does that mean?"

"It's supposed to mean peace and unity, but it's also been stolen at times for other uses."

"What else, Bay?" Landon was determined to keep me on task as the medical examiner focused on the body. It wouldn't work. I'd already seen the horror. I didn't want to needlessly upset him, though, so I did my best to refrain from looking in that direction.

"The rest of these symbols don't seem to mean anything in any context I can understand," I said. "You have the Elven Star, the horned god, the triple crescent, the triple goddess, the triquetra and then ... whatever these are." I knelt next to what looked to be chicken scratch. It was purposely done, although I had no idea what the squiggles and lines were supposed to represent. "I don't know these."

"That's okay." Landon moved to my side. "Good job."

I ignored the compliment and dug for my phone.

"What are you doing?" Chief Terry asked, lifting his hand. "This is a crime scene, Bay. I can't let you take photos."

"I need to take photos of this," I argued. "I need to compare it to the books we have at home."

Chief Terry opened his mouth to argue, but Landon shook his head to still him.

"Let her take the photos," Landon said. "She'll be able to figure out what these symbols mean a lot faster than we can."

"Okay, but ... I don't want that photo in the newspaper, Bay," Chief Terry said. "If it shows up in The Whistler I'm going to be angry."

I shot him a dark look. "Do you really think I'm going to splash a photo of bloody symbols on the front page of the newspaper?"

Chief Terry balked. "I ... that's not what I meant."

"Whatever." I couldn't hold back my irritation as I snapped several photographs. "I'll see what I can find in the books."

"That sounds like a good idea." Landon moved closer. "You should probably be done here."

I knew what he was getting at, but his tone – that "I'm going to protect you whether you want me to or not" tinge to his voice – grated. "Fine. Whatever you want."

"Bay, I didn't mean I thought you would print the photos in the newspaper," Chief Terry said. "I didn't mean to hurt your feelings."

"I know." I kept my voice even. "I'm going to head over to the newspaper office to see if I can start tracking down some information."

Landon balked. "It's the middle of the night, sweetie. You should go home, get some sleep."

"Are you going home to sleep?"

"No, I'm on this now. It's different for you, though."

Of course he would think that. "I'm going to the newspaper office. I'll be fine." I pulled away from him, shifting my attention to the curious shadows watching from the sidewalk. Hemlock Cove was a small town and it was only a matter of time before the crime scene drew a crowd. Already I recognized three faces – all of whom worked in bakeries, which meant they were up early. A fourth face, though, watched from the corner, her arms crossed over her chest. Even though I'd met her only once, I recognized Scarlet Darksbane immediately.

I could've been mistaken – I was tired, after all – but she looked beyond interested in the scene. No, she wasn't a curious onlooker. She wasn't horrified by what was happening. She looked … smug. That was the only description I could come up with.

"I'll come over and get you for breakfast in a few hours," Landon called to my back as I trudged toward The Whistler. "You have a couch in your office, Bay. Try to use it."

"I'll get right on that."

"Crap," Landon muttered. "This is going to turn into a thing."

I wasn't sure if he knew I could hear him, but I opted not to comment. This had already turned into a thing. He simply didn't realize it yet.

SIX

J was numb when I got to the newspaper building, my
fingers shaking as I unlocked the front door and
headed toward my office. The automated environmental controls
kept the building cold overnight, not warming until shortly before
eight in the morning. I manually overrode the thermostat and
started the heat flowing. It would be a while before the building
felt cozy. Thankfully I had a small space heater in my office,
which I immediately turned on before using my teeth to yank off
my gloves.

I jolted when Landon walked into the room, briefly shutting my
eyes and pressing my lips together to collect myself. I knew why he
was here. He didn't deserve to be yelled at because I was on edge.

"I don't need a babysitter."

"That's good because that's not why I'm here." Landon knelt in
front of the heater, grabbing my hands and pressing them lower to
make sure I got most of the blast. "I came to make sure you're all
right."

"You mean babysit me, right?"

Landon growled, the fierceness in his eyes causing me to flash a
genuine smile.

"I'm sorry." I was. "I didn't mean to worry you. I just … wasn't expecting that."

"I don't think anyone can ever expect that," Landon noted. "You're okay, right?"

"Yes. I'm a little weirded out, but I'm okay. You have a job to do. I'm not here to take you away from that."

"Oh, I'm not here because of that." Landon leaned closer to the heater. "I just want to warm up for a bit, and you just happen to be inside the only open building."

I snorted. "I see where I rank in your priorities this morning."

"At the top. You're always at the top. It's cold, though, and we can't do anything until the medical examiner is done. Besides that, I wanted to make sure you locked the door behind you."

I chewed my bottom lip. "I think I might've forgotten to do that."

"I figured you probably would. I'll lock it on my way out. You need to be careful."

"Because we have a murderer running around?"

Landon nodded. "We have a murderer running around who either believes in the occult or wants everyone to believe that pagan enthusiasts are to blame. That could mean trouble for you, and because you're an important part of the team – the most important member of my team – that means I want you safe."

"Don't you say I'm always in trouble?"

"Yes, but whoever did this is a monster," Landon replied. "You need to be careful. I'll keep in touch and tell you what we find. You watch your back."

"I always do."

Landon shot me an amused look. "Do a better job than usual, okay? I don't want you to end up alone with whoever did this. As resourceful as you are, this guy means business."

My mind drifted to Scarlet Darksbane and her odd expression. "What makes you think it's a man?"

"You're right. It could be a woman. Whoever strung up Adele Twigg, though, needed upper body strength. That means we might be dealing with more than one culprit."

That hadn't occurred to me. "A team?"

"Possibly," Landon cautioned. "We don't have any evidence yet. Just ... be careful."

"I promise. You be careful, too."

"I'm always careful," Landon said. "You're the one I'm worried about."

"I'm always careful, too. No matter what you think."

Landon studied me for a long moment. "Don't make me cuff you to me. I will if I think you're in danger of running off to find a murderer."

"You always threaten that. You never do it."

"Hey, we're starting a new life. That means we're starting new traditions. I'm more than happy to make cuffing you to me one of those traditions."

Something about his expression told me he was serious. "I'll be careful."

"Good. Now, do you have anything to eat around here? I'm starving."

Only Landon could think about food at a time like this. "I have candy in my drawer."

"And that's why you're my favorite witch."

I DID MY BEST to tune out the murder investigation outside. I scanned the town square on occasion – the activity continued to increase as Hemlock Cove denizens woke to find terror on their streets – but mostly I managed to focus on my work. What I came up with was disheartening.

"What are you doing here?"

Viola Hendricks, my new ghost buddy, popped into existence next to my desk, causing me to cry out. I wasn't expecting her and she didn't seem to understand that ghosts appearing and disappearing willy-nilly was frightening.

"We need to come up with a way for you to announce your arrival without scaring the bejeesus out of me," I complained, wiping a hand over my forehead. "Maybe we can find a bell and you can ring it before just dropping in like this."

"I can't ring a bell. I'm a ghost."

She had a point. "Then maybe we can teach you to do something else so I don't lose a year of my life whenever you decide you want to hang out," I suggested.

"I could sing before appearing," Viola offered. "I've been listening to a lot of rap and I really enjoy the music."

That sounded more terrifying. "We'll play it by ear." I flicked my eyes back to the computer screen before continuing. "Have you noticed what's going on outside?"

"Yeah. What's that about?" Viola threw her ghostly form into the chair across from my desk. She was getting better at miming human actions. When she first returned from the dead – a bloody death I happened to witness – she had trouble acting normal. Viola had been something of a kook in life, so "normal" was a relative term. She seemed to seamlessly fit in now. It was something of a relief.

"Mrs. Little hired a renaissance troupe group to perform at the new festival," I replied. "It's an after-Thanksgiving-but-before-Christmas festival. I have no idea what she's going to call it."

"If she can find a way to put her name in it, she will," Viola pointed out. She'd been one of Mrs. Little's cohorts while alive. Now, in death, she held nothing but disdain for the woman. "She will probably want to turn it in to her own little shop of horrors. Get it … because her last name is Little and she's a total horror."

Viola's sense of humor was an acquired taste. I much preferred her to the former ghost who used to haunt The Whistler's hallways – Edith was a racist bully who refused to believe she did anything wrong and instead embraced the idea that everyone else was to blame for her unhappiness. But I also found my patience wearing thin where Viola was concerned relatively quickly on most days. "I get it." I forced a smile. "You're very clever."

"I could've been a comedian if I wanted to be," Viola confirmed, her eyes drifting to the window. "There are a lot of cops out there. What happened?"

"Oh, right." I remembered I was in the middle of telling a story when Viola sidetracked me. "The woman in charge of the renaissance group was killed last night. Whoever did it strung her up in the middle of town and exsanguinated her."

"Is that some ... perverted ... thing?" Viola wrinkled her nose.

"I guess it depends on how you rate your perversions. It means someone drained her blood."

"Oh, gross!"

"Definitely gross," I agreed, rubbing the back of my neck. Lack of sleep was starting to catch up with me and I was ready for a nap. Landon and Chief Terry were toiling toward dawn outside, so I was determined to remain awake. "Whoever did it used the blood to draw symbols on the pavement."

"What kind of symbols?"

"Pagan symbols."

"Like witch symbols?"

The last thing I wanted was to confirm that, but there was no reason to lie. It wasn't as if Viola could start a panic in the middle of town. Aunt Tillie and I were the only ones who could interact with her. "I guess you could call them witch symbols," I hedged. "They're pagan symbols, though, and they make absolutely no sense."

"Maybe that's what the murderer wanted," Viola suggested.

"What do you mean?"

"Maybe the murderer wanted to confuse people."

"I've considered that," I supplied. "The symbols make absolutely no sense as they are now. They don't lead in to one another. Most pagan symbols are peaceful, turned into something ugly only when co-opted by those who don't understand what they mean."

"Isn't that how the Salem witch trials started? People didn't understand something innocent and they turned it into a weapon of sorts, right?"

Sometimes I think I woefully underestimate Viola. She's smarter than I give her credit for. "Exactly."

"They turned it into a witch hunt," Viola continued. "Hey, wait.

They turned it into a witch hunt. I wonder if that's where they came up with the term."

And sometimes she's dumber than I give her credit for. I have to remember that, too. "I think that's a definite possibility," I said dryly. "I recognized most of the symbols, but these squiggles are giving me fits. I can't identify them."

"Let me see." Viola drifted behind my desk and stared at the photos I'd uploaded to my desktop. "It looks like a different alphabet."

Hmm. That was interesting. "Like Greek?"

"I've seen Greek letters on the sides of fraternity houses," Viola countered. "This looks like something else."

"Maybe like ancient Sumerian or something," I muttered, my mind busy. "I wonder if I can draw some of the letters and then scan them into the computer and run a search that way."

"I have no idea about that." Viola reclaimed her chair. "I don't know anything about computers except they have unlimited porn."

I arched an eyebrow. "You spend a lot of time looking at porn on computers, do you?"

"Not any longer. I can't make my fingers work the keyboard." Viola wiggled her ghostly fingers for emphasis. "I kind of miss it. I was a big fan of the alien stuff."

"Alien stuff?"

"Yeah. You know ... probes and stuff."

That was way more information than I needed. "Anyway ... I'm going to try to track down these symbols. I should be in town most of the day. I rode with Landon and now I'm kind of stuck."

"He's your long-haired FBI agent lover, right?"

Viola had a delightful way with words. "I guess you could say that."

"He's extremely hot," Viola enthused. "He reminds me of those hair bands from the eighties."

I pursed my lips to keep from laughing. Landon wouldn't find that funny in the slightest. "His hair isn't that long."

"Yeah, but he's got that look," Viola said knowingly. "I can totally see him swinging his hips, his butt covered in black leather as he ...

sings about giving love a bad name." Viola looked lost in some rather lascivious thoughts.

"Okay, well ... I will take that under advisement." Landon wouldn't find the idea of Viola fantasizing about him as he crooned power ballads very entertaining. "I don't suppose you heard anything last night while you were hanging around, did you?" I wanted to change the subject, and returning to conversation about the murder seemed the best option.

Viola took me by surprise when she immediately nodded. "People were arguing outside, behind the library. It was pretty loud."

"What time?"

"Um ... ." Viola mimed tapping her bottom lip. "It was late. I was watching infomercials. They have a new pajama that essentially allows you to wear a blanket with feet. Did you know that? It's called the Snuggie."

"I've seen the commercials. Get back to the fight. Did you look outside?"

Viola shook her head. "I didn't know it was a big deal."

"Did you hear what they said?"

"I wasn't really interested," Viola replied. "I only know two people were arguing."

I thought about what Landon said regarding the body. "Are you sure it was two people? Could it have been three?"

"I'm pretty sure it was two."

That didn't mean that three people weren't involved. That simply meant that two people were talking. "Was it two women?"

"I honestly have no idea." Viola had clearly lost interest in the conversation. She focused on the window. "I'm going to see what they're doing."

"Wait!" It was too late. Viola, who I was convinced had some form of Attention Deficit Disorder, was already gone. "Well ... crap."

It wasn't as if she had information anyway, I told myself as I shifted to the couch. Exhaustion was about to overwhelm me and I needed to close my eyes. I told myself it would be for only a few minutes, but I slipped under relatively quickly. I needed a quick power nap to recharge myself. Landon said I was part of the team and I had work to do. I would get to that work as soon as I could hold open my eyes.

I WOKE TWO HOURS LATER to find Landon on the couch with me, his winter coat draped over us as a blanket, his body wrapped around mine. I had no idea when he joined me, but his breathing was regular in my ear and he slept hard. I was comfortable to let him rest a bit longer until I noticed movement in the doorframe between my office and the hallway.

Chief Terry, his face lined with weariness, smiled when he caught my gaze. "There are times I want to smack the boy upside the head for being … well … him. There are other times, like now, that I find him kind of endearing. I can't explain it."

I smiled at Chief Terry's fond expression. I wasn't sure if it was aimed at me, Landon, or both of us, but I was happy to see it. "Did you sleep at all?"

"I got two hours in my office. That's what we agreed to."

Two hours. Hmm. "I think that's when I fell asleep," I admitted ruefully, rubbing my cheek. "I didn't mean to do it. I was researching the symbols, but … ."

"You don't owe me an explanation," Chief Terry said. "You were wakened in the middle of the night. You need your sleep. Frankly, after seeing what you saw, I'm glad you can sleep."

"Did you sleep okay?"

Chief Terry's lips curved. "You don't have to worry about me. I slept fine. Your boyfriend obviously slept fine, too."

I risked a glance over my shoulder and found Landon stirring. "Did you sleep okay?"

"Like a rock," Landon replied, stretching. "I was too tired to even drool on you."

I giggled as Chief Terry scowled.

"See, that's why I prefer him sleeping to awake," Chief Terry said. "I hate to push you, but we need to notify the renaissance people."

I knit my eyebrows. "You haven't made notification yet?"

"We wanted to wait for a preliminary report from the medical examiner."

"And?"

"And she's dead," Chief Terry supplied. "We're not sure about cause of death. All the medical examiner can say at this point is that she was alive very close to when the killer started taking her blood, but he's not sure if that's how she died. We have to wait for that, but we can't wait to notify the family."

"That's the toughest part of your job, huh?" My heart went out to him.

Chief Terry shrugged. "It goes with the territory. Get up, Romeo."

Landon made a growling sound in the back of his throat. "Just a minute. I'm warm and comfortable. That means Bay is warm and comfortable, too. Do you want her to stop being warm and comfortable?"

"I want you to get up." Chief Terry refused to be distracted. "We have a full day."

"Yeah, yeah, yeah." Landon pressed a kiss to my cheek. "I was planning to buy you breakfast, but we have things to do. How about we meet for lunch and compare notes then?"

I nodded. "That sounds like a good idea."

"Good."

"Oh, speaking of ghosts, I talked to Viola," I said.

"When were we speaking about ghosts?" Chief Terry asked.

"We weren't, but there's never a good segue way for that."

Chief Terry snickered. "Good point."

"Anyway, she was watching television last night and said she heard people arguing outside," I supplied. "She didn't see who it was, but she was convinced it was only two people and they were close to the library. She also doesn't know if it was a man and a woman, two women, or two men, so … it's not a lot of help. You might want to look around outside the building for potential clues."

"Good tip." Chief Terry smiled. "What are you going to do with your morning?"

"I'm taking these photographs to Clove and Thistle," I replied. "I can't figure out what they are."

"Do you think it's wise to involve them?"

"I don't think it's ever wise to involve them," I replied. "But they have a better selection of books than I do."

"Oh." Realization dawned on Chief Terry. "I guess that makes sense. Be careful when you're with them. You girls seem to lose your heads when you decide you're going to investigate."

"I'm pretty sure I should be offended by that."

"I'm pretty sure you recognize the truth when you hear it," Chief Terry corrected. "Come on, lazybones. It's time to get to work."

Landon groaned as he rolled out from behind me. "He's kind of a tyrant."

I shrugged. "You guys work well together and you know it."

"I'm not admitting anything until I have some coffee." He gave me a quick kiss. "We'll meet you at the diner for lunch. Stay out of trouble."

"I always do."

Chief Terry scowled. "You never do. Why do you think we always tell you to stay out of trouble?"

"Because you're compulsive busybodies."

Chief Terry made a disgusted sound in the back of his throat. "Your sense of humor is only funny half the time. You know that, right?"

I smiled. "Which half?"

"Be good," Landon ordered, shuffling his feet against the floor as he snagged his coat. "Stay safe."

"You, too."

SEVEN

*J*grabbed three breakfast sandwiches and to-go cups of coffee from the bakery before winding my way to Hypnotic. It was early, but Thistle and Clove were already working. I had a few ideas to bounce off them and I figured bribing them was probably my best option.

"Something smells good." Clove, her brown eyes gleaming, smiled when I entered. The expression slipped quickly, though, upon scanning my face. "Are you sick?"

"Oh, that's that cousinly love I've come to expect," I teased, resting the drink carrier on the counter. "Is that your way of saying that I look like crap?"

Clove shook her head, her dark hair brushing across her shoulders. She was solemn. "No. You're really pale, though."

"I didn't get enough sleep." I rummaged in the bakery bag until I found my sandwich and then grabbed my coffee before planting myself on the couch in the middle of the store. "I'm sure you've noticed what's going on in the town square."

"Oh, we've noticed," Thistle said dryly. "It's hard to miss."

"We heard there was a murder." Clove talked around the lip of her coffee cup. "Thelma Hanson stopped in and said it was one of the renaissance people."

"It's the head woman," I corrected, wiping the corners of my mouth with a napkin. "Adele Twigg. That was her name. Landon got the call in the middle of the night."

"Who found her?" Thistle asked.

That was a very good question. "I don't know. I didn't think to ask. It was probably one of the people coming to town to open the bakeries. I'm meeting Landon and Chief Terry for lunch. I'll ask them to be sure."

"What happened to her?" Clove asked, her voice small. "Was it ... bad?"

"It was about as bad as it gets," I replied. "I don't think I've seen anything that bad since the body in the corn maze." My mind drifted back to the corn maze. It was more than a year ago. That's where Landon and I met. He was undercover, and I hated him on sight. Okay, I kind of wanted to kiss him before hating him, but it was an awkward situation all around.

"It was worse than the corn maze?" Thistle was understandably dubious as she took the chair at the edge of the sitting area. "What happened? The body was long gone by the time we got in."

"Thelma said they took the body away quickly because they didn't want anyone to see it," Clove added.

"I don't doubt that." I described the location of the body for them, refraining from going into grisly details. When I got to the part about the symbols, Thistle was eager for further explanation. "None of the symbols seemed to mean anything in the configuration I found them. Here." I handed over my phone. "I took photographs."

"I don't want to see them." Clove made a face. "I think I'll have nightmares if I do."

"No one will think less of you if you don't want to see them," I offered. Clove was the most sensitive Winchester so I wasn't surprised by her reaction.

"I'll think less of you," Thistle argued, furrowing her brow as she swept through the photos. "Oh, geez." Thistle made a horrified face. "I can't believe you didn't warn me this was on here."

"I told you that the symbols were written in blood," I snapped.

"Not that. I can handle that." Thistle held up the phone, revealing a selfie Landon took several days earlier. We were in bed – everything covered – but we looked comfortable and happy. "Now I'm scarred for life."

I snatched back the phone and openly glared. "Why can't you leave him alone?" I whined. "You're poking at him just to poke at him. It's not a good trait."

Thistle shrugged, unbothered. "He's extremely easy to unravel. I think it's funny. Marcus never freaks out. He's always calm."

"That's why you're a good match," Clove said sagely. "Sam and I never freak out either. That's why we're a perfect match."

Thistle and I shot her twin looks of doubt.

"You and Sam freak out over stuff," Thistle corrected. "You're like nervous dogs in a thunderstorm. It's beyond annoying."

Clove narrowed her eyes to dangerous slits. "Take it back."

"No."

"Take it back or I'll make you eat dirt," Clove warned. "I don't care how hard the ground is. If I have to go to the store and buy dirt for you to eat, I'll totally do it."

"Whatever." Thistle's expression was smug as she turned her attention back to me. "Landon and I will argue as long as we're sharing a roof. You know that. It won't change, so I don't see why you're whining about it."

I raised a finger in warning. "If you're not careful I'll let Landon off his leash and let him go to war with you. Right now you're the only one engaging in war. Landon hasn't been because he doesn't want to upset me."

"Oh, whatever," Thistle scoffed. "He's been a crying tool."

"Fine. You two are on your own." I held my hands up in a placating manner. "I have other things on my mind, including finding out what these other symbols are."

Thistle was blasé as she turned her attention to more serious matters. "I think it's some sort of alphabet."

"That's what I thought," I said. "Do you recognize it?"

"No, but we might be able to track it down." Thistle carried the phone to the counter and grabbed a pencil from the cup near the register. "I'm going to copy them and we'll go through the books this afternoon. We might get lucky."

"If that doesn't work, we could always ask Aunt Tillie," Clove added, earning horrified looks from Thistle and me. "What?"

"Why would we possibly want to involve Aunt Tillie in this?" I challenged. "She'll take over the investigation and get us in trouble."

"She'll also focus all of her energy on Mrs. Little," Thistle added. "As much as I hate Mrs. Little, I don't think she did this. Aunt Tillie blames everything on her."

"Well, the thing is, I do kind of need to talk to Mrs. Little," I said.

"Why?" Thistle was more curious than accusatory.

"Because I think there's something wrong with that Scarlet Darksbane woman."

"Of course there is," Thistle said. "You knew that the minute you heard her name. Darksbane. I mean ... only a freak looking for attention would choose that name."

"It's not just that." I told them what I witnessed when leaving the scene before dawn. "The thing is, what was she doing out there? I mean ... I understand why Mrs. Gunderson was out and about. She bakes for two hours before she even opens her shop. The same with the other bakers. What was Scarlet doing out there, though?"

"That's a pretty good question," Thistle said, rubbing her chin. "Did she look at you?"

"She did. She had a ... smug ... look on her face. I don't know how else to describe it."

"Smug like she just killed someone and pointed the finger at witches?" Clove asked.

I shrugged, noncommittal. "Smug like she was happy about something," I clarified. "I can't say she looked happy about murder as much as she looked intrigued by all of the activity."

"We definitely need to find out more about her," Thistle said. "Did Landon run the search he promised you?"

"I think he has a few other things on his mind," I pointed out.

"True." Thistle tapped her bottom lip. "You said Aunt Tillie was following her, right?"

I nodded. "I guess. She could've been following Mrs. Little. It wouldn't be the first time. She was acting odd – even for Aunt Tillie – so I think she was more interested in Scarlet."

"I hate to say it because it goes against every self-survival instinct I have, but we should probably talk to Aunt Tillie about this," Thistle said. "She might know what the symbols stand for."

"She might," I conceded. Going to Aunt Tillie for help seemed wrong, and not just because she was prone to dramatic fits. She would lord it over us for years if we asked her to join in on our cause. "Let's talk to Mrs. Little on our own first," I suggested. "She won't talk to us if we have Aunt Tillie with us."

"She won't talk to us anyway," Thistle argued. "She's still ticked about that wishing well thing."

"Which was not our fault."

"No, but we ultimately embarrassed her in the end, and she's still steaming," Thistle said. "She's not going to give us what we want."

"No, but she might let something slip," I pointed out. "She's not good at hiding things."

"That's true." Thistle cocked her head to the side. "Okay. I'll go with you. Clove can watch the store."

"Good." Clove let loose with a relieved sigh. "The last thing I want to do is have Mrs. Little focused on me. She can focus on the two of you."

"You're so brave," Thistle intoned. "You're like a superhero, you're so courageous. Has anyone ever told you that?"

"Not only am I going to make you eat dirt, but once I'm done you're totally going to be dead to me," Clove warned.

"Like that's a bad thing," Thistle scoffed. "Come on, Bay. We might as well track down Mrs. Little now. She won't be easy to deal with no matter when we approach her. I'd rather get it over with."

She wasn't the only one.

MRS. LITTLE STOOD BEHIND the counter in her ostentatious unicorn shop. She seemed distracted, intent on a sheet of paper next to the cash register. She lifted her head when she heard us enter, a welcoming smile on her face. The smile slipped when she realized who she was dealing with.

"What do you want?"

"Oh, it's so good to see you, too, Mrs. Little," Thistle cooed, her voice positively dripping with faux sugar. "I can't tell you how much I appreciate your welcoming energy and giving heart."

"Cut the crap, Thistle," Mrs. Little barked. "We all know I like you girls about as much as you like me. What are you doing here?"

Mrs. Little wasn't in the mood to play games. That was good. I wasn't in the mood either. "We're here about the dead body in the town square," I said. "It was Mrs. Twigg, the woman you introduced at the meeting last night."

Mrs. Little's expression was hard to read. I was almost positive she was surprised, though. "Mrs. Twigg? Are you sure?"

I nodded. "She's dead. Someone killed her and strung her up in the middle of the square. Then they drained her blood and used it to draw symbols on the pavement."

Thistle leaned closer. "Are you supposed to be spreading that around?"

"Mrs. Gunderson was there and saw everything," I whispered back. "It will be common knowledge by lunch."

"Good point."

I kept my eyes on Mrs. Little. "Do you want to say something?"

"I don't know what you want me to say, Bay," Mrs. Little said, regaining a bit of her lost composure. "It's terrible news. I didn't know Mrs. Twigg that well, but she seemed like a nice woman."

"I didn't get a chance to talk to her at all," I said. "I was hoping to interview her for a story regarding the festival, but … I guess that's up in the air now."

"What's up in the air?" Mrs. Little was obviously distracted.

"The festival," I replied.

"Why would the festival be up in the air?" Mrs. Little snapped. "We have a signed contract. The renaissance group can't back out for any reason. That includes death. I'm very thorough when I draw up the contracts."

"But . . . ."

"No." Mrs. Little shook her head to cut me off. "The festival will go on just the way I said it would. If the renaissance people try to break that contract I'll have them in court so fast they won't know what hit them."

"Wow." Thistle made a horrified face. "You're all heart, Mrs. Little."

"I'm a businesswoman, Thistle. I don't have the option to have a heart."

"Yes, she's in the cutthroat world of unicorn sales, Thistle," I drawled. "We have no idea how competitive that world can be. Cut her a little slack."

Thistle snorted at my sarcasm. "Whatever."

"If that's all, girls, I have work to do." Mrs. Little turned her attention back to the sheet of paper she was studying when we entered.

"That's not all," I said, drawing Mrs. Little's eyes back to me. "We have some questions about Scarlet Darksbane."

This time, rather than registering surprise, Mrs. Little puffed out her chest and beamed. "I thought she would get your attention."

"What is that supposed to mean?"

"It means that you're threatened and I knew you would be," Mrs. Little replied, not missing a beat. "I found a real witch, someone to fight the Winchester family, and she's going to be popular in this town. You all have reason to be afraid now, don't you?"

Hmm. That wasn't the response I expected. "Well . . . ."

"Why should we be afraid?" Thistle challenged. "We don't even know this woman."

"More importantly," I added. "Does she realize that you brought her to town to start a war with us?"

"Scarlet is her own person." Mrs. Little adopted a prim tone that was more telling than she wanted it to be. "She makes her own decisions. If you're wondering whether or not I warned her about your family, I did. She told me not to worry. She's handled dark witches in the past."

Thistle snorted, catching Mrs. Little off guard. "We're not dark witches, you ninny. I mean … how many times have we saved you even though we can't stand you?"

"That's neither here nor there," Mrs. Little countered, tugging down her blouse to smooth it. "You only saved me because you didn't want the police asking questions you can't answer. I'm onto your game. You practice dark magic. You talk to ghosts and … do other terrible things like dance naked in a field."

"We do all of those things," I confirmed. "That doesn't mean we're evil."

"And Tillie?" Mrs. Little challenged. "How can you even pretend she's not evil?"

"Because she's saved our lives more times than we can count," Thistle replied. "Aunt Tillie is … unique. She's not evil. She has evil tendencies, but she's not outright evil unless you're related to her."

"I should've known you would stand up for her," Mrs. Little muttered.

"And we should've known this whole Scarlet Darksbane thing was a dig at us," I shot back. "I don't really care why she's here. I need some information, though, and you're going to provide it."

"What kind of information?"

"Well, for starters, what's her real name?"

Mrs. Little balked. "Scarlet Darksbane."

"That's not a real name," Thistle argued. "She made that up. How can you even pretend to think that's a real name?"

"Your name is Thistle," Mrs. Little pointed out.

"I wish people would stop bringing that up," Thistle grumbled under her breath.

"We need background information on her," I said, remaining on point. "You must have something."

Mrs. Little's expression was unreadable as she stared me down. "Why do you really want to know?"

"Because I think it's a bit too coincidental that we had a murder that seems to point toward pagan leanings right after Scarlet Darksbane hit town."

Mrs. Little's eyes widened to saucer-like proportions. "You can't be serious. You're going to blame this murder on her?"

"I didn't say that," I cautioned. "I merely said I wanted more information on her."

"Well, I'm not going to share that information." Mrs. Little folded her arms over her chest, defiant. "I won't help you hurt that poor woman."

"Especially when you're hoping she'll hurt us," Thistle said, shaking her head. "I hope you know what you're doing, Mrs. Little. Making enemies of us isn't a smart move."

"When have you ever been anything but my enemy?"

"I guess you'll find out." Thistle grabbed my arm and yanked me toward the door, waiting until we were on the sidewalk to speak again. "So ... we need to talk to Aunt Tillie over dinner tonight."

I expected the reaction. I couldn't argue with it. "She'll go nuts on Mrs. Little before this is all said and done."

"It's hardly the first time that's happened. Besides, Mrs. Little deserves it. She's losing her mind or something."

Sadly, Thistle had a point. "Okay. But once we unleash Aunt Tillie it'll be up to us to watch her."

"Oh, what's the fun in that? Let's unleash her and see what happens. That sounds like fun."

Well, she wasn't wrong.

EIGHT

"There you are."

Landon and Chief Terry were already seated at a table when I entered the diner.

"Hi." I took the open seat between them. "How was your morning?"

"Long," Landon replied, sliding his arm over the back of my chair as he regarded me. "How was yours?"

"Well, I bought breakfast sandwiches for Clove and Thistle so we could chat over a few things – I had bacon on mine, in case you're interested – and then we talked to Mrs. Little."

"Bacon, huh? I only got a doughnut. I'm jealous."

"You had three doughnuts," Chief Terry corrected. "That's cop food, by the way. You should love it."

"I like a doughnut as much as the next person, but I much prefer bacon." Landon leaned closer. "Give me a kiss."

"Why?"

"Because I want one."

"You just want to see if I smell like bacon." I gave him a quick kiss despite Chief Terry's dark expression and then leaned back in my chair. "Better?"

"I'm totally getting a bacon cheeseburger for lunch," Landon muttered. "I need the protein."

"Yeah, because you would've steered clear of the bacon otherwise," I teased, earning a poke in the ribs for my lame joke.

"Why did you go to see Margaret?" Chief Terry asked.

I shrugged, noncommittal. "I just had a few questions."

"That's not going to work," Landon argued. "You must've had a specific reason to see Mrs. Little."

"I wanted to see what she knew about Mrs. Twigg." That wasn't a total lie. I did want information on Mrs. Twigg. I simply wanted information on Scarlet Darksbane as well.

"Did she give you anything?"

"Not really. She was full of herself."

"She always is." Chief Terry extended his long legs under the table as he reclined. "We notified the family, but we didn't get anywhere questioning them."

"Why?"

"Because they're a little dramatic," Chief Terry replied. "They're ... loud."

"What does that mean?" I was honestly curious.

Landon snorted, amused. "Let's just say that the Twigg family makes the Winchester family look sedate. They were ... wailing and stuff."

That was a frightening thought. "So you have to go back and interview them after lunch?"

"We do, and I want you to come with us," Landon said, causing me to jerk my head in his direction.

"You want me to go with you?"

Landon nodded.

I narrowed my eyes, suspicious. "Why?"

"Because you've got a solid investigative mind," Landon replied. "You read people well and you're good when it comes to asking intuitive questions."

"Why really?"

Landon made an exasperated sound in the back of his throat. "That is why. Really and truly."

I was dubious. "You usually try to keep me out of investigations unless you think you can use me," I argued. "You must think I can help you in some way."

"I think that statement reflects badly on me as a boyfriend," Landon groused.

"No, the kiss because you wanted to see if she tasted like bacon reflected badly on you as a boyfriend," Chief Terry argued. "In this instance, you're being straightforward and she's being a pain. You guys confuse emotional responses sometimes. I don't get it."

I pursed my lips. "You really want me to go with you to read people?"

Landon shifted on his chair, uncomfortable. "Yes."

"And?" I prodded.

"And they're a little off, and you live in a family full of off people," Landon replied. "The entire troupe is made up of Twiggs."

"I'm not sure what that means," I hedged.

"It's one family," Chief Terry supplied. "We're talking sons, daughters, in-laws, cousins, nieces, nephews. They're all related, and I'm a little confused at how they're related. They all said how they were related, but it seems a little confusing unless you have a family tree in front of you."

"They started this wailing when we told them about Adele's death," Landon said. "It was like one of those funeral scenes you see in movies with a bunch of braying women throwing themselves on the ground to get attention."

"Yeah, you probably shouldn't give the eulogy." I patted his arm and smiled. "Just for the record, I would totally bray for you."

"Aw, how sweet." Landon grinned. "It wasn't normal grief, at least as far as I could tell. They wanted time to regroup before questioning and they were loud in arranging it. That's the feeling I got, anyway."

"We found the response strange," Chief Terry said. "Now, no two people grieve exactly the same way, but the entire family fell apart when we told them. It wasn't the sort of thing that I can easily describe ... and it's certainly not something I want to experience again."

"Okay, so you want me to go along and ... what?"

"See if they're faking."

"How am I supposed to know that?" I challenged.

"You read people," Landon repeated. "You see things that we don't. Plus, well, they're all wearing pagan jewelry and stuff. I recognize some of the symbols from the square this morning, but others I don't. I figured you might know what they mean."

"So you do have an underhanded reason for wanting me with you."

"I always want you with me, because I'm a good boyfriend," Landon countered. "Every moment without you is hell."

"You're laying it on a bit thick."

"I knew that the second I said it." Landon's smile was flirtatious. "Will you go with us?"

I nodded without hesitation. I was curious to meet the family. This way I wouldn't get in trouble for sneaking around behind Landon's back to get the goods on the Twiggs.

"I'd love to go with you," I said. "I don't have much else to do anyway. Thistle is trying to track down those symbols I couldn't identify. She thinks they look like they come from an alphabet, too. We're trying to figure it out."

"That sounds like a solid plan." Chief Terry leaned forward. "How did Margaret react to Adele's death? I planned to talk to her myself, but you stole my thunder."

"I'm sorry." I wasn't really, but I batted my eyelashes so he'd refrain from barking at me for interfering. Chief Terry rarely lost his temper, but when he did it was almost always because I stuck my nose in where it didn't belong. "I thought she'd probably heard by now, but she had no idea on the identity of the victim."

"Was she upset?"

"Yeah. She looked shocked at first. She recovered pretty quickly, but I could tell it surprised her. Then she did a big song and dance about how the troupe can't back out of the festival because they signed a contract."

"Really?" Chief Terry arched an eyebrow. "That's interesting."

"I thought it was kind of mean."

"Oh, it's definitely mean," Chief Terry confirmed. "It's also helpful. If the contract requires the Twiggs to stay in town that gives us more time to sort through all of the weird threads in their relationships."

That sounded ominous. "Do you think they're suspects?"

"Stranger murders are pretty rare," Landon pointed out. "They're the exception rather than the rule."

"So that means you think Mrs. Twigg knew her killer," I mused. "It would be easier for everyone to swallow if an outsider was the culprit."

"We don't know anything yet," Chief Terry said. "Hopefully we'll know more this afternoon."

"Yeah, that would be nice." I flicked my eyes to the diner door when the bell overhead jangled, cringing when I caught sight of Scarlet Darksbane. I exhaled heavily as I sank in my chair, hoping she wouldn't look in our direction. Landon slid me a sidelong look as I did, suspicion lining his face.

"What did you do?"

"What are you talking about?" Chief Terry asked.

"She did something," Landon replied. "She's shrinking in her chair."

"That is a horrible thing to say about the woman you supposedly love," I hissed.

"Oh, that won't work on me," Landon countered. "You did something. Spill."

I didn't get a chance to answer, because Scarlet picked that moment to stalk to our table. She didn't look happy as her gaze bounced among our faces.

"Can we help you, Ms. Darksbane?" Chief Terry asked, his tone amiable.

"I don't know," Scarlet replied, pinning me with a gaze. "I was looking for Ms. Winchester because I have a few questions."

"What questions?" Landon asked.

I briefly wondered if I could escape without him noticing. The odds weren't great, but if I moved fast enough ... .

"I want to know why she was questioning Mrs. Little about me and insinuating that I might be a murderer," Scarlet said.

Crap. So much for escaping.

"Oh, well, fun." Landon gripped my wrist to make sure I didn't flee. "I think someone left a little something out of her story when telling us about her day. What do you think, Terry?"

Chief Terry's eyes sparkled. "I think we should all have lunch together so we can get caught up," he said. "How does that sound to you, Bay?"

It sounded terrible. I was caught with no hope of evading the question, though, so lying was my only option. "That sounds great," I gritted out.

"I thought you'd think so."

SCARLET SAT ACROSS FROM ME, Landon and Chief Terry to either side. Her gaze was heavy as it pored over my face. She waited until we all ordered to speak again.

"So, you think I'm a murderer, huh?"

That was a loaded question. "I have no idea what you're talking about," I lied. "I said nothing of the sort."

"That's not what Mrs. Little said." Scarlet's tone was accusatory.

"Mrs. Little is mentally unbalanced," I supplied. "I don't like to speak ill of the crazy, but she's three feet shy of a balanced cauldron."

Landon shot me a warning look. "Mrs. Little isn't a fan of the Winchester family." He chose his words carefully. "She's ... um ... a bit anxious at times."

"That's code for crazy," I added.

"Bay." Landon shook his head to quiet me. "You'll have to excuse Bay, Ms. Darksbane. It's been a long day and we're exhausted."

The look Scarlet shot Landon was full of flirtatious energy. "Please. Call me Scarlet."

I fought to keep from throwing up in my mouth. "Oh, gag me."

Chief Terry flashed me an amused grin before smoothly taking over the conversation. "Tell us a bit about yourself, Scarlet. What made you decide to move to Hemlock Cove?"

"Well, this area is famous in certain circles," Scarlet enthused. If I had to guess, she was in her early thirties. The way she reacted to the question made her seem much younger. "I've always been a proponent of the craft, and when I had a chance to move to a community that not only doesn't frown on my lifestyle but embraces it, well, I couldn't pass up the opportunity."

"The craft?" Landon knit his eyebrows. "I'm not sure I understand."

"Witchcraft," Scarlet supplied. "I'm a witch … just like everyone else in town."

If she thought everyone in Hemlock Cove was a real witch, she had another thing coming. "Someone said you wanted to move to town earlier, but because we didn't have any open retail space you were forced to wait. Why didn't you settle someplace else instead?"

"Because I wanted to live in Hemlock Cove," Scarlet replied. "This place is magical. You're a witch, right? Tell me you don't feel the magic."

I was a witch pretending to be a person pretending to be a witch, so that was a difficult question to answer. "I feel a lot of things here," I replied, narrowing my eyes when I caught Chief Terry's gaze roaming Scarlet's long legs. "Right now I'm bordering on an ulcer."

Chief Terry forced his eyes to me, surprised. "Do you feel sick?"

"She's just being Bay." Landon rested his hand on my knee under the table. Whether he meant for the contact to bolster or quell me, I wasn't sure. "Where did you grow up, Scarlet?"

"Ohio."

"Where in Ohio?"

"Oh, around." Scarlet was being purposely vague. "But I'm happy to be here now."

"Even though we just had a brutal murder?" I asked pointedly.

Scarlet met my gaze. "That's certainly a tragedy. Still, I've been to several big cities. The crime rate in Hemlock Cove is surely smaller than places like Chicago or Detroit, right?"

"You might be surprised," I muttered.

"It's a pretty safe area," Landon said. "There will be issues wherever you choose to live, but Hemlock Cove is warm and wonderful."

"How long have you lived here?" Scarlet asked, effectively cutting me out of the conversation as she focused all her attention on Landon.

"I've only technically lived here about two weeks," Landon replied. "During the past year, though, I've come to think of Hemlock Cove as my home."

"Because you visit a lot?"

"Because Bay is here." Landon's simple answer caused my growing anger to abate. Er, well, at least a little.

"You're lucky," Scarlet said, flicking her eyes back to me. "You caught yourself a good one."

"I didn't really catch him," I said. "I like to think we caught each other."

Landon smiled indulgently. "Actually, I believe I caught her. I'm the lucky one."

Scarlet didn't look convinced. "Even though she accuses random newcomers of being murderers?"

"I didn't say you were a murderer," I snapped, agitation taking over. "I merely asked about your background."

"You asked Mrs. Little about my background," Scarlet corrected. "You could've asked me about my background and saved both of us a little effort."

"Meh. I believe anything worth doing is worth doing right."

"What does that mean?"

"It means that Bay's blood sugar is low and she needs lunch," Landon answered for me. "She's had a rough day. I brought her with me to the crime scene this morning, and I'm starting to think it was a bad idea. She seems a bit ... upset."

"Really? You took your girlfriend to a crime scene?" Scarlet seemed intrigued. "Why would you do that?"

Wait a second ....

"Because I wanted her help," Landon replied, ignoring the tilt of my head as I stared at Scarlet. "She's very good at figuring things out.

She's the smartest woman I know, and when Chief Terry explained that there might be ritual aspects to the scene I thought she might be able to help."

"You seem to admire her a great deal," Scarlet noted. "I can't say that I'm not a little jealous."

"I do admire her," Landon confirmed. "She's very good at what she does, and most of the time she has impeccable manners."

"I must bring out the worst in her." Scarlet licked her lips in what I assumed she thought was a tempting manner. That was about all I could take.

"Why did you act so surprised when Landon said he took me to the scene?" I asked, catching everyone off guard.

"I'm sorry." Scarlet adopted a blank expression. "I'm not sure what you're getting at."

"You seemed surprised," I pressed. "You acted as if you didn't know I was there ... or that there were ritual aspects to the scene."

"I still don't understand," Scarlet hedged. "Why wouldn't I be surprised? I've never heard of an FBI agent taking his girlfriend on cases."

"Bay ... ." Landon was confused.

I held up my hand to still him. "It's just ... you were there this morning," I prodded. "I saw you on the sidewalk. You were behind Mrs. Gunderson and you were watching the scene."

"You were there?" Landon leaned forward, intrigued. "What were you doing up at that hour?"

Scarlet's face twisted into something hideous for a split second before she smoothed her expression and forced a smile. "I couldn't sleep. It's a new town and I'm excited to be here. When I heard all of the hoopla, I had to see what was going on."

"I see." Landon darted a curious look in my direction, clearly waiting to see if I would press her further.

I had every intention of pressing Scarlet Darksbane. I wanted more information before I did it, though. "Oh, well, it must've been quite the midnight extravaganza for you."

"It was terrible."

"Hmm. The thing is, you looked right at me," I reminded her. "I know you saw me."

"Of course I saw you." Scarlet forced a smile. "I simply forgot you were there."

She was lying. For what reason, I couldn't say. "Well, I'm sure it was hard for you to wrap your head around. No one expects to wake up to murder right after they move to a small town."

"Definitely not." Scarlet played with her empty straw wrapper before turning to Chief Terry. "Tell me about the town."

"What do you want to know?" Chief Terry asked.

"Anything you can think to tell me. I want to know everything about my new home."

Scarlet purposely stared at Chief Terry while Landon watched me. When I shifted my eyes in Landon's direction, I found overt curiosity staring back. He knew better than questioning me in front of Scarlet. He would wait until we were alone to do that.

Scarlet was definitely up to something. That didn't make her a murderer, of course, but she told a lie that was easy to disprove. How could that possibly benefit her?

NINE

"*W*here are we going?"

I hopped in the back seat of Chief Terry's official vehicle and fastened my seatbelt as Landon and Chief Terry got settled.

"The husband is out at The Dragonfly," Chief Terry replied. "The troupe members are spread out, but the immediate family is there, so that's where we'll start."

"Great. I can see Dad at the same time." I was making a concerted effort to spend more time with my father, smooth the frayed edges of our relationship. This would allow me to get a visit out of the way and I wouldn't look suspicious to the guests at the same time.

"I'm glad it worked out for you." Chief Terry's response was muted, although I couldn't decide if that was because we were heading out to question the family of a murder victim or the fact that he disliked my father. They had a bit of a competition going. It was probably inevitable given the fact that Chief Terry picked up my father's slack after my parents divorced when I was a kid.

"So, do you want to talk about lunch?" Landon asked as Chief Terry navigated toward the main highway.

I knew he wouldn't let that slide. "I had a really good Reuben," I said. "I liked it."

Landon made a face. "Not that."

"Oh, well, you'll have to be more specific."

In truth, lunch was a tedious affair. Scarlet did her best to act sweet and innocent, flirting with Landon and Chief Terry whenever the opportunity arose. She also evaded questions like a pro. I figured I was the only one at the table to notice, but it was fairly obvious – and unbelievably aggravating. That was on top of the fact that she kept "accidentally" rubbing her foot against mine. I couldn't help but wonder if she was aiming for Landon and catching me instead, but I kept the suspicion to myself. Of course, by the end of the meal I came off looking aggressive and obnoxious despite my best attempts to appear friendly. Being a Winchester, I was used to that.

"Why didn't you mention that you saw Scarlet at the scene last night?" Landon caught me off guard with the question.

"I didn't know it was important. There were several people on the sidewalk watching when I left."

"Yes, but you specifically noted Scarlet's presence," Landon noted.

We were back to that pesky "feeling" business again. "I don't know. Maybe because whenever I'm around her I can't help being suspicious."

"Why?" Chief Terry asked, drawing my attention to him. "You clearly don't like her. You generally wait to get to know someone before disliking them. It's not like you."

"I can't explain it. Whenever I'm around her it's like someone is running fingernails across a blackboard. She makes me want to punch someone."

"Her?"

"And Mrs. Little."

Chief Terry smirked. "Well, if you don't like her, there must be a reason. Do you think she's the real deal?"

I shrugged. "How should I know?"

"You're a witch," Chief Terry pointed out. "I thought maybe it was like dogs or something. I thought you could identify a witch just by sight ... or smell ... or something."

That was the most ridiculous thing I'd ever heard. "It's not as if we walk around sniffing each other's butts."

"I'm pretty sure I didn't suggest that," Chief Terry said dryly. "I only thought you would, you know, recognize one of your own."

For some reason, the fact that he singled me out as something other than human irked me. It was probably the remnants of a lunch gone bad, but I was annoyed. "Whatever." I crossed my arms over my chest and stared out the window.

Chief Terry opened his mouth to say something – I'm sure it was an apology – but Landon made a throat-clearing sound and shook his head. I didn't miss the exchange, but it infuriated me all the more.

By the time we pulled in at The Dragonfly I was in a righteous snit. Landon opened my door and helped me out, giving my face a searching look before resting his hands on my shoulders.

"You don't do well with a lack of sleep," he said after a moment. "I know you're cranky, but there's no reason to take it out on Terry."

Guilt swamped me. "I'm not." I scratched the side of my nose before leaning over and poking at my ankle. "I just ... I don't know what's wrong with me."

"You're tired. I'm going to make sure you get a solid ten hours of sleep tonight."

"Yeah, maybe." I wasn't convinced weariness was the cause of my annoyance. When my fingers brushed over something clinging to my sock I wrinkled my nose as I pulled out a small straw figure of some sort. I had no idea where it came from. It certainly wasn't there when I dressed in the middle of the night.

"What is that?" Landon asked, peering closer.

"It looks like straw," Chief Terry said, moving up next to me. "Were you two rolling around in straw or hay?"

"Not last time I checked," Landon replied. "Straw makes Bay break out in itchy fits."

I stared long and hard at the figure. It looked like a small poppet, something witches imbued with occasional magic when they wanted to pass along an ill wish. We didn't use them in the Winchester household as a rule because my mother and aunts didn't like them. That didn't prevent Aunt Tillie from sneaking in the occasional poppet when she really wanted to mess with someone. This did not look like her work.

"Do you guys have one of those evidence bags?"

Chief Terry gave me a considering look. "Why?"

"I just ... I need one."

"Okay." Chief Terry retrieved a small bag from his glove compartment and handed it to me so I could secure the poppet inside. I placed it on the floor of Chief Terry's vehicle, and the minute I released it I felt better, more like myself.

Hmm.

"What is that thing?" Landon asked, his eyes heavy on mine. "You look ... freaked out."

"I don't think 'freaked out' is the correct term," I said. "However, I think that's an ill wish."

"What does that mean?"

"Like a voodoo doll?" Chief Terry asked, confused.

"Kind of," I confirmed. "It's a poppet of some sort. It was clearly made by a witch."

"Aunt Tillie?" Of course Landon automatically assumed that. Aunt Tillie wasn't above a good curse. "I prefer it when she makes you smell like bacon. I'll talk to her about it."

I opened my mouth to argue the point and then snapped it shut. "I'll talk to her."

"Why keep it?" Chief Terry asked. "I'd think you'd want to destroy it. Is that what was making you so cranky?" He tried to make a joke of the question, but I could tell he was serious.

"Yeah. The thing is ... I have no idea how I ended up with it poking out of my shoe."

"Aunt Tillie is devious," Landon noted.

"She is," I agreed, "but I haven't seen her since lunch yesterday."

"Well ... maybe she sneaked into the guesthouse and put it in your shoe," Landon suggested.

That seemed a remote possibility. "Or maybe another witch put it there during lunch," I countered, remembering the way Scarlet's foot kept brushing against mine.

Landon's expression was somber. "Do you really think she did that?"

"I know you don't want to believe it because she's so pretty and bubbly, but I think it's a distinct possibility."

"Would that doll play into the symbols next to Adele Twigg's body?" Chief Terry asked. "Do they have anything in common?"

"I guess, in a roundabout sort of way," I answered. "I'm not sure, though. I want Aunt Tillie to look at it."

"Will she know what it is?" Landon asked.

I nodded. "She knows everything, and for once I'm not saying that simply because she's browbeaten me into it."

Landon cracked a smile. "It's okay, right? This isn't anything serious, is it?"

I immediately shook my head. I didn't want to worry him. "Poppets are usually considered kid magic. Aunt Tillie whipped one out when dealing with Mrs. Little a few times over the years, but they're not especially dangerous."

"That's good." Landon's eyes roamed my face. "What aren't you telling me?"

"Nothing. It's just ... poppets are generally created for one specific person," I explained. "If someone created that one specifically for me, it means Scarlet purposely sought us out over lunch."

"You don't know that she's the one who placed it on you," Chief Terry argued.

"Who else?"

"I don't know, but ... we don't have proof," he cautioned. "You need to be careful."

I cast another look at the baggie before forcing a smile. "Careful is my middle name. Come on. Let's talk to the Twiggs. Landon is right about me being tired and cranky. I'm not especially proud of it. I'm also sorry for snapping at you."

Chief Terry slung an arm over my shoulder. "It's okay. You were much worse as a teenager."

I was pretty sure that was an insult. "You said I was an angel when I was a teenager."

"Yes, well, I lied to you back then because I didn't want to hurt your feelings."

"Good to know."

"BAY! I DIDN'T know you were coming."

Dad greeted us in the lobby, gracing me with an energetic hug before tipping up my chin.

"You look tired. Why does she look tired?" he turned a set of accusing eyes toward Landon. My father's relationship with Landon was hardly easy, but they'd been making progress in recent weeks.

"We woke early because of the murder," Landon said. "I tried to make her go home and sleep, but she doesn't always obey orders like a good girlfriend should."

I made a face. "Nice."

Landon's lips curled. "At least you seem to be back to your old self. I guess that poppet thing was causing the PMS confusion, huh?"

My cheeks colored as Dad glanced between us. "Can you not say 'PMS' in front of my father?"

Landon was chagrined. "I'll do my best."

"I never understand half of what you guys are talking about," Dad said. "Still, while Landon and Chief Terry are questioning everybody, why don't we have some tea and catch up?" He was so earnest I could hardly say no, yet Landon wanted me close when he questioned people so I could read them.

"Well ... ."

"That sounds like a good idea," Landon interjected smoothly. "You guys can sit at one end of the table and we'll question people at the other. It will give you a chance to spend time with your father, sweetie, without being bored by the questions."

I realized right away what he was suggesting. He wanted me to watch but not draw attention to myself. That was no problem. "Sure."

It took my father only five minutes to get everyone settled, making sure that Landon and Chief Terry had a full pot of hot water as they worked through various family members before placing a cup of herbal tea in front of me and sitting to my left.

"So, what are you really doing here?" Dad kept a smile on his face as he lowered his voice.

I stilled, surprised by the change in his demeanor. "What do you mean? I'm here to see you."

"Seeing me might be an added bonus, but you're here to help Landon and Chief Terry," Dad countered. "I understand the scene downtown was brutal. Why are you involved in this?"

He didn't understand why Landon and Chief Terry brought me along for official questioning. He couldn't wrap his head around the nature of our investigative relationship. Heck, he had a difficult enough time understanding the myriad facets of our personal relationship.

"It's hard to explain," I dodged.

"Try me."

"Well, for starters, someone used Mrs. Twigg's blood to write a bunch of symbols on the pavement by where her body was dumped." I kept my cup in front of my lips to make sure no one could read them. Thankfully, the Twigg family seemed focused on Landon and Chief Terry. They also broke into occasional wails, so they paid very little heed to me.

"What kind of symbols?"

"They were a hodgepodge of pagan and Wiccan symbols," I replied. "It's as if someone Googled 'pagan symbols' and then used whatever popped up."

"Have you considered that's an actual possibility?"

"Of course. There were other symbols that seemed familiar, but I couldn't quite remember where I'd seen them before. Thistle is researching them."

"But you think you've definitely seen them before?" Dad seemed intrigued by the investigative play-by-play.

"I do," I confirmed, bobbing my head. "It's weird."

"The whole thing is weird," Dad said. "Not to get into an argument with you and Landon or anything, but do you really think it's a good idea for him to take you to a crime scene?"

It was a normal, and completely reasonable, question for a father to ask. It grated a bit all the same. "Landon and I are a team."

"I know you are. But this was a particularly brutal scene. Why did you have to see it?"

"He wanted me to look at the symbols."

"You're not an investigator."

"No," I agreed. "I'm not. Landon and I work together occasionally, though. He asked for my help, and I would never hesitate to offer it. If you want to know the truth, I like that he considers me part of his team."

"Bay, I get that and I think it's nice," Dad said. "But you didn't have to see that body. You'll be haunted by it."

Haunted was an interesting word. "I don't think she was killed there." I was talking more to myself than my father. "I think there would've been more of a mess if she was killed in the town square."

"It sounds like there was plenty of mess," Dad noted. "I heard there was blood everywhere."

"There was," I said. "It was used to make the symbols. It's not as if there were puddles of blood everywhere." I flicked my eyes to the end of the table when an older man – he looked to be in his late sixties, maybe early seventies – broke into body-wracking sobs as he talked to Landon. "Who is that?"

"Arthur Twigg," Dad replied. "The dead woman's husband."

I shifted my eyes to a sobbing woman standing in the corner. "And her?"

"Denise," Dad replied. "She's Adele's daughter."

"Did you spend any time with Adele before her death?"

"Not really." If Dad was bothered by the purposeful shift in the conversation, he didn't show it. "They were only here for a few hours before she left to go to the festival meeting," Dad explained. "Margaret Little picked her up."

"Did she drive her back?"

"I ... hmm." Dad broke off, tilting his head to the side. "I don't know. I can't say that I remember her returning, But I wasn't really looking. Once we got everyone settled, we retired to our private library upstairs and left them to have the run of the inn."

"So you don't remember her coming back?"

Dad shook his head. "That doesn't mean she didn't come back. I simply didn't see her return."

Hmm. I focused on Arthur as he talked to Landon.

"I don't know what happened," Arthur said. "I don't know how anyone could hurt my wife. She was the sweetest and nicest person who ever walked the planet. She was ... a giver. She was a nurturer. Why did this happen?"

"We're trying to figure that out, Mr. Twigg," Landon said. "We don't have any answers for you yet. I'm sorry."

"Then what are you doing here?" Arthur challenged. "Why aren't you out looking for the monster who killed my wife? It's someone who lives in this town. You should be able to figure it out."

"We're trying," Landon said, his eyes bouncing to me before returning to the grieving husband. "I swear we'll find answers. We won't rest until we know who did this."

"That won't bring her back," Arthur lamented.

"No, but it will allow you to put it behind you," Landon said. "We're looking for answers. As soon as we know something, we'll share those answers with you. You have my word on that."

TEN

*L*andon and I returned to the guesthouse once we were finished at The Dragonfly. By unsaid agreement, we both tumbled into bed for a nap before dinner, rolling against one another and falling asleep within minutes.

I woke before him, smiling when I felt his breath on my face. I left him to sleep, carefully climbing out of bed and closing the door before joining Thistle in the living room. She was intent on her laptop and barely looked up when I entered.

"What are you looking at?"

"Well, for starters, I figured out what those symbols are," Thistle replied.

I arched an eyebrow, impressed. "That was fast. How did you figure it out?"

"Don't bend over backward giving me accolades," Thistle said, placing the laptop on the coffee table before grabbing a book from the floor. "Here." She handed the book to me and I opened it at the spot where she'd left a bookmark.

"Oh." Realization dawned. "It's the Theban alphabet."

"We should've recognized it, right?" Thistle rubbed the back of her neck. She looked as tired as I had felt two hours ago. "Aunt Tillie tried to make us learn it when we were kids."

"Yeah, we put the effort in for about a week because we thought it would mean we could write back and forth in code." I smiled at the memory. "Then we realized Aunt Tillie could read it so it wasn't really a code."

"Yeah, then you suggested we learn Klingon and we studied that for a week," Thistle said. "Sadly, Aunt Tillie can read Klingon, too. Who knew she was multilingual?"

I chuckled as I leaned back on the couch. "Have you figured out what the symbols indicate?"

"I'm working on it right now," Thistle replied. "I got distracted by something else."

"What?"

"A chatroom."

I pursed my lips. Thistle wasn't exactly the chatroom type. Okay, if they had a chatroom for people who like agitating other people, she'd be the moderator. Random chatrooms certainly weren't her thing, though. "What were you doing in a chatroom?"

"I didn't specifically set out to find a chatroom," Thistle replied. "I was Googling Scarlet Darksbane."

Oh, well, now we were getting somewhere. "What did you find?"

"Well, she doesn't seem to have an online store," Thistle started. "I found that odd. One of the first things Clove and I did when we opened Hypnotic was create a website. We sell as much online as we do in person now. I even checked Etsy because we're broadening our horizons there in the next couple of weeks, but I couldn't find anything."

"I had no idea. That's good for you guys."

"Yeah, I'm going to create a page just for my artwork," Thistle added. "I'm hoping to start selling paintings and sculptures."

"You're very talented."

Thistle smirked. "You're just saying that because you don't want to instigate a fight."

"No, I'm saying it because it's true."

Thistle waited.

"I also don't want to deal with a fight," I added after a beat. "It's been a really long day. I've even taken two naps. I can't remember the last time I took two naps in one day."

"You needed the sleep. I wouldn't worry about it." Thistle returned her attention to the laptop screen. "So, when I couldn't find a shop I started looking for Wicca boards. A lot of the younger people think being a witch is fashionable and I thought I might be able to find mention of her if I searched those boards."

"Did you?"

"It took a bit," Thistle replied. "On something called Wicca 411 I found an entire thread devoted to her."

The way Thistle was dragging things out – something she picked up from Aunt Tillie – told me she'd found something of interest. "You get more like Aunt Tillie every single day. You know that, right?"

"That won't make me tell you what I found," Thistle warned.

Daughter of Hecate, she was a pain in the rear end! "Thistle, I've rested up," I warned. "I will totally drag you outside by your hair and make you eat dirt."

"The ground is hard. Good luck with that."

"I'll find a way."

Thistle snorted. "We both know I'm stronger than you. In the end, you'll be the one eating dirt."

I wanted to argue, but she had a point. "Whatever. You suck."

"You suck more."

"You both suck," Landon announced, shuffling out of the bedroom. His black hair was tousled from sleep and he wore an old T-shirt from his high school days that was a bit too small in the shoulders. I thought he looked kind of cute, but the look Thistle shot him said the exact opposite.

"Please don't start," I begged. "I cannot deal with a big fight here when I know there's going to be another big fight up at the inn for dinner tonight."

"What fight are we having at the inn tonight?" Landon asked, placing a blanket over both of us as he settled on my other side. "Did I miss a Winchester argument?"

"Not yet, but the day is young," Thistle replied.

"So why is there going to be a fight?" Landon is often slow when he first wakes.

"Because Aunt Tillie will be there," I answered simply. "You could've slept longer."

"I missed you in the bed." Landon grinned as I shot him a dubious look. "What? I did. I also heard you two talking and am curious what you're up to."

"Thistle found out what those symbols I couldn't recognize were. They're part of the Theban alphabet – which is a pagan alphabet of sorts – although we're still trying to figure out what the message was."

"Hey, that's something." Landon snagged my hand. "That hardly sounds like something to fight about."

"We weren't fighting," Thistle said. "We were simply discussing the finer points of dirt eating."

"That sounds … normal."

"We were also discussing Scarlet Darksbane," I added. "Thistle found mention of her in an online chatroom."

"Do I even want to know what you were doing looking for Hemlock Cove's newest witch in a chatroom?" Landon asked.

"It's always good to know your enemies," Thistle pointed out.

"I didn't realize you'd both decided that Scarlet was your enemy."

"You saw what I found in my shoe," I protested. "How can you say that she's not our enemy?"

"I'm not suggesting that we shouldn't watch her," Landon clarified, refusing to let go of my hand when I tried to draw it back. "I'm simply saying that she hasn't done anything yet to invoke the Winchester family ire stick."

I was taken aback. "Ire stick?"

"You know. It's a stick that you use to beat people who irk you." Landon mimed hitting Thistle with an invisible stick for emphasis.

"Oh, I totally want an ire stick now," Thistle enthused.

"You and me both." I giggled when Landon shot me an amused look. "You brought it up."

"Yes, and now I wish I hadn't." Landon shifted to face me. "You don't know that Scarlet Darksbane is doing anything nefarious."

"She put a poppet in my shoe," I reminded him.

"See, you say that thing is a poppet," Landon argued. "To me it looks like a small clump of straw."

"You had a poppet in your shoe?" Thistle was intrigued. "Do you still have it?"

"Yeah." I retrieved the baggie I grabbed from Chief Terry's vehicle from the table by the door – I was so tired upon returning home that I'd almost forgotten about it – and wordlessly handed it to Thistle.

Landon held up the blanket so I could get comfortable a second time, his gaze never leaving Thistle's face. "What do you think that is?"

"It's not naturally occurring," Thistle replied immediately. "Someone tied string to it to make it look like a person. How do you explain that?"

"I don't know." Landon slid a sidelong look in my direction. "She was acting odd before she found it."

"How?"

"She was ... cranky."

Thistle barked out a laugh. "She's always cranky. She gets that from Aunt Tillie."

"That's rich coming from you," I muttered under my breath.

"Let's not lose focus," Landon interjected quickly. "If this is a poppet, what was it supposed to do?"

"It could be anything," I replied. "The second I locked it in the bag, though, I felt better. Before that I thought I was going to have a pounding headache and I was massively irritated with Chief Terry. I never get irritated with Chief Terry."

"That's true. He seems oblivious to your anger."

"He would never risk a beating with the ire stick," Thistle teased. "Why do you think Scarlet Darksbane put it on you?"

"Because she just happened to show up at lunch," I said. "She heard we were questioning Mrs. Little about her and she wanted to confront me."

"Did you rip her hair out of her head?" Thistle asked. "By the way, that's totally a weave. I saw her walking down the street and there's no way her hair is real."

"Her boobs are fake, too," I added.

"Geez. You two sound like jealous mean girls." Landon pressed the heel of his hand to his forehead. "Bay, I was sitting right next to you throughout lunch. Scarlet was across from you. She didn't have a chance to slip that thing on you."

"She could've done it when we were distracted," I argued. "Her foot brushed mine several times. I thought she was trying to play footsies with you. I wasn't around anyone else who could've put that poppet on me today. I woke up with you. I drove to a crime scene with you. I spent hours in my office alone. Then I went to Hypnotic. Then I went to Mrs. Little's shop with Thistle, but she stayed behind the counter and we were the only ones there. Then I met you for lunch. When else could it have been put on me?"

"I don't know," Landon said, shifting uncomfortably. "It's just ... she seemed friendly."

"You only think that because she spent the entire meal fawning all over you and Chief Terry," I groused. I knew I sounded petulant, but I was convinced Scarlet Darksbane was going to cause a lot of trouble. "You think she's too pretty to be evil."

"Oh, give me a break," Landon said. "I happen to think you're much prettier, and I know there are times when you're evil."

"Like when?"

"Like when you don't have a good night's sleep and regular meals," Landon answered, not missing a beat. "I can't wait until you get a full night's sleep tonight, because you're extremely cranky."

"Whatever." I didn't bother to hide my scowl as I directed my attention to Thistle. "Just tell me what you have."

Thistle placed the baggie containing the poppet on the table and tapped a few buttons on the laptop keyboard. "It's kind of weird – and I think Landon is going to think I'm playing into your feverish delusions – but what you just said makes sense given what I found in the chatroom."

I puffed out my chest and zinged Landon with an "I told you so" stare, which he promptly ignored.

"Just tell us," Landon said. "At this point, I want her to be right, otherwise she's going to do something kooky."

"I don't do kooky things," I snapped.

"Says the woman who conducts séances and goes on adventures with her great-aunt, who just happens to wear a combat helmet while swinging a big stick and blowing a whistle."

"Oh, well, when you say it like that … ."

Landon grinned as he grabbed my hand. "You need to chill a bit, sweetie. I get that you're worked up with everything that's happened, but there's no reason to jump to conclusions – at least not yet."

"That's very wise." I squeezed his hand. "You're totally full of crap, though." I turned to Thistle. "Lay it on me."

"Well, it seems that Scarlet – and I can't find any mention of a real name, so we're going to need Landon and Chief Terry to get that information for us – was part of some Wicca circle in Grand Rapids several years ago."

"Grand Rapids?" I rolled my neck. "Didn't she say she was from Ohio?"

"I can't remember exactly what she said, but that sounds right," Landon said. "She kind of evaded that question."

"I wasn't sure you'd noticed."

"Cops and FBI agents make people nervous, Bay," Landon said. "I've found most people don't want to talk about themselves when law enforcement is around. They think it's a form of entrapment or something."

"I never cared about stuff like that even after I found out you were an FBI agent," I pointed out.

"Yes, but you're a unique woman." Landon traced his fingers over my palm. "Hmm. That's weird. Now that I think about it, you did talk all of the time even after you found out who I really was."

"That's because she's chatty," Thistle said.

"That's because she reads people well," Landon corrected.

"Which means I'm reading Scarlet right," I pressed.

"Fair enough." Landon nodded. "What did you find, Thistle?"

"Well, it's hardly proof that you guys would use, but it's interesting all the same," Thistle replied. "Three different women in this chatroom claim they hired Scarlet for a personal cleansing, but it was only after she offered her services and they turned her down."

"What's a personal cleansing?" Landon asked.

"It's kind of like ... um ... a spa visit for your aura." Explaining magic to someone outside the circle was often difficult. "For people who suffer from runs of bad luck ... or family tragedy ... or even a series of nightmares, cleansings can help."

"Okay, go on."

"The thing is, all three of these women – and from what I can tell, they're lipstick witches at best – claim that they didn't have problems until Scarlet offered cleansings," Thistle said. "They accused her of creating the bad luck and then offering to swoop in to get rid of the bad luck."

"So it's kind of like a scam," Landon noted. "Wait ... what's a lipstick witch?"

"One in name only," I replied. "Aunt Tillie coined the term. It's for witches who dress up like witches but don't wear the underwear to match the ensemble."

"Yeah, you're just confusing me now." Landon stretched. "So the beef with Scarlet is that she offered her services for a fee, was turned down, created a situation where these people would have no choice but to say yes and then essentially collected the fee after all. Am I understanding what you're saying correctly?"

"That's basically it," Thistle acknowledged.

"I guess I can see where that would work," Landon said after a few moments of contemplation. "It's not as if these women could go to law enforcement and claim that a witch put a curse on them. They would've been laughed out of the building at best and locked up for a psych evaluation at worst."

I patted his knee. "Welcome to our world."

"I never really considered it that way." Landon chewed on his bottom lip. "I'll run a search on Scarlet if I get time tomorrow, but don't get your hopes up."

"That's all we ask." I forced a sugary smile. "I promise to reward you for your efforts if you come up with anything good."

Landon snickered. "You're rewarding me regardless." He shifted his eyes to the clock on the wall. "Starting right now, too. We have an hour and a half before dinner. That means you can wash my back in the shower."

"Is that a euphemism for something else?"

Landon's smile was lazy. "When are you going to learn that everything I say is a euphemism for something else?"

"I don't know. I'll give it serious thought, though."

Thistle made a derisive sound in the back of her throat. "He just told you that he's a pervert and you encouraged him to keep at it. You guys make me sick sometimes."

"Right back at you." Landon grabbed me around the waist as he swung me up from the couch. "Just think, soon you won't be here for us to make you sick."

"I'm really looking forward to that."

"So am I."

That made three of us. "No fighting," I ordered. "I'm too tired for fighting."

"I'll fix that right up," Landon promised. "In an hour, you'll forget you were even tired."

That sounded like an impressive feat, one I looked forward to.

ELEVEN

We decided to walk to The Overlook for dinner. The guesthouse was situated on a parcel of land that had been in my family for ... well ... as long as I knew. The walk took only ten minutes when the weather cooperated. It wasn't exactly warm out, but we were running out of time to enjoy the great outdoors. Within two weeks or so, winter would invade and we would have no choice but to hunker down and wait it out.

"It's not so bad." Landon wrapped his hand around mine as we walked. "It's a little brisk, but not unbearable."

"Yeah." My mind was elsewhere, so I kept only half an ear on what he said. I couldn't get the idea of Scarlet Darksbane trying to curse me out of my head. Sure, it seemed farfetched when you looked at it from an analytical point of view. Why focus on me, after all? Still ... the suspicion was right there and I couldn't shake it.

Landon, seemingly oblivious, kept babbling. "And then I'm going to join the circus and run off with the bearded lady so we can live happily ever after."

"That sounds fun," I said mindlessly.

"Hey, Bay?"

"Hmm."

"If you don't start paying attention to me I'll be the one to make you eat dirt."

The threat was enough to cause me to jerk my head in his direction. "What?"

"You haven't listened to a word I've said," Landon pointed out. "I've been a delightful conversationalist, too. You're hurting my feelings."

I didn't miss the hint of mischief floating in his eyes. "Sorry. I ... was thinking."

"About Scarlet Darksbane?"

I saw no reason to lie. "Yeah."

Landon's face was serious. "Do you think she's trying to hurt you?"

"I don't know. Maybe she's running the same scam she did before. Maybe she was just trying to irritate me because she thinks I believe she's a murderer."

"Do you believe she's a murderer?"

That was an interesting question. "I don't know. We don't know enough about Adele Twigg to come up with a motive. We need more information. Plus, you said it yourself. The way Adele's body was strung up, it either had to be a man, more than one person or Wonder Woman."

Landon smirked. "We'll figure it out. I don't want you driving yourself crazy with the notion that Scarlet is guilty, though. I'm starting to regret taking you to the scene."

"You wouldn't have the information you already have if it wasn't for me."

"True." Landon squeezed my hand. "I like working with you, but I'm not a fan of you putting yourself in danger. Be extra careful for me while this is going on, okay? Whoever did this ... ."

"Is a monster," I finished, exhaling heavily. "I've got it."

"Then we'll let it go for now." Landon and I lapsed into comfortable silence as we walked, Landon breaking it first. "When are you going to move into the big office at The Whistler?"

The question took me by surprise. "What do you mean?"

"Sweetie, you're going to be the owner in less than a month. That means you get the big office."

I hadn't really considered that. Several weeks ago, thanks to a twist of fate and Landon's determination to get my boss Brian Kelly out of my life, I signed a purchase agreement to take over The Whistler. We would close on the sale right after the holidays and, come the first of the year, I'd be a business owner rather than an editor and reporter.

"You think I should move to the big office?"

Landon smirked. "Yeah. That's your office. You can even fit a bigger couch in there for when we need naps."

I chuckled. "Only you would focus on that."

"That's not what I'm focused on," Landon corrected. "I only thought of it this afternoon when we were both crowded onto that small loveseat. Still, you deserve the big office. You should be happy to move into it."

"It's a lot to think about," I admitted. "I never thought I'd be the one in charge."

"Really?" Landon cocked a dubious eyebrow. "You've enjoyed bossing me around from the beginning."

"Ha, ha." I sucked in a breath. "I'm kind of excited. I know it sounds lame because I'll be doing the exact same job I was before – plus I'll have to handle the advertising – but it still seems like a big deal."

"That's because it is a big deal, Bay." Landon slowed his pace as we approached The Overlook's back door, the entryway that led to the family living quarters. My family waited on the other side, but he clearly needed one more moment of privacy. "I want you to be happy. I think this is something you've always wanted. It's okay to be excited."

"I know. It's just ... in a few weeks I'll be the boss. It's all going to be on me. I'll be making all of the decisions."

"Does that worry you?"

I opened my mouth to answer, but nothing immediately came out. I wasn't sure what to say. "I guess 'worry' isn't the word I would choose," I said after a moment. "I am excited ... and nervous ... and a little bit freaked. It's a big deal. Other than you moving in, it's the biggest thing that's happened to me since I moved back to Hemlock Cove."

Landon smiled. "Things are coming together for us quickly. I like that. It's important that you take a moment to enjoy what's about to happen. You'll remember this for a very long time.

"The work will always be there," he continued. "This excitement will change over time. I think you'll always love being the boss. It won't always be new, though. Take some time to enjoy what's about to happen."

"I will." I leaned forward and planted a firm kiss on the corner of his mouth. "Thank you."

"You're welcome. Now ... shall we place a bet on whether or not Aunt Tillie is in a mood?"

I grinned. "She's always in a mood."

"Let's see what the mood du jour is, shall we?"

We didn't have to look far. My great-aunt, who just happened to be dressed in a pair of dragon leggings that I knew for a fact my mother confiscated months ago, sat on the couch glaring at the television.

"What is the Declaration of Independence," she yelled at Alex Trebek.

"What is the Louisiana Purchase," one of the television contestants said.

"Correct."

"Son of a ... what a load of crap!" Aunt Tillie muttered. "What are you two doing? I see you over there loitering."

"We weren't loitering," Landon countered quickly. "We were merely taking cover from the dragons."

"Yeah, I thought Mom took those leggings away from you." I slipped out of my jacket and hung it on the coatrack. "I believe the term 'dire consequences' was bandied about if you tried to wear them again."

Aunt Tillie was blasé. "I'm not afraid of your mother."

That's not exactly how I remembered the conversation. While it was true that Aunt Tillie didn't normally fear anyone, if she kowtowed to anyone it was Mom. My mother had a certain way of bending wills that was both uncomfortable and truly frightening.

"Yeah, but I watched her throw those away," Landon noted. "She said they were obscene. Given where the dragon is hiding his gold when you bend over, I can't help but agree."

"That shows what you know," Aunt Tillie shot back. "I'm wearing a sweater that covers the dragon's cave."

"Even when you bend over?" I challenged.

"I'm old. I don't bend over very often."

"That's what I thought." I made a tsking sound as I rounded the couch, digging in my pocket to retrieve the poppet and tossing the baggie in Aunt Tillie's direction. "What do you make of that?"

"You brought it?" Landon rolled his eyes. "You're going to get her going."

That was the plan. He simply didn't need to know it. "I found that in my shoe today. It was actually kind of attached to my sock."

Aunt Tillie narrowed her eyes as she stared at the baggie. "Did anything happen before you discovered it?"

"Landon said I was mean to him."

"I said cranky," Landon corrected. "You were cranky."

"Oh, I'm kind of sorry I missed that." Aunt Tillie opened the bag and sniffed. "Hemlock."

"Isn't hemlock poisonous?" Landon asked, concern flooding his handsome features.

"Yes, and this is water hemlock, to boot. But she didn't ingest it. She's okay." Aunt Tillie flipped over the baggie. "It doesn't have a face."

"What does that mean?" Landon asked.

"It means it probably wasn't made for Bay," Aunt Tillie replied. "It looks generic, as if someone decided after the fact to point it at her. Did you have a headache while it was on you?"

I nodded. "How did you know?"

"It's a sloppy effort," Aunt Tillie replied. "Whoever did it doesn't know what they're doing."

"What are you talking about?" Thistle asked, walking through the back door with Marcus on her heels. "Is that the poppet?"

I nodded. "She says it's laced with hemlock."

"Well, that would explain the headache you were complaining about." Thistle moved closer. "Did you tell her where you think it came from?"

"Not yet."

"Where did it come from?" Aunt Tillie's eyes gleamed. "Please say Margaret Little. If she's finally dipping into the occult I don't have to hold back. I've been waiting for this day since long before you two were born."

"Oh, geez." Landon shook his head and moved toward the kitchen. "I'll be in the dining room. I've heard this story a few too many times today."

"I'll go with you," Marcus offered. "I'm just not in the mood to plot."

"That's why you two are better off as men than women. You're not adventurous enough to be women," Aunt Tillie shouted after them.

"Oh, that's the sweetest thing you've ever said to me," Landon drawled.

Aunt Tillie ignored his sarcasm. "We'll be at the table in a few minutes. Tell Winnie not to complain. Don't tell her what I'm wearing, by the way. I want it to be a surprise."

"Great. I'm looking forward to it."

I waited until Landon and Marcus disappeared through the door to speak again. "It's the new witch," I volunteered. "Landon thinks I'm crazy, making stuff up in my head, but I know it's her."

"Who?"

"Scarlet Darksbane. Mrs. Little's new witch. She's the only one I was near today who could've done it."

"If it's her, she doesn't know what she's doing," Aunt Tillie noted. "It's as if she found a book and decided to let that lead the way."

"You were following her last night," I noted. "Why?"

"I was technically following Margaret last night," Aunt Tillie corrected. "I didn't hear about the new witch until I was already downtown. Once I did hear, though, I had to follow."

That sounded about right. "Thistle looked her up. She's been accused of running a scam. It's probably one you've heard about before."

Thistle repeated what she found for Aunt Tillie's benefit. "If she's here, she has to be worried about real witches finding out what she's doing."

"That's only if she believes witches are real," Aunt Tillie countered. "From her perspective, she might believe everything is a game. I mean ... come on. Everyone in Hemlock Cove takes on a witch or warlock persona at some point. Scarlet might believe that's the extent of it."

"She does treat it like a game," Thistle conceded. "Why else would she pick that stupid name?"

"I don't think you have room to talk, Thistle," Aunt Tillie said. "I've often wondered what your mother was smoking when she named you. I think it had to be something much stronger than what you can find in my special garden."

I pursed my lips to keep from laughing. "I think she's a scam artist, but Mrs. Little had to tell her about us, because Scarlet seems keen to make inroads with me."

"She wants to be friends with you?" Aunt Tillie was understandably dubious. "Why? If she knows we're real witches, why would she want anything to do with us?"

"I'm not saying she knows," I clarified. "I'm saying that Mrs. Little told her we're real witches and she probably thinks that Mrs. Little is nutty. Still, she wants to be tight with Mrs. Little, because she probably thinks that Mrs. Little has a lot of say when it comes to businesses and promotions around here."

"That's very good thinking." Aunt Tillie wagged a finger in my direction. "Margaret probably brought in this Scarlet because she thought she was a real witch. Scarlet probably convinced her of it. Margaret is such an idiot; she wouldn't recognize a real witch if one cracked her over the head with a broomstick.

"Scarlet probably has her own agenda," she continued. "She wants to ingratiate herself into Margaret's world, get a feel for the town, and then run the curse scam on residents and tourists. She could clean up, because the tourists are predisposed to believe that nonsense."

"Why move against Bay so fast, though?" Thistle challenged. "That would draw attention."

"Because Mrs. Little is telling her we're real witches," I said. "Scarlet probably doesn't believe in real witches – just what she reads in books – and thinks we're her competition. She probably wants to take us out."

"Exactly." Aunt Tillie bobbed her head. "She thinks she can intimidate us. I can't wait to explain to her why that won't work."

I snorted. "And how are you going to do that?"

"We need to find out her real name," Aunt Tillie replied. "Can't you make your FBI honey find out?"

"He's going to look, but he's more interested in solving a murder right now."

"Well, that's just ridiculous," Aunt Tillie muttered. "Doesn't he know that we could be dealing with a dark witch here?"

I furrowed my brow. "You just said she was a fake witch."

"A fake witch with a book who managed to make a curse work," Aunt Tillie clarified, shaking the baggie for emphasis. "That means she has some sort of power. If she's coming here, that means she wants to take over the town."

"Oh, geez. Here we go." Thistle pinched the bridge of her nose. She was used to Aunt Tillie's theatrics. "Let's focus on finding out Scarlet Darksbane's real name first, huh? If we can't bug Landon to do it for us, then we'll have to do it ourselves."

Uh-oh. I sensed trouble. "What do you have in mind?"

"We have to break into her shop and go through her paperwork," Thistle replied, as though burglary was part of our everyday repertoire.

"We can't do that," I protested, internally cringing at how Pollyannaish I sounded. "It's against the law."

Aunt Tillie and Thistle exchanged amused looks.

"I guess Bay is out," Aunt Tillie said. "She's a good girl now that she's living with the fed."

She was trying to manipulate me. It wasn't going to work. Er, well, it probably wasn't going to work. "I didn't say that."

"We'll do it ourselves," Thistle said. "We'll take the risk and have all the glory. Bay is a good girl now. We mustn't corrupt her."

Son of a … ! "Fine." I blew out a sigh. "I'll go with you. How do you suggest we do it without Landon and Marcus finding out?"

"That's easy," Aunt Tillie replied. "You need to sneak out when they're sleeping."

I balked. "That's a terrible idea."

"No, it's a good idea," Thistle argued. "We can sneak out, break in, and get back without them even knowing."

Thistle has a strong personality, but every once in a while she does something asinine. She lets Aunt Tillie talk her into absolutely ridiculous adventures and then we all end up caught and in trouble. By the way, we almost always get caught.

"I don't know." I made a face. "Landon will be angry if he finds out."

"Well, if you need to do what Landon says then we fully understand." Aunt Tillie's tone was sickeningly sweet. "You're Landon's girlfriend first now, and a witch second."

"I hate you," I muttered under my breath. "Fine." I was resigned. I couldn't let them go without me. "If we get caught, though, I'm totally blaming you guys."

"We need to get Clove in on the plan, too," Thistle said. "She'll be ticked off if we leave her out."

"She'll also complain the entire time," I pointed out.

Thistle shrugged. "That's her way."

"It's definitely her way," Aunt Tillie said. "I'll pick you up outside the guesthouse at midnight. Marcus and Landon won't even know you're gone. Trust me."

I didn't trust her. That was the problem. "Okay, but you can't wear those leggings."

"Definitely," Thistle said. "If you wear those leggings, someone will see us."

"I'm not new." Aunt Tillie rolled her eyes. "Good grief. You'd think I'd never broken into a store with you before. I know what I'm doing. I have everything under control."

"Yeah, we can have that engraved on our tombstones," I muttered. "Landon will definitely kill me if he catches us."

"You leave Landon to me," Aunt Tillie said. "I know exactly how to handle him."

Those were frightening last words.

TWELVE

J found Thistle waiting for me in the living room after I crept out of my bedroom shortly before midnight. True to her word, Aunt Tillie came up with an idea to make sure Landon and Marcus didn't wake. She planted a lullaby in their heads – something that magically sang them to sleep, so to speak – and Landon was so deeply entrenched in slumber when I slipped out from beneath the covers I worried he might drown in his own drool.

I had dressed in all black, stalling by the front door to tuck my blonde hair beneath a knit cap before tugging on a pair of dark boots. Thistle watched, her face impassive.

"Do you feel guilty about this?"

Thistle shrugged. "Yes. Mostly because Marcus wouldn't have stopped me from going. He would've complained a bit, offered to come with me, and then let me do what he knew I was going to do anyway. What about you?"

"Oh, Landon would've tried to stop me," I replied. "He can't willingly encourage me to break the law. He won't be happy when he finds out what we've done."

"Finds out? How will he find out?"

"I'll tell him."

"Oh, you're the worst criminal ever," Thistle complained, making a face. "If you keep this up I'm cutting you from my crew."

"What crew?" I hauled on my mittens and followed Thistle out of the house, casting a wistful look over my shoulder as I thought about Landon sleeping alone in our bed.

"My robbery crew." Thistle said it as if I was the slow one for not understanding what she was getting at. "I mean … when the apocalypse comes, we'll need a crew of capable robbers so we can steal stuff. I'm certainly not doing the bulk of the work myself."

She had a point.

Aunt Tillie was in her idling truck when we got to the end of the driveway. She, too, was dressed in black, a dark combat helmet covering her silver curls. She clenched a cigar in her mouth, ignoring the way Thistle let loose an exaggerated cough before climbing into the truck.

"You look like a bad movie cat burglar," Thistle announced, glaring as she fastened her seatbelt.

"And you look like a witch pageant reject," Aunt Tillie shot back, purposely blowing a smoke ring in Thistle's face.

I coughed, lowering the window despite the cold. "Since when do you smoke cigars?"

"Since I decided that's my new business venture," Aunt Tillie replied. "I'm going to start manufacturing my own cigars. Actually, I have a few business ventures in the works. This is simply the first."

I narrowed my eyes, instantly suspicious. "What do you put in these cigars? By the way, if the answer is pot I'll need to drive."

"Oh, stop being such a kvetch," Aunt Tillie said, shifting her truck into gear. "Did you see I got my new plow on?" She gestured toward the front of the ancient vehicle. The only way Mom allowed her to plow was if she had something old and sturdy to drive around town. The old Ford could take a good jolt and barely rattle, and with Aunt Tillie behind the wheel there was a lot of jolting. "I'll be loaded for bear as soon as the snow flies."

"Yes, we always look at you and think 'loaded,'" Thistle said dryly. "Are we picking up Clove or is she meeting us there?"

"She's meeting us there," Aunt Tillie replied. "She said she didn't trust me to come out to the Dandridge. Apparently Sam is afraid of me or something. I don't get it. I've never been anything but nice to the boy."

I let loose with a derisive snort. Sam Cornell was Clove's live-in fiancé. None of us trusted him when he first hit town. We slowly grew to like – and even trust – him. Aunt Tillie held out longer than most of us, though.

"You're kind of mean to him," I pointed out.

"I am not."

"You are, too."

"I am not."

"You are, too," Thistle snapped. "You know you are. Stop denying it. I hate it when you deny the obvious."

"You're on my list," Aunt Tillie warned, pulling onto the main highway that led to Hemlock Cove. "You're so on my list."

I ignored her tone and stared out the window. "What lullaby did you put in Landon's head?"

"I selected a little something special for him," Aunt Tillie replied. "I believe it includes something about fighting the law and the law winning. I thought that would make him happy."

"Oh, geez. Now he'll be stuck with that song in his head for the entire day tomorrow."

Aunt Tillie wasn't bothered by the charge. "That's what happens when you're 'The Man.'"

"One of these days 'The Man' is going to lock you up," I warned.

"I can't wait for that day." Aunt Tillie's smile was serene. "That's the day pigs will fly out of my behind. Guinness will come calling to put me in the record books that day, too. It'll be glorious."

Sadly, she was probably right.

THIS WASN'T THE FIRST time we'd broken the law with Aunt Tillie. This wasn't even the first time we'd broken into a store with her. She used to like to mess with Mrs. Little and she used us to help her when we were younger. Even as teenagers and adults, she often included us. It was something of a ritual.

Because this wasn't our first time, Aunt Tillie opted to park in the alley behind Hypnotic without prodding. If someone should see us, we could always claim Thistle and Clove forgot something at the store. It was after midnight, so the town was dead. Even the police station was empty, the county taking over 911 duties after nine.

Aunt Tillie killed the lights and deftly hopped out of her truck. She was so much more spry when she was about to break the law. I took a moment to search the alley for Clove, glancing over my shoulder and back before meeting Thistle's eyes in the murky light behind the Hypnotic door.

"Where is she?"

Thistle shrugged. "She probably backed out. She's a real baby when she wants to be. She probably complained to Sam and he talked her out of coming. That would be just like her."

"I heard that!" Clove, her expression mutinous, stepped out from behind the trash receptacle on the other side of the narrow alley. She was tiny – not even five feet tall – so I missed her when I originally searched. "I'll make you eat trash if you're not careful."

Instead of having the grace to be abashed, Thistle snickered. "You're such a baby."

"And you're an evil ... witch."

"You were going to switch out that W for a B, weren't you?" Thistle wasn't bothered by Clove's tone. "It's okay. I can handle it. Lay it on me."

"I'm done talking to you." Clove held up her hand and focused on me. "By the way, I'm not talking to Thistle, but I blame you for this late-night excursion, Bay. If you weren't obsessed with the new witch we wouldn't have to do this."

"You didn't have to come," Thistle reminded her.

"Oh, right." Clove wrinkled her ski-sloped nose. "It was either come and complain the entire time or stay home and complain all day tomorrow while listening to you guys tell stories about your grand adventure without me. You know I don't like being left out."

"That's exactly why we invited you," Aunt Tillie said, patting her shoulder. "That and the back window for the former cauldron shop is really tiny. You're the only one who can fit through it and open the door for us."

Clove's mouth dropped open. "Excuse me?"

"The last time I checked that store had an alarm on the front door and a security chain on the back," Aunt Tillie replied, unruffled. "We need you to go in through the back window and slide the chain. Generally we could use magic to unlock the door, but that won't work on the chain."

I stared so hard at Aunt Tillie she was forced to return my gaze. "What?"

"You know an awful lot about the security system in that store," I noted. "Would you care to share with the class how you learned these things?"

"Not even remotely." Aunt Tillie clapped her hands. "Get moving, Clove. The sooner you get the door open the sooner we can take on the pervasive evil threatening our small town and rid the world of dark witches."

"Wait … I thought we were operating under the assumption that Scarlet was a fake witch, not a dark witch," Clove said.

"We are." Thistle gestured toward me and herself. "Aunt Tillie is in her own little world."

"And proud of it," Aunt Tillie said. "Now get that door open, Clove. I don't have all night to waste. I need my beauty sleep." Aunt Tillie looked Thistle up and down. "And so does your cousin."

"You make me want to kick you sometimes," Thistle muttered.

"I'm fine with that."

After much grumbling, a few kicks and a loud screech when she fell through the window, Clove yanked open the back door from inside and scalded us with her best "I hate you and I'm going to make you pay" look. "I hope you're happy," she growled.

Aunt Tillie used her hip to prod Clove to the side as we entered. "I'm always happy. I'm a genuinely happy person."

"And we're back to Aunt Tillie being loaded again," Thistle intoned, causing me to snicker.

"If you want to be loaded, all you have to do is ask." Aunt Tillie pressed a flask into Thistle's hand as she presented me with a flashlight. "Find everything we need to find."

I made an exaggerated face. "Why me?"

"Because you're a reporter and know what we need to look for," Aunt Tillie replied. "I'll watch Thistle while you work. It will be fine."

Thistle shot me a triumphant look as she belted back a shot of whatever Aunt Tillie had in her flask. On a whim, I grabbed it from her and took a drink – liquid courage never hurts – and then I flicked on the flashlight. The alcohol had quite a kick. I couldn't identify it, and I sputtered as I tried to swallow.

The store was in disarray, boxes scattered from one end of the display area to the other. Numerous folders rested on the counter, so that's where I headed first.

"Keep an eye on the front window," I ordered Clove. "If you see any headlights, tell us. We'll duck. Hopefully this won't take too long."

"You heard her," Aunt Tillie said, reclaiming her flask from Thistle when Clove turned a complaining look in our great-aunt's direction. "You're the lookout."

"Just for curiosity's sake, what is it that you and Thistle are doing this evening?" Clove asked, taking up position by the front window. "Why is it that Bay and I are doing all of the work?"

"Because in every group there's only one leader," Aunt Tillie explained. "I'm your leader."

"Oh, puh-leez," Thistle scoffed. "I'm the leader. You used to be the leader, but you retired."

"I haven't retired. Retirement is for old people."

"You are old," Thistle shot back. "You're as old as … well … old gets."

"I'm in my prime." Aunt Tillie's eyes flashed, causing me to watch her for a long moment. If she decided to pick an argument now, things would get out of hand quickly. Someone would definitely hear us, and we'd be in cuffs before we could escape the store.

"Prime what?" Thistle challenged.

"Condition," Aunt Tillie replied. "I'm middle-aged at best."

"Oh, are you listening to this?" Thistle grabbed the flask and took a long swig. "She's delusional. I think that cigar had more than nicotine and tar in it."

"It did," Aunt Tillie confirmed. "It had a bit of magic, too."

"I'm guessing magic is code for pot," I said, focusing on the top file. "That means she can't drive home. One of us will have to."

"I've got it." Thistle took another drink from the flask.

"Yeah, I think I'll be the one driving," I muttered, narrowing my eyes. "This is the purchase agreement for the property."

"For the record, no one is driving my truck," Aunt Tillie snapped. "It's mine, and you'll be walking home before I allow that."

"You deserve to walk home," Clove grumbled. "I wish I was home right now. Sam is warm in our bed and I'm stuck here with you people."

"Shut up, kvetch," Aunt Tillie ordered. "What does the purchase agreement say?"

"It's … interesting." I couldn't think of a better word. "Seymour Walton owned the property and he was pretty far behind on his payments when he decided to sell. Scarlet got this place for a song."

"What's a song?" Clove asked.

"Twenty grand."

"Are you kidding?" Thistle was flummoxed. "If I'd known that was all he was asking I would've bought it."

"Why do you need another store?" I asked, genuinely curious.

"Because our store isn't very big and this one is right next door," Thistle replied. "We could've put in a door and turned this into an art gallery."

Huh. That actually made sense. "Well, maybe you'll get lucky," I said. "We might be able to chase off Scarlet Darksbane. Then you can buy the space and expand."

"Definitely," Aunt Tillie agreed. "Does that purchase agreement give you Scarlet's real name?"

"She's listed as Scarlet Darksbane." I closed the file. "She might've legally changed her name. If so, we'll probably have to rely on Landon to get us the information."

"I don't want to do that," Aunt Tillie said. "He's unbearable when he has information we want."

"He's not unbearable," I argued, opening the next file. "He's ... cute. He's also at home ... alone ... and sleeping without me. I feel a little guilty about leaving him behind."

"Does anyone remember when we didn't have boyfriends to leave behind?" Thistle asked. "It used to be that we could sneak out whenever we wanted and never risk getting in trouble. I miss those days."

I snorted. "Whatever. You would cry without Marcus around to rub your feet."

"Oh, I would definitely miss him," Thistle agreed. "It was simply easier when we could break the law without wondering if we were going to get yelled at."

She had a point. I scratched my nose as I read the next file. "This is all purchase orders. She's ordering skull candles and Ouija boards, by the way. I think she's trying to copy your inventory."

"That slut!" Thistle looked to be one shot away from drunk.

I lobbed a pointed stare at Aunt Tillie. "How much has she had?"

"A little more than is probably healthy, but she'll live." Aunt Tillie wasn't bothered. "In fact ... did you hear that?" Whatever Aunt Tillie was about to say was forgotten as she tilted her head to the side.

"What do you hear?" Clove asked, her voice going shrill. "Is it the cops? Are we going to be locked up forever?"

"Get down!" I hissed, motioning with my hand. I'd yet to see or hear anything, but I didn't want to take chances with my freedom. It was going to be hard enough to explain my actions to Landon. If he had to bail us out of jail first, it would be even harder. "Just ... shh."

Everyone went silent, Clove hunkering close to the floor near the front window while Thistle and Aunt Tillie hid behind a box.

"Stop leaning on me," Aunt Tillie ordered. "You're drunk."

"You're drunk," Thistle shot back. "I'm completely on top of things. In fact ... whoops." Thistle toppled to the side, laughing hysterically as she hit the floor. "Okay, maybe I'm drunk."

"You're a pain in the butt is what you are," Aunt Tillie snapped. "I can't believe how much of a pain you are."

"Really? Because I can't believe what a pain all of you are."

The new voice caused me to swivel, my eyes going wide when I saw the figure in the doorway. I recognized Landon's voice right away, the tilt of his head signaling his annoyance. He didn't sound happy.

"I knew it was the fuzz," Aunt Tillie complained.

Landon took a step forward, standing under the emergency light along the back of the wall as he met my gaze. "You're in so much trouble."

Well, the best laid plans ... .

THIRTEEN

"The Man' is here. Run for your lives!"

Aunt Tillie wasted no time scrambling to her feet and trying to push past Landon. For his part, my boyfriend didn't look at all happy as he snagged her by the back of her shirt and held her at arm's length.

"Knock it off," Landon ordered, his voice weary.

"Run for your lives!" Aunt Tillie repeated. When none of us did as she ordered, she scorched each of us with a dirty look. "You're all on my list."

"You only wanted us to run so Landon would try to grab us and you could get away," I shot back. "Don't bother denying it."

"I would never deny it," Aunt Tillie supplied. "That's a great plan."

"You've run that plan on us, like, thirty times," Clove complained. "We got in trouble each and every time."

"That's why it works," Aunt Tillie pointed out. "A classic is a classic for a reason."

"Shut up," Landon ordered, his eyes never leaving my face. "So ... I woke up expecting to find you in bed with me but guess what happened."

"You woke up and found me gone," I replied without hesitation. "I'm ... ."

"Don't." Landon held up a finger to silence me. "If you apologize right now it'll mean absolutely nothing and only serve to further infuriate me."

I pursed my lips, unsure. "Well, then ... um ... I'm not sorry."

It was hard to gauge Landon's expression given the limited illumination, but I was almost positive he smiled slightly. That couldn't be right. It had to be a trick of my imagination.

"None of us are sorry." Aunt Tillie squirmed as she tried to get away from Landon. He refused to let go of her shirt. "Are you trying to get fresh with me or something? Is that why you're pulling on my shirt that way? You've already seen my boobs during solstice celebrations. I don't understand why you're being so shy now."

Instead of releasing her, Landon merely lowered his gaze. "I know what you're doing and it won't work. I do have a question, though."

"Shoot." Aunt Tillie smiled, clearly trying to placate him.

"Don't shoot," Thistle countered. "I'm too drunk to run and I don't want to die."

Landon shook his head. "How is she already drunk?"

"Aunt Tillie brought a flask," I answered, cringing at the expression on his face. "Don't look at me. I only had one sip."

"And I had none because they made me crawl through the window and then act as lookout," Clove groused.

"Yeah, good job on that," Thistle said dryly. "You're the lookout, and we got caught by the FBI. That's so much worse than getting caught by the regular cops."

She wasn't wrong, especially in this case. "Landon ... ."

"Shh." Landon lifted his free hand to his lips. "I need to talk to Aunt Tillie first, Bay. Don't worry, I'll get to you."

Oh, well, that was comforting. Or not.

"Tell me why you picked that song," Landon prodded. "That's what you did, right? You planted a song in my head."

"Kind of," Aunt Tillie hedged. "It's a lullaby. It's supposed to make you want to stay asleep."

"Hmm. That means you had this planned. When did you decide you were going to do this?"

"Before dinner."

"Technically, I never wanted to do this, but I'm my own worst enemy at times," Clove offered. "If they don't invite me I complain because I hate being left out. If they do invite me I complain because I'm a kvetch. Yeah, I said it. I'm a kvetch, and proud of it."

This time I was certain Landon's lips quirked. He was enjoying himself. That couldn't be right.

"Well, Clove, the good news for you is that you're done here for the night," Landon said. "I noticed your car is parked about a block down the street. You can go home now."

"Really?" Clove visibly brightened. "You're not going to arrest me?"

"Not tonight."

"Great." Clove happily blew past me, stopping long enough to shoot Aunt Tillie a haughty look before disappearing through the door. "For once being the kvetch works out."

Landon leaned back so he could stare out the door and watch her go. It took me a moment to realize what he was doing. Once Clove's headlights flashed in the alley, he turned his full attention back to us. "So ... where were we?"

"You made sure she got safely to her car," I noted.

Landon arched an eyebrow. "There's still a killer out there, Bay. Of course I made sure she got to her car. I'd expect someone to do the same for you."

"What about me?" Aunt Tillie asked.

Landon answered without hesitation. "You're on your own. Any killer would have to be crazy to go up against you."

Aunt Tillie beamed. "That's the sweetest thing you've ever said to me."

Landon rolled his eyes. "Whatever. Now, tell me why you picked the song that you did."

"Because you're 'The Man,'" Aunt Tillie replied simply. "I thought hearing a song about fighting the law and the law winning would make you sleep like the dead."

"Well, that backfired," Landon said. "It made me feel all excitable and manly instead. Guess what happened when I reached for my girlfriend."

Aunt Tillie was understandably disgusted when she realized what he meant. "You're a sick man."

"If you're just figuring that out you're not nearly as smart as I thought you were." Landon relaxed his grip and heaved a sigh. "What are you doing here?"

"It's a case of mass sleepwalking," Aunt Tillie answered. "It's freaky, but nothing to worry about."

"Really? You're all sleepwalking?"

"And drinking." Thistle looked around with blurry eyes. "What happened to the flask?"

"You're done with the flask," Landon said.

"You're definitely done with the flask," Aunt Tillie agreed. "I only have one belt left, and that's for me when it's time to go to bed. You're a little lush."

"Whatever." Thistle rolled her neck. "I want to go home. I'm tired. Is Marcus still there? Is he asleep?"

"He is," Landon confirmed. "I tried to shake him to find out where you guys had gone, but I couldn't wake him. Then I heard him humming. I recognized the song as a lullaby and realized what probably happened."

"How did you find us?" I asked, finding my voice.

"It wasn't that hard," Landon replied. "You've been obsessed with Scarlet Darksbane since she hit town. Where else would you go?"

"Are you angry?"

"Angry?" Landon furrowed his brow. "I haven't decided yet." He released Aunt Tillie completely. "Take Thistle home. You're okay to drive, right?"

Aunt Tillie made a disgusted face. "Of course I'm okay to drive," she said. "I'm not a drunkard like Little Miss Keg Stand here."

"Little Miss Keg Stand." Thistle snickered as she followed Aunt Tillie to the door. "That was a good one."

"Oh, geez. I prefer you so much more when you're surly with a lot of attitude," Aunt Tillie complained. "By the way, I'm not stopping completely at the guesthouse. You'll have to jump out when we get close. I'm tired and I want to go to bed."

Thistle mock saluted. "That sounds like a plan to me."

Landon watched them go, his arms folded over his chest. When he turned his gaze to me, his expression was hard to read.

"If it's any consolation, I knew it was a bad idea from the start," I offered. "I was against the lullaby, but ... you can't stop Aunt Tillie when she gets an idea in her head."

"Really? Are you going to stick with that story?" Landon's expression was mild.

"Fine. I didn't want to do it, but they basically called me a chicken until I did."

"Aunt Tillie and Thistle?"

I nodded.

"And you'd rather put a spell on me and lie than be called a chicken?"

Oh, well, if he was going to look at it that way ... . "On a normal day, no. I had to know, though. Scarlet Darksbane is driving me insane. I think that's what she wants. I need to know more about her."

Landon ran his tongue over his teeth as he regarded me. "Did you find anything?"

The question caught me off guard. "Just that she spent only twenty grand on this building, and Thistle is worked up because if she'd known she could get it so cheaply she would have expanded the store to include an art gallery."

"Well, buck up," Landon drawled. "At the rate you guys are going, you'll run Scarlet Darksbane out of town within the week and Thistle can have another shot."

"That's what I said."

This time there was no doubt. Landon's smile was reflected in the beam of my flashlight.

"Come here," Landon muttered, opening his arms.

I took a hesitant step in his direction. "Are you going to cuff me to you?"

"Not right now."

I slid into his embrace, sighing as he gave me a brief hug. "Wait … you're not angry?"

"I'm not happy, but I should've seen this coming," Landon replied. "You can't help yourself. When you add Aunt Tillie and Thistle to the mix, you're susceptible to suggestion."

"I think that makes me sound weak," I complained.

"You're not weak. You're just … excitable."

"You're excitable, too," I pointed out. "That's why the lullaby had the opposite effect on you and you woke up expecting action."

"Yes, well, you're going to fight the law later and the law is going to win."

Now it was my turn to smile. "You're really not angry?"

"I'm not happy, Bay," Landon cautioned. "But I honestly can't decide if I'm more upset with you or myself."

"Why would you be upset with yourself?"

"Because I saw it coming and did nothing to stop it," Landon replied. "You can't help yourself. It's in your blood."

"So … we're good?"

Landon shook his head. "You're going to owe me a freaking long massage and I'm going to make you rub yourself in bacon grease before you do it."

"That sounds kinky."

"That's how I roll." Landon moved away from me and focused on the folders he'd caught me going through. "Anything?"

This could be a trap. "What do you mean?"

"Don't be a pain," Landon chided. "We're already in here. We might as well look around."

I was flabbergasted. "Are you suggesting that we break into Scarlet's shop?"

"Absolutely not. You already broke into her shop. I happened to catch you. If Terry catches us, I'm totally blaming you. In fact, if anyone catches us I'm totally blaming you."

That sounded more than fair to me. "Deal." I used my hip to edge him away from the counter. "I'm looking through the files. See if you can get that safe open over there."

"What safe?" Landon grabbed my flashlight and tilted it in the direction of the wall. "Huh. You're right. She has a safe."

"It's one of those older ones," I pointed out. "You can usually get inside if you just listen while turning the dial."

"You know a lot about breaking into old safes," Landon noted.

"Aunt Tillie taught us when we were kids," I explained. "She was making plans to start her own female gang at the time and thought that turning us into bank robbers was the way to go."

Landon chuckled. "She sounds like the worst babysitter ever. I'll bet you had fun hanging out with her, though." Landon pressed his ear to the safe as he turned the dial, seemingly intent on what he was doing.

"You look like you already know how to break into a safe," I pointed out.

"I watched western movies, too. Now ... shh." Landon closed his eyes and listened as he turned the dial. His hair was messy from sleep – he hadn't bothered to brush it – and he looked ridiculously handsome. It wasn't the time to consider it, but the massage and the bacon grease didn't sound half bad.

It took everything I had, but I shook myself out of my reverie and returned to the folders. Unfortunately, they didn't offer much. Everything had to do with the purchase of the store and order forms for items not yet delivered. I couldn't find anything that pointed to the truth about Scarlet's past.

"Ha!" Landon reveled in his victory, doing a little dance as the safe door swung open. "You may bow to my superior safecracking skills, my dear."

"I might do that later," I said, shuffling to his side. The safe was nearly empty, except for a lone journal sitting on the middle shelf. "What's this?"

"Bay, wait."

It was too late. I had my hands on the journal before Landon could stop me. I flipped it open, narrowing my eyes when I realized the writing was in another language, perhaps even some sort of code.

"Huh."

"What is that?" Landon abandoned his earlier qualms about reading the journal and scanned the writing over my shoulder. "Is that the Theban alphabet you mentioned?"

"Maybe." I honestly wasn't sure. "I can't see it that well. If it is Theban, I think she modified it somehow. Aunt Tillie might know."

"Aunt Tillie is probably home in bed," Landon pointed out. "There's no way we can get her back here before people start showing up for work in the bakeries."

"We don't have to bring her here. We can take the journal to her." I moved to shove the notebook under my arm, but Landon snatched it back and scowled.

"You can't steal it."

"Why not?"

"Because I'm an FBI agent, and that's against the law."

"It's also against the law to break into a store in the middle of the night," I said.

"Yes, but I didn't do that," Landon argued. "I happened to stumble across you breaking the law. There's a difference."

"How? We're still in here."

"Yes, but I have plausible deniability if I need it. What? It works for me."

"You're an odd man."

"You love me anyway." Landon licked his lips as he stared at the journal. "Do you have your phone?"

I bobbed my head. "Yes."

"Take photos of the pages." Landon rested the journal on top of the safe and took the flashlight from me, aiming it at the pages. "Be quick. We need to get out of here soon."

"I still can't believe you're helping me break the law," I said, steadily snapping photos as Landon flipped pages and held the light. "This is the coolest thing we've ever done together."

"You're only saying that because I haven't gotten out the bacon grease yet."

I snickered ... and then sobered. "I'm sorry about the lullaby. I didn't want her to do it. I felt guilty, but ... well ... I had to look."

"I know that, Bay." Landon turned somber. "I don't know what I would've done in your position. I believe in following my gut. I also believe in following your gut. Your gut is telling you that there's something wrong with Scarlet Darksbane.

"I don't like it when you lie and cover your tracks, but in this case I don't know if I should be angry or relieved that I can pretend it was nothing more than a bad dream when we get home," he continued. "I need to give it some thought."

"So ... you're not going to yell?" His reaction was almost too good to be true.

"I guess we'll see when we're safely away," Landon said, turning to the last page of writing. "Got it?" I nodded and watched as Landon returned the journal to the safe and shut the door, twirling the dial before locking gazes with me. "It's time to go. In fact ... ." Landon broke off when a set of headlights flashed against the front window. A car pulled into one of the spots on Main Street. Landon reacted quickly, grabbing me around the waist and dragging me toward the back door.

"Who ... ?"

"Shh." Landon was quick, jerking me through the opening and shutting the door without making a sound. Before he could drag me down the alley I pointed toward the still-open window.

Landon nodded in understanding, pushing the pane shut at the same moment the interior store lights flashed on. He grabbed me, pressing me to him as he hunkered below the window. We were tight against the wall in case someone looked out. Whoever it was would have to open the door to see us.

"Scarlet?" I mouthed, uncertain.

Landon shrugged. "I don't know." He clutched me tightly as we waited to see if someone would come to the door. Explaining what we were doing would be nearly impossible.

I bit the inside of my cheek when I felt Landon's hands wandering. "Really?"

Landon grinned. "If we're going to get caught, we might as well be doing something fun when it happens."

"Or we could just leave," I whispered. "We have a chance to get away."

"Okay, but I'm still going to need you to fight the law when we get home. I've had certain … ideas … for the past hour and I can't shake them."

"Fine." I blew out a sigh. "You're extremely weird."

"I can live with that."

FOURTEEN

*L*andon was in a good mood the next morning. I wasn't sure what to make of it. He'd yet to melt down over the break-in and he kept humming bars from his lullaby as we got ready to walk to the inn for breakfast.

"If you're going to yell ... ." I started as we hit the pathway that led to The Overlook.

"Why would I yell?" Landon cast me a sidelong look.

"I broke the law."

Landon beamed. "And you've been properly punished."

"If that's your version of punishment, sign me up."

Landon snorted as he grabbed my hand. "I hope they have pancakes this morning. I'm in the mood for a huge stack of them."

"I want eggs and hash browns."

"Maybe we'll both get lucky."

I shrugged. "I think we already did."

"Ha. You're funny this morning." Landon had an added spring in his step. "Have you given any thought to what I said about moving into the big office? I can help you move furniture and stuff."

"Don't you think I should wait until Brian is officially out?"

"I don't really care either way what Brian does," Landon replied.

"He's already gone as far as I'm concerned. We can start moving your stuff today if you want."

The idea was both exciting and daunting. "I think we should wait until Brian is gone. It seems somehow rude to do it while he's still there."

"Okay, but have you even seen Brian in the last week?"

That was a fair question. "No, but I've been doing most of my work from home," I admitted. "I don't want to see him. He's been surly since the agreement. He acts like I've stolen something from him."

Landon's eyes flashed with something I couldn't quite identify. "You already did all of the work at that place. He spent all his time coming up with ideas to do less work himself while heaping it on your shoulders. You didn't steal anything from him. You earned that newspaper."

"I know that. I'm not sure he does, though."

"Do you want me to talk to him? Quite frankly, I've been looking for an excuse to have another conversation with that rodent before he leaves town."

If I thought I disliked Brian Kelly – which I did – Landon outright loathed him. I'd never fully ascertained why, but I think it had every-thing to do with me and the perceived value of my work. "You're good for my ego. You know that, don't you?"

Landon's smile returned. "You work hard, Bay. You deserve to get the accolades for a change. You've been telling me about your ideas for The Whistler since I met you. Now you get to do what you want."

"I might fail."

"Do you really think so?"

"Probably not," I conceded. "The newspaper has a solid advertising base and there's not so much work that I can't keep up with it. Still, I'd be lying if I said I wasn't a little worried that things might completely fall apart the moment I walk in and take over."

"I think that's normal to worry about." Landon squeezed my hand. "You'll be fine. In fact, you'll be better than fine. I have faith."

"I think that's because you're sweet on me."

"I'm definitely sweet on you," Landon confirmed, pausing by the back door. "I also know you're good at what you do and everything will be fine. Don't make yourself sick over this. You'll do a great job."

"And you're not angry about last night?" I couldn't quite let it go.

"I'm not happy about last night, but it's done with," Landon replied. "If you ever let Aunt Tillie plant a lullaby in my head again we're going to have problems. As for the other stuff, ... I'm pretending it was a dream and nothing more."

"That sounds a bit passive. You're not known for being passive."

"Thank you."

"You're welcome. I guess." I stepped through the door before him, waiting until he was inside to speak again. "So ... you're really not angry?"

"Not yet," Landon answered. "If you keep pushing me I might get there."

"Then I guess I'll let it go."

"Good plan."

The main living quarters were empty, so Landon and I headed straight for the kitchen. Only Twila remained, gathering a platter of bacon and sausage before shuffling toward the swinging door that led to the dining room.

"You're late," she announced.

"And you're my new favorite person in the world," Landon said, grabbing a slice of bacon and grinning. "I've often wondered if this is what Heaven looks like."

"You're nothing if not predictable," Twila smiled, shaking her head. "You guys look well rested. I'm a little surprised given your late-night excursion."

Uh-oh. "What have you heard?"

"Aunt Tillie has been telling the thrilling tale of her victory over 'The Man' for the past twenty minutes," Twila replied.

Aunt Tillie was the first person I saw when I walked into the dining room. She sat in her regular seat, at the head of the table, and regaled the breakfast guests – who were thankfully made up of only our family and friends – with the terrifying tale of our evening.

"And then he said he wasn't going to bother arresting me

because he knew I would transform into a horrifying vision of his doom," Aunt Tillie explained. "I swear, he looked as if he was going to cry."

Landon crossed his arms over his chest as he regarded Aunt Tillie. She barely spared him a glance before continuing.

"Then Clove started crying and begging Landon not to take her to jail, but I told her everything was going to be okay," Aunt Tillie continued.

Clove balked. "I did not start crying. You're making that up." She turned to Sam, her face red. "I didn't start crying."

"It's okay, honey." Sam patted her hand. "I know you were brave."

"I was totally brave," Clove confirmed.

"She was a kvetch, like she usually is," Aunt Tillie corrected. "I was the one who saved the day. Bay kept whining about feeling guilty because she left Landon behind – that's an unattractive quality, by the way – and Thistle turned into a total drunk, so I have no idea what she was doing."

Thistle sat at the far end of the table, her head in her hands. "I have no idea what you had in that flask, old lady, but it was a lot more than liquid courage. I had like four sips and I have the worst hangover I've ever had."

"That's because you're a lush," Aunt Tillie fired back. "If you're a lush, of course you're going to have a hangover. Now, where was I?"

"I believe you were about to tell the part of the story where you terrorized me into not arresting you," Landon supplied, moving around the table and taking his regular spot next to Aunt Tillie. "That's not exactly how I remember things, so I'm dying to hear your take on it."

Aunt Tillie's expression was hard to read. She clearly thought she was going to get away with her story. Maybe she figured Landon and I were still arguing and we wouldn't show up for breakfast. Of course, she's Aunt Tillie. She doesn't care about being caught in a lie. That happens daily at The Overlook.

"So how was the rest of your night?" Aunt Tillie turned her full attention to me. "Your boyfriend must have been a bear after my thrilling and complete victory. Did he take out his anger on you? Did he threaten to lock you in a room and never let you out?"

I exchanged a brief look with Landon before sitting. "No."

"What did you do?" Mom asked Landon, legitimately curious. "You two don't look like you're fighting."

"We're not fighting," Landon said, grabbing the pancake platter. "We had a nice night."

That was one way of looking at it.

"You had a nice night even though you caught Bay, Clove, Thistle and Aunt Tillie breaking and entering?" Mom was understandably dubious. "Did someone slip you a lobotomy when no one was looking?"

I tried to hold back a giggle … and failed.

Landon patted my knee under the table. "I don't believe you can slip someone a lobotomy, but I get what you're saying. As for the rest … I'm not angry."

"I think someone switched out our Landon with one from another dimension," Clove said. "They look exactly the same but they act completely different."

"Eat your breakfast, Clove," Landon ordered, keeping his focus on Aunt Tillie. "I believe you were telling a story about how you terrorized me into letting you go. Please continue."

"Oh, well, I'm old," Aunt Tillie hedged. "I forget what I'm saying half the time. It comes with the territory. Can someone please pass me the syrup?"

"That's what I thought," Landon muttered.

I pursed my lips to keep from laughing as I looked Thistle up and down. She looked worse than the night we stole three bottles of Aunt Tillie's wine as teenagers. We'd had no idea what kind of kick the wine had and passed out on the bluff behind the house. Twila thought we were dead when she happened upon us. Once Aunt Tillie found out, we wished we were dead.

The hangover lasted three days. No joke.

"How are you feeling, Thistle?"

"Shut up, Bay," Thistle growled.

"I was merely asking after my sick cousin," I teased. "I'll try to refrain from doing that from here on out."

"That would be great."

Landon snickered as he added sausage and bacon to his plate. "What does everyone have planned for the day?"

It was a simple question, but I knew it was pointed at me. Maybe Aunt Tillie, too.

"I'm going to plan for another night of law enforcement games," I said, grabbing a sausage link from his plate.

Landon leaned forward and bit one end of the link before I could draw it away. "Keep saying stuff like that and you'll never get in trouble again."

He was in far too good of a mood. I couldn't help but wonder if Aunt Tillie had cast a second spell without telling me. I was about to ask when the sound of someone clearing his throat drew my attention to the doorway behind me.

"Chief Terry! Come in."

"I don't want to interrupt."

"You're not interrupting," Mom said, hopping to her feet. "Sit down next to Bay. I'll grab an extra plate."

"And then I'll fill the plate with food," Twila offered, winking.

My mother and aunts were embroiled in a never-ending attempt to turn Chief Terry's head. It was all about the competition. If one of them actually won – which Chief Terry didn't seem keen to let happen – I was convinced they wouldn't know what to do once he was caught.

"How was your night?" I asked, smiling as Mom patted Chief Terry's shoulder after delivering his plate. The triumphant look she shot Marnie was straight out of a *Desperate Housewives* rerun. "Stop crowding him, Mom. He's trying to eat."

Mom shot me a dark look. "Do you want me to start singing about fighting the law? I hear that gets Landon going and it might make for an uncomfortable breakfast, but if it shuts you up … ."

I narrowed my eyes as Chief Terry slid me a curious look. "I'll eat my breakfast and be quiet," I gritted out.

Mom was haughty as she spun on her heel and headed for the other side of the table. "That's what I thought."

Chief Terry forked three pancakes onto his plate, adding bacon and sausage before reaching for the syrup. "Do I even want to know what's going on?"

"No," Landon replied. "It's typical Winchester crap."

"I heard that," Aunt Tillie snapped.

"I wasn't whispering."

"Don't make me put you on my list."

"Don't make me put you on my list," Landon shot back. "Given your story this morning, I think you should be worried about me for a change."

"Whatever." Aunt Tillie rolled her eyes. "I'm so over this breakfast."

"That makes two of us." Thistle had barely touched her food in lieu of rubbing her forehead. "I feel as if I've been hit by a runaway broom."

"Why?" Chief Terry asked, focusing on Thistle's drawn features. "Are you sick?"

"Hungover," Aunt Tillie supplied. "The girl has turned into a lush. It's sad."

"Yeah, I can tell already that I don't want to know what's going on," Chief Terry said. "Let's talk about something else. Who wants to hear about my night?"

Mom, Marnie and Twila shot up their hands at the same time, all three of them gracing Chief Terry with flirty smiles.

"I always want to hear about how you spend your time," Mom said.

"I always want to hear about it, too," Twila added.

"I always want to show you a better way to spend your time," Marnie said, taking control of the conversation. "I think you should take me up on that offer one day."

"Oh, geez," Chief Terry muttered under his breath. "What exactly did I walk in on this morning?"

"Just the beginning of the winter wilds," I replied. "You know how stir crazy we get when we can't spend a lot of time outside and away from one another."

"Yes, I remember when you were seventeen and your mother dropped you and your cousins at my house for a slumber party," Chief Terry said. "Most other mothers would not drop three teenagers on a single man because it would cause talk, but your mother didn't care."

"Yes, well, you knew us when we were teenagers," I pointed out. "She needed a break."

"I have a feeling I'll need a break pretty soon," Chief Terry said. "What were we talking about again?"

"You were going to tell us about your night," Clove prodded helpfully. "Your night has to be better than our night."

"Right." Chief Terry bobbed his head. "So, I get a call shortly after one in the morning. Guess who it was." He continued, not waiting for us to answer. "Margaret Little called. She was convinced someone broke into the new magic store."

Uh-oh. I risked a glance at Landon and found him calmly eating his breakfast. He didn't look bothered in the least.

"I tried talking her down, but she wouldn't listen, so I had to drive to the store in the middle of the night." Chief Terry was oblivious to the growing tension at the table. "Apparently she has an extra key to Scarlet Darksbane's store and let herself in, which is technically against the law. I confiscated the key."

"Huh." I had no idea what else to say. "Did you find anything?"

"Who knows," Chief Terry replied. "The store is a mess because she's unpacking things. It looked normal to me. Margaret swore up and down she heard noises in the alley, so I guess I'm going to have to force someone to patrol that alley regularly. It's going to take a bit out of my budget, but what else can I do?"

Crap on a cracker. "Well … ." I didn't want Chief Terry to get in trouble for something we did.

"Zip your lips, Bay," Aunt Tillie whispered. "If you don't … ." She mimed drawing an invisible knife over her neck.

"What's going on down there?" Chief Terry asked, focusing on Aunt Tillie. "Am I missing something?"

"Well … ."

"I will make you cry if you're not careful, Bay," Aunt Tillie warned.

"You're not missing anything," Landon interjected smoothly, murdering Aunt Tillie with a harsh look before shifting his gaze. "Bay and I were in the alley last night. You don't need to increase security. It was us."

"You?" Chief Terry was flabbergasted. "But ... why?"

"Well ... ." Now it was Landon's turn to flounder.

"They were playing a sex game," Aunt Tillie announced before I could think up a lie. "They were muttering something about fighting the law and the law winning this morning. I know. I think it's disgusting, too. They should both be flogged."

Chief Terry's expression was incredulous. "You went to the alley behind Scarlet Darksbane's store to play a sex game?"

"No, we went to the alley behind Hypnotic," Landon corrected. "She's exaggerating about the sex game stuff."

Only barely. By the time we got to Landon's vehicle we were most certainly playing a game of sorts. "Definitely exaggerating," I echoed.

"Yeah, I don't want to know." Chief Terry held up his hand to stop further discussion. "Whatever you were doing, keep it to yourselves and don't let Margaret Little know. She'll make a big deal out of it if she finds out, and she already thinks this entire family is made up of demented perverts."

"I worked hard to make her believe it, too," Aunt Tillie said, flashing a smile for Landon's benefit. "So ... everything is fine, right?"

Chief Terry shrugged. "Why wouldn't it be?"

"No reason." Aunt Tillie's smile didn't falter, instead growing more evil as she pinned Landon with a gaze. "See. Everything is perfectly fine. There's no reason to get your panties in a twist."

"I feel like twisting something," Landon said.

"Oh, you know exactly how to flatter me." Aunt Tillie took a huge bite of sausage and then continued to speak with her mouth full. "So ... what is everyone doing today?"

I didn't know about everyone else, but I was considering finding a hole to hide in. That was the only way Landon wouldn't bring this up later.

FIFTEEN

"**A**re you coming back to the guesthouse with me?"

Landon found me in the library shortly after breakfast. I left him to chat with Chief Terry, both out of respect for him and the need to mess with Thistle and her hangover. I knew he'd track me down before leaving.

"I think I'm going to stay here for a bit," I replied. "I want to talk to Aunt Tillie."

"Why? I think she's already done enough damage for twenty-four hours, don't you?"

"If you think that's the best she can do, you're in for a big surprise." I couldn't help but smile. "That's normal Aunt Tillie stuff. You were around a bit last winter, but you weren't a regular guest until after Christmas. She goes stir crazy in winter. She'll be much worse in a few weeks."

"I was around last winter," Landon argued. "I came back right when she was getting into her plowing groove for the year."

I smiled at the memory. "That was funny. You threatened to revoke her license."

"You didn't think it was funny when I first came back."

"No. I didn't know what to think then," I conceded. "I was glad to see you, but I was afraid you would take off again."

"And now?"

"And now I know you're addicted to me and will never take off again."

"Good answer." Landon smacked a loud kiss against my lips. "What are you going to do today? I tried to ask in an unobtrusive way, but you kind of blew me off over breakfast."

"I didn't blow you off. I simply don't have an answer. I'm not sure what I'm doing."

"But you're staying here?"

"I'm staying here to show Aunt Tillie the photos of the journal," I explained. "After that, I'm not sure. What are you doing?"

"Getting back to the basics," Landon replied. "We have a dead woman and no idea what happened to her. She's in a town full of strangers. When dealing with murder, it makes more sense to look at immediate family. The ritual nature of those symbols adds a certain edge to things that I'm not entirely comfortable with, though."

"Meaning?"

"Meaning, if I go with my gut, I believe that someone she knows killed her and tried to make it look like a ritual murder so people would jump all over the residents," Landon supplied. "She was strangled, by the way. I'm not sure I told you that."

"Strangled?" That didn't seem to fit the tableau in town square. "Not that strangulation isn't violent, but I thought you might find another cause of death. I don't know why. It's stupid really."

"It's not stupid," Landon argued. "It's hard to reconcile what you saw with strangulation. I get it. The thing is, strangulation is one of those things that's generally not premeditated unless you're a serial killer and want to get up close and personal with your victim."

"Which we're likely not dealing with."

"No. Strangulation is one of those heat-of-the-moment murders."

"But someone clearly gave what they did after – draining the blood and drawing the symbols – a lot of thought."

"Did they? You said yourself that the symbols made no sense."

"I guess." I rolled my neck, uncertain. "What happens now?"

"Now we're going to spend some time questioning the troupe members who weren't as close with Adele," Landon replied. "They're all family members in some way, but the closer the family member, the more likely they are to gloss over certain things about a loved one that they believe might not be flattering."

"Like if Adele dressed up as Lady Gaga and moonlighted at a strip club?"

"Exactly." Landon tapped the end of my nose. "I know you're convinced that Scarlet Darksbane had something to do with this, but the odds aren't in favor. That doesn't mean we'll overlook her or ignore your gut. It simply means we have to look everywhere."

"I know. I never said that Scarlet was a murderer, by the way. I only said she was up to something."

"What?"

I shrugged. "I don't know. Hopefully Aunt Tillie will be able to decipher this and find out."

"Do you think that's possible?"

"Anything is possible."

"Including you accidentally finding trouble," Landon said. "Be good and be safe. If you get anything, don't hesitate to call."

"You do the same."

"I should be home in plenty of time for dinner. Maybe, once we're finished, we can play another rousing game of 'I Fought the Law.'"

I didn't want to encourage him, but I couldn't stop myself from laughing. "This time the sultry robber is going to win."

"I'm perfectly fine with that."

I FOUND AUNT TILLIE in the family living quarters, her attention diverted by the television.

"I don't understand why we need five hours of morning shows these days," she complained. "In my day we had one hour of morning shows and it was called the news."

I snickered. "I didn't picture you as a *Today* show fan."

"I'm not, but there's nothing else to watch," Aunt Tillie complained. "I already binged the entire new season of *Stranger Things*, and *The Walking Dead* doesn't come back on until February. I'm going through withdrawal."

"Total bummer." I sat on the couch and handed her my phone. "Tell me what you see when you look at these photos."

Aunt Tillie made a strange face. "If you're about to show me something sexual from your night in the alley with Landon I will curse you to within an inch of your life."

"If you make me smell like bacon again you'll only make Landon more powerful."

"And he has enough power," Aunt Tillie groused. "What food does he hate? The boy inhales food as if we're about to be overcome by zombies and he's going to spend the rest of his life on the run."

"He doesn't like chocolate chip cookies," I lied. "Try making me smell like that."

"Whatever." Aunt Tillie made a face even a great-niece couldn't love. "I'm not a rookie. If I make you smell like cookies we'll never see you again. Landon will finally follow through and cuff you to him permanently."

She had a point. "The photos aren't of Landon and me. They're of a journal we found in Scarlet Darksbane's safe. It's written in some sort of code or another language I don't think I've ever seen. I don't recognize it."

Aunt Tillie's eyebrows flew up her forehead. "Wait a second ... are you telling me that 'The Man' not only stuck around after catching you breaking and entering, he also helped you open a safe?"

"I was equally surprised. He didn't even yell."

Aunt Tillie was tickled. "He's coming along nicely."

"What is that supposed to mean?"

"I worried about him at first," Aunt Tillie said, her finger busy as she looked through the photos, occasionally stopping to enlarge something for a better look. "I thought he was too much of a straight arrow to fit in with us. He's not a straight arrow any longer.

"I thought there was a time he'd choose duty over protecting our family secret, but he's done the exact opposite," she continued. "He's done nothing but put you first. There are times ... well, it's weird to say, but there are times he reminds me of your Uncle Calvin."

And that right there was the greatest compliment Aunt Tillie could bestow upon Landon. By all accounts, Uncle Calvin was some sort of a saint for putting up with her. No one else ever would. Wait ... if Uncle Calvin was Landon in this scenario, does that mean ... ? Ugh!

"Are you saying I'm you?"

Aunt Tillie grinned at the question. "That's your worst fear realized, isn't it?"

"Landon isn't Uncle Calvin," I said after a beat, determined to prove her wrong. "He's not a saint. He has saint-like qualities at times – like when he puts up with family dinner and whatever shenanigans you're embroiled in – but he's no saint. Now Marcus is a different story. He's totally a saint. He's Uncle Calvin and Thistle is you."

"That's a definite possibility." Aunt Tillie wrinkled her nose as she stared at the photos. "I don't recognize this. Whatever it is, she either made it up or stole it from a book I'm not familiar with. It's definitely not Theban ... or Klingon."

"Is there a way we can determine what it is?"

"I'm emailing the photos to myself," Aunt Tillie replied. "I have a few places I can check. I saw you talking to Landon in the library. He looked serious. Do you really believe this new witch is a murderer?"

"I didn't say that."

"Hey, if you believe it, I believe it." Aunt Tillie held up her hands to placate me. "I'm predisposed not to like her. Disliking someone and believing they're capable of murder are two entirely different things, though."

"You sound like Landon."

"I'm going to help you even though you said that." Aunt Tillie got to her feet. "Just think about what I said. I know you're spouting the standard party line that you don't believe she's capable of murder, but deep down inside I'm not sure that's true."

"Landon said that Adele Twigg was strangled," I said. "He said that strangulation is a method of murder when two people know each other well and are arguing. Do you believe that?"

"I'm not a cop."

"For which every cop I know is forever thankful. I'm having trouble understanding how someone who knew Adele Twigg could do what they did with the symbols."

"There's a lot of ugliness in the world, Bay. You'll never be able to understand all of it."

"Yeah, I get that." I heaved out a sigh. "If you can find anything on this code she's using, give me a call. I'm heading into town."

"To do what?"

"Work."

Aunt Tillie wasn't convinced. "What are you really going to do?"

"See if I can spy on Scarlet Darksbane or shake answers out of Mrs. Little," I answered sheepishly.

Aunt Tillie chuckled. "You're coming along nicely, too. You get more and more like me with each passing year."

"That's the meanest thing you've ever said to me."

I PARKED IN FRONT of Hypnotic. I considered heading straight to the newspaper office, but Brian Kelly's Ford was parked in front, and I wasn't keen on exchanging bitter looks and biting sarcasm with him. I'd much rather irritate Thistle, who was stretched out on the couch when I entered the store.

"Good morning, cousins!" I yelled the greeting much louder than necessary because Thistle is fun to mess with when she's hungover.

"I will kill you if you don't shut up," Thistle growled, never moving her arm from shielding her eyes.

"She's crabby," Clove said apologetically as she organized herbs behind the counter. "I told her to go home and sleep it off, but she told me to stuff it and now we're not speaking."

"And yet I can still hear you talking," Thistle complained. "Why are you talking?"

"I'm talking to Bay, not you."

"Whatever."

I managed to bite back the urge to mess with Thistle further and instead joined Clove at the counter. "Did you get in trouble with Sam last night?"

"I told Sam what we were doing before I left," Clove replied. "He thought it was a dumb idea, but he didn't try to stop me. He's not an FBI agent, so he doesn't really care when I break the law."

"What about Marcus?" I flicked a curious look to Thistle. "Did he care?"

"He said he had a great night's sleep because I wasn't hogging the covers," Thistle mumbled. "He didn't even know I slept on the bathroom floor."

"You slept on the bathroom floor? You barely drank anything."

"Yes, well, Aunt Tillie is clearly upping her game," Thistle said. "By the way, when we got here Mrs. Little was outside talking to members of her angry flock. She told them that she was certain someone was loitering last night. She swears up and down she heard people in the alley."

"Landon and I were in the alley, but I doubt very much she heard us," I countered. "Landon was in a … unique … mood because of the song Aunt Tillie planted. It's weird what gets him going."

"Yes, bacon and bad music," Thistle said dryly. "Marcus doesn't care what we do. He warned me that he wouldn't bail me out if I got arrested, but we all know he's blowing smoke."

"True. Landon wasn't nearly as angry as I expected him to be," I said. "I thought for sure he would blow a gasket eventually – he played it really cool right from the start – but he seems fine. He's in a good mood and everything."

"Maybe he's mellowing," Clove suggested.

"Maybe. Aunt Tillie says that he reminds her of Uncle Calvin."

Thistle snorted, finally removing her arm from her face. "That means you're Aunt Tillie. You realize that, right?"

"I pointed that out. We then agreed that Marcus is the most like Uncle Calvin."

"Which means you're the most like Aunt Tillie," Clove said, her eyes sparkling.

"You're both dead to me," Thistle announced, stretching her arms over her head as she planted her feet on the end of the couch. "If you ask me, Landon has simply realized that picking a fight over our antics isn't worth it. Plus, well, when he really gives it some thought he knows that he fell in love with you because you're wacky. He has no reason to want to change you, so he's decided to be easier to get along with."

She had an interesting theory. "He hasn't been easier for you to get along with."

"That's because he wants me out of the guesthouse," Thistle explained. "He's ready to play house with you. To do that, he needs some alone time. Don't worry. I'm ready to get out of there, too. I mean … I'll miss it, but it's time."

"You'll miss it?" That was the first time she mentioned anything of the sort. "I thought you hated it in the guesthouse because it was so close to the inn."

"I thought that, too." Thistle took on a wistful expression. "When we all moved in together, I thought I'd hate it. But we've had a lot of good years there. We've had a lot of fun … and chocolate martini nights … and general mischief was part of the deal.

"I'm ready to move forward with Marcus," she continued. "It really is time. That doesn't mean I won't miss the fun we had. Heck, last night was fun. Sure, I regret the hangover this morning, but last night was fun."

"We'll still have fun," I pointed out. "We'll simply have to sneak around to do it."

"Which makes it even more fun." Thistle mustered a smile. "We're all adults now. I'm not sure when it happened, but we are. We're all going to live with our boyfriends in a few weeks. We'll be truly separated for the first time in … years."

"It's weird," Clove said. "I like The Dandridge and I love Sam, but I still think of the guesthouse as home sometimes. I wonder when I'll outgrow it."

"It is your home," I pointed out. "If you ever need or want to come back, it's still your home."

"Oh, Landon will love that," Thistle said.

"Landon will be fine with it." Upon reflection, I knew that to be true. "Maybe that's what last night was about. He knows we need the occasional adventures with one another to be happy."

"That's altogether frightening and funny," Thistle said. "Either way, everything will be fine. It'll be different, but fine."

I didn't just believe her, I felt the truth in the words. "Yeah. I love spending time with you guys."

Clove preened. "Me, too."

"Oh, geez." Thistle flopped her head back on the couch. "And now we're the schmaltz family."

"Fine. I only like spending time with Clove," I shot back.

"And I only like Bay," Clove added.

"Much better."

I looked to the window, pursing my lips when Scarlet Darksbane's obviously identifiable red hair appeared in front of the store. She didn't look inside as she hurried along the sidewalk in the opposite direction of her store.

"And, as much as I like spending time with you, I have something to do," I said, striding toward the door.

"Are you going to stalk the new witch?" Thistle asked.

"Stalk is a harsh word."

"Okay. Are you going to accidentally follow the new witch?" Thistle corrected.

"No. I'm totally going to stalk her."

"Have fun."

"Oh, I intend to."

SIXTEEN

*S*carlet stared at her phone as she walked. I remained far back, keeping a full block between us. The sidewalk and streets weren't busy, so it was easy to keep an eye on her, but she would easily spot me if she turned around.

At first I thought she was heading toward Mrs. Gunderson's bakery. She blew past the building, though, without so much as a glance through the window. It was frustrating, because now that I'd seen the bakery I really wanted a doughnut.

Scarlet kept her pace even but unhurried, casting a quick look at the police station as she passed – perhaps looking for Landon and Chief Terry so she could continue flirting with them, I internally sneered. She kept going, skipping past all the shops and the diner, heading toward the cemetery.

What newcomer to a town spends time in a cemetery? Okay, true, I'd been known to hang out in cemeteries. I almost always had a reason, though. Usually I was looking for a ghost. Something occurred to me and I slowed my pace, staring hard as a ghostly figure detached from the barren weeping willow at the edge of the cemetery. I had to squint to make out the spirit's features from this distance, but the moment she turned her head I recognized Adele Twigg.

Well, that was interesting.

I ducked behind a maple tree, knowing the trunk was wide enough to hide me, and watched as Scarlet picked her way through the memorial markers. She seemed to be reading the tombstones, her gaze focused on each monument rather than the ghost following her. Her lips moved, and for a moment my heart stuttered because I was certain that she was talking to Adele Twigg. After a few moments, though, I realized she never once looked at the ghost. Adele may have been following her, but Scarlet didn't notice the ethereal being tracking her.

I remained where I was, watching Scarlet for a full fifteen minutes. I stayed behind when Scarlet exited the far end of the graveyard, my mind busy. What was she doing? Why did she care about the tombstones? What was she saying to herself as she studied them?

Adele didn't follow Scarlet. Her face appeared downtrodden as she mimed kicking at the pathway between the tombstones. I risked coming out when I was certain Scarlet was gone, keeping my focus on the ghost as I approached. "Mrs. Twigg?"

She jerked up her head, surprise evident over her white features. My stomach twisted at the look of hope on her face, things coming together in my head. She didn't realize she was dead. Or, perhaps she did and the fact that I called out her name gave her hope that she wasn't dead. She was still adjusting to her new reality – and it didn't look as if it was going well.

"You see me?"

"I see you," I confirmed. "What are you doing here?"

"I don't know," Adele replied. "I woke up here."

"In the cemetery?" I glanced around, searching for signs of a struggle or evidence that might help Landon and Chief Terry move forward. I was fairly certain they didn't think to search the cemetery.

"No, in the middle of town," Adele replied. "I woke up there and … I don't like this town. I don't want to be here any longer. I want to go home."

Her expression was pitiable, but I'd learned a long time ago that coddling displaced spirits rarely ended well. Most were prone to feeling sorry for themselves rather than looking at the bigger picture. Sure, it might not seem like there's a bigger picture when you're dead, but there's something beyond this world. I have no idea what it is, but it must be better than remaining behind and growing bitter while watching family and friends move on without you. Quite frankly, nothing could be worse than that.

"Mrs. Twigg, do you know what happened to you?" I kept my voice even as I regarded her. "Do you know who ... hurt ... you?"

Adele jerked her shoulders, the question making her scowl. "Hurt me? Why would anyone hurt me? I've never done anything to hurt anyone, so why would someone want to hurt me?"

"Some people are just like that," I replied. "I guess that means you don't remember what happened to you, huh?"

"All I remember is waking up in this place – this stupid, hateful place – and now I want to go home," Adele snapped. "Why can't you understand that?"

I had no idea if the woman was mentally unbalanced because her death was too much to deal with or because she was simply born that way. "I do understand. I'm trying to help you. I can't do it without information, though."

"What information?" Adele challenged, her eyes flashing with fury. "I want to go home. I need you to call my husband so he can pick me up. Then I'm going home."

"You can't go home."

"But I want to go home."

"Yes, but ... you're dead." Part of me thought I was being cruel – and the overwhelming distress that flitted across Adele's face told me she thought the same – but it was clear that bluntness was in order. "You died, Mrs. Twigg. You can't go home."

"But ... I can't be dead," she sputtered. "That's impossible."

"Nonetheless, it's true."

"Really?" Adele cocked a challenging eyebrow. "If I'm dead, how can you see me?"

That was a very good question. Er, well, at least from her perspective. "I'm a witch." There was no reason to lie to her. It wasn't as if she could tell anyone. She couldn't ring the church bell and scream "witch" while trying to gather the townsfolk to burn me at the stake.

"You're a witch?" Adele's face twisted. "Just like that, huh? 'I'm a witch.'" She imitated me to the best of her ability. She wasn't half bad. Maybe that came from her renaissance training. "You can't blurt stuff out like that, girl. You need to dress it up a bit, soften the blow."

"I've tried softening the blow," I explained. "You're not the first ghost I've dealt with. It doesn't work. I've found it's easier to simply tell the truth and let spirits deal with it as they will."

"Oh, well, you're a professional, I see." Adele adopted a haughty manner. "So I'm dead, you're a witch and I can't ever go home again. Is that what you're telling me?"

I held my hands palms up and shrugged. "Pretty much."

"Well, this just bites the big one."

I bit back a laugh. Adele's attitude reminded me of Aunt Tillie. I kind of liked it. She wasn't whining and crying as much as bitching and moaning, so it was a mild relief to know I wouldn't have to coddle her.

"It definitely bites the big one," I agreed. "The thing is, we don't know who killed you."

"Killed me? I … killed me? Are you saying I was murdered?"

"Yes. Someone strangled you." I decided to omit the part about the bloody symbols and the way her body was strung up for display next to the town clock. She probably wouldn't enjoy the visual and, now that I'd admitted to being a witch, she might even suspect me and stop talking. "I don't suppose you can remember back to the night of the festival meeting, can you? Do you remember what you did after the meeting?"

"I … um … don't know." Adele screwed up her face in concentration. "I don't understand any of this. I'm a good person. I try to be a good person. I do things the right way. I make others in my employ follow the rules. Why would someone want to kill me?"

"That's what we're trying to find out." I offered up a wan smile. "If you remember who did this to you, I promise to help. I can make sure the police know what happened. We'll make sure that justice is served."

"But I don't remember," Adele snapped. "I don't remember anything."

I felt helpless. "I'm sorry."

"You're sorry?" Adele's attitude roared back with a vengeance. "You're sorry? Oh, well, that makes everything so much better. You're sorry. I'm dead and you're sorry. If this is what it's like to be a witch you should choose another profession."

"I'm also a newspaper reporter," I offered helpfully. "I'll be a newspaper owner in a few weeks. I'm still wrapping my head around that. It's a little weird."

Adele made a disgusted face. "We're talking about me, not you."

"Right. Well ... maybe if you walk around town something will jog your memory," I suggested. "I'm guessing you won't be able to move on until you remember what happened and the guilty party is punished. That's how it usually works."

"Move on? Why would I want to move on?"

"Because you'll go crazy if you stay here."

"I'm already going crazy," Adele barked. "You know what? I'm done talking to you." She held up her hand to quiet me. "You're either crazy or I'm dreaming. I have no idea which. But you can't help me, so I'm done."

"Mrs. Twigg." I adopted a pragmatic tone, but Adele made a screeching sound to get me to stop talking.

"I'm done," she repeated. "I'm going to find my family."

"They won't be able to see you."

"Says you. I think we've already established that I don't believe you."

"But ... ."

"No! Did you not hear me when I said I'm done? Stop talking to me."

I opened my mouth to argue further even though I knew it would do no good, but it was already too late. Adele was gone and I was alone.

"Well, she's going to be fun," I muttered.

BY THE TIME I MADE it back to Main Street, the activity level in the downtown area had ratcheted up a notch. Scarlet was back, standing in front of Mrs. Little's store with the unicorn peddler and a couple other cohorts, their heads bent together. They looked as though they were plotting. Sure, I disliked both of them with a fiery passion, so that could've skewed my observation, but I had serious doubts they were discussing the weather.

The renaissance troupe was the center of attention, a bunch of unhappy workers unloading a truck and carrying items toward a huge tent that was being erected on the lawn in front of the library. I sat on the bench in front of Hypnotic, my eyes busy as they bounced between faces. I couldn't decide if I wanted to focus on Scarlet or the renaissance folks.

In the end, I split my attention.

That's where Landon found me an hour later, still frowning as I watched the hustle and bustle and internally debated exactly how evil Scarlet really was.

"I usually love your face, but right now you look as if you're up to something," Landon announced, taking the seat to my right as Chief Terry landed on my left.

"I'm pretty sure that was an insult," I said dryly, narrowing my eyes as I watched two of the younger generation of renaissance workers slip into the woods behind the library. They made a big show of looking over their shoulders, as if they were trying to make sure no one followed, and then they disappeared.

"It wasn't an insult," Landon countered. He was more interested in the activity near the tent than what was going on in the woods. "I love your face regardless."

"No need to lay it on so thick," I said. "I'll keep living with you regardless."

"Good to know." We lapsed in to companionable silence for a few moments, Landon focusing on the workers while I stared at the woods. "How have you spent your morning?" He tried to keep his voice light, but I knew he was checking up on me.

"Aunt Tillie didn't recognize the thing I showed her in the photos, but she's researching it."

"What did you show her?" Chief Terry asked, curious.

"You honestly don't want to know," I replied. "Trust me."

Chief Terry looked to Landon for confirmation.

"You don't," Landon agreed.

"Fine." Chief Terry let loose a growl. "You guys are up to something. I can feel it."

"That's funny," I said, "I was just thinking the same thing about Mrs. Little and our newest witch."

Landon followed my gaze as I looked toward Mrs. Little's shop. "They do look pretty happy with one another, don't they?"

"I don't suppose you've managed to find her real name?"

"I've been a little busy, Bay."

"Don't worry about it." I was agitated, but knew he couldn't very well drop everything to do as I asked. "You have a job to do. I'll handle Scarlet."

"That's a terrifying thought," Landon muttered. "What else did you do today besides talk to Aunt Tillie?"

"I went to Hypnotic and made Thistle's hangover worse by taunting her."

Landon snickered. "She deserves it. What else?"

"I followed Scarlet Darksbane."

"Oh, geez." Landon's smile slipped. "You followed her? Why?"

"Because she's up to something and I'm pretty sure it's something terrible," I replied without hesitation. "I just can't figure her out. She spent a good thirty minutes wandering around the cemetery. I thought she was talking to Mrs. Twigg for a bit because her lips were moving and the ghost was hanging out by the willow tree, but she was merely talking to herself. That's a sign of mental instability, by the way."

"You talk to yourself all the time," Landon pointed out.

"Thus proving my point."

Landon pressed the heel of his hand to his forehead. "Sweetie, have you considered that you're starting to go off the rails regarding Scarlet Darksbane? She hasn't done anything wrong … at least not yet."

"She will."

"How can you be sure?"

"Because she's evil."

"Oh, well, good," Chief Terry muttered. "You've clearly been spending time with Aunt Tillie. That sounds like something she'd say. You'll end up just like her if you're not careful."

I jerked my eyes to Chief Terry's face. "That's the meanest thing you've ever said to me."

"Yeah, that's not going to work on me." Chief Terry was unruffled. "You said you saw Adele Twigg's ghost in the cemetery – I can't believe I said that out loud. Did she say anything?"

"She was ticked off when I told her she was dead. Then she said she wanted to go home, told me I was a bad witch and then said she was going to find her family. She's not down here right now as far as I can tell, but I'm sure she'll be back. She's kind of mean."

"You spent eighteen years living with Aunt Tillie," Landon pointed out. "She's definitely meaner than Adele Twigg ever dreamed of being. I'm sure you'll survive."

"Good point." I was back to staring at the woods. The workers had yet to return. "I'll be right back." I got to my feet.

Landon followed suit. "Where do you think you're going? If you're going to make a scene with Scarlet, turn your cute little butt around and sit."

"I have no intention of talking to Scarlet right now," I said. "Talking to her gives her power, and I have no intention of doing that."

"Yup. She's turning into Tillie." Chief Terry graced Landon with a sympathetic look. "Your life is about to take a sudden swerve. Run while you can. Save yourself."

Landon scowled. "Don't encourage this madness. You're making her think it's okay when you feed into her delusion."

"I'm not delusional," I shot back. "I'm right. You'll see I'm right eventually, and when you do I'm going to make you do a little dance when you apologize."

"Oh, well, I'm looking forward to that," Landon said dryly. "If you're not going after Scarlet, where are you going?"

"Two of the workers went into the woods," I replied. "I want to see what they're doing."

Whatever Landon expected me to say, it wasn't that. He recovered quickly. "Okay, I'll go with you."

"Don't do anything dirty in the woods," Chief Terry called out. "I'll arrest you for indecent exposure."

"It's too cold to do anything indecent in the woods," I said. "That's what spring is for."

"You make me feel old, Bay."

"You're young in spirit."

Landon and I set a brisk pace as we headed toward the trees. The fact that the two workers hadn't yet returned made me suspicious.

"Was it two men? Two women?"

"A man and a woman," I replied.

"Maybe they're doing something dirty," Landon suggested.

"You told me they're all related," I reminded him. "If they're doing something dirty, well, then there might be some old laws on the books that you can use to hold them."

Landon made a face as we stepped into the trees. "That's really gross, Bay."

"Don't tell me you weren't thinking it."

"I wasn't."

"Then you're slow on the uptake."

I truly didn't expect to find family members making out in the woods. I enjoyed seeing Landon's twisted expression due to his obvious discomfort with the subject matter. What I found when I turned to my right, though, was straight out of a V.C. Andrews book. You know, the ones about siblings going at it in the attic? Yeah, that's pretty much what we came upon when we moved closer to a large pine.

"Oh, my ... gross!"

"That's putting it mildly," Landon grumbled. "I'm going to have nightmares about this. I blame you, Bay."

"No one made you come."

"Yeah, well, it's too late now. I just ... I can't look."

He wasn't the only one.

SEVENTEEN

"*I*'m blind!"

I slapped my hand over my eyes.

"What are you doing out here?" The man – although he didn't look a day over twenty-one – hopped to his feet, his cheeks flaming. "Are you spying on us?"

"Not intentionally," Landon replied. "We just wanted to see what you were doing."

"That means you were spying on us," the man barked, his face mottled with embarrassment.

"I guess, from your perspective, that's true," Landon conceded. "We certainly didn't expect to find you doing this, Greg. That's right, isn't it? You're Greg Twigg."

"I am." The man smoothed the front of his shirt, doing his best to act self-righteous even though we'd just found him making out with his sister … or cousin … or even a second-cousin was kind of gross. "You're the FBI agent who questioned us about Mama's death, right?"

"Mama?" The word was out of my mouth before I could think better of uttering it. What kind of grown man calls his mother "mama?" Apparently the type who makes out with a relative.

"Yes, she was my mama," Greg snapped, his glare landing on me. "Who are you?"

"Never mind that," Landon answered for me. "She's ... a consultant with the FBI."

That was a gross exaggeration.

"What are you doing out here with your ... sister?" I couldn't stop myself from asking the obvious question.

"I'm not his sister." The woman, who looked to be even younger than the man, scrambled to her feet. "I'm his cousin."

"That doesn't make it better," I pointed out.

"We weren't doing anything," she protested. "I dropped a contact lens and he was helping me look."

"In your mouth?"

"Bay, let's not take this to a disgusting place," Landon ordered. "I'll ask the questions. Did you drop the contact lens in your mouth?"

I held back a snicker, but just barely.

"Oh, man." Greg ran his hand through his blond hair, frustrated. "We're going to get in so much trouble for this, Tess. I told you it was a bad idea. You just couldn't stop yourself."

"Oh, don't blame this on me," Tess shot back, her green eyes flashing as she pulled a twig from her brown hair. "You're the one who kept grabbing my butt in the tent. You started it."

"I kind of want to grab something myself," Landon said. "I believe it's called a barf bag."

"You'd better get two," I muttered.

"Okay, I know what you're thinking, but it's not as bad as it seems," Greg said. "Tess isn't really my cousin. Not by birth, at least."

"That doesn't make it much better in my book," I said. "You're basically owning up to pseudo incest rather than regular incest. If you're raised with someone, spend your whole life looking at them as a cousin, you should not be sneaking off into the woods as adults to get a little over-the-clothes action when you think no one is looking. Blood or no blood, it's still gross."

"Wow, and I thought this town was full of witches," Tess drawled. "It seems like it's full of puritans instead."

"Don't make things worse, Tess," Greg snapped. "They don't understand. If I was in their position, I'm not sure I would either."

"Oh, please," Tess scoffed. "He might refer to her as his consultant, but he's clearly sleeping with her. Look at the way he positions himself in front of her. They're more than FBI agent and consultant."

"Yes, but she's not my cousin," Landon pointed out.

"He's not really my cousin either," Tess explained. "It's all an act."

"I don't think you can pretend to make out," I argued. "Once tongues get involved, you're really doing it."

"Not that." The look Tess shot me was full of pure loathing. "I mean we're not really cousins. We weren't raised together. We didn't play together as children. We didn't meet each other until six months ago."

Huh. I wasn't sure what to make of that. "So you were raised apart? That still doesn't make it okay to smooch your cousin."

"Oh, geez. Are you slow or something?" Tess's voice whipped past fury, banked at irate, and slammed into me with the force of a thousand daggers. "We're not cousins! We weren't raised in the same family. We're actors."

Huh. That was ... different.

"Wait, so you're saying that you're not really Twiggs?" Landon asked.

"Ding, ding, ding. We have a winner!" Tess barked. I thought I was sarcastic, but she made me look like an amateur. "I'd give you a prize for figuring it out, but it took you far too long."

"Well, it's not exactly easy. You didn't volunteer this information when I interviewed you guys at The Dragonfly," Landon pointed out. "You acted like family during interviews."

"That's because Arthur told us we had to," Greg supplied. "We thought we should tell you the truth, but the Twigg Troupe – and no, we're not okay with the name – has a reputation to uphold. That's what he told us."

I scratched an itch on the side of my nose. "And Arthur is the husband, right?" Landon gave me a brief rundown of the family tree the day before, but it was so large and scattered I didn't retain much of it.

"Yeah." Landon rubbed his chin. "Were they really married?"

"Yes." Greg said. "They were married, but the rest of it is utter crap."

"None of you guys are their kids?"

"My understanding is that they couldn't have kids," Tess supplied, her tone easier now that the truth was out and we didn't think she was playing some sort of weird incest game in the woods behind the library. "The way they explained it to us when we auditioned – well, at least the way they explained it to me anyway – was that they always wanted a bushel of kids so they could travel the country putting on shows."

"Renaissance shows?" I asked.

"They never said," Tess replied. "They just said shows. I always assumed it was renaissance stuff, because they're really into it. They like the horses and pageantry. Arthur loves playing with swords."

"Is that a euphemism for something?" I asked.

"Like what?" Tess's face was blank.

"Never mind."

Landon slid me a smirk before continuing. "I need you guys to run this down for me. We assumed that you were all related. Now you're telling me you're not. How does it work?"

"Well, it's pretty simple," Greg replied. "The Twiggs started with a group of about ten people, I think. I wasn't around then, so you'll have to ask Arthur about it."

"Don't worry," Landon intoned. "I will."

"By the time we got involved, they'd been doing it about seven or eight years," Greg said. "They had a lot of turnover, so you could almost always find a spot."

"And they held auditions?"

Tess nodded. "In Orlando, the third Thursday of every month. They keep their home base in Orlando. They usually travel the first two weeks of the month and then head home for the last two weeks."

"Okay, but I still don't understand," Landon pressed. "How did you hear about them?"

"There aren't that many traveling renaissance festivals," Greg supplied. "If you want to make a living doing this – and there are a lot of people who do – then you have to get in with one of the better troupes. I wouldn't say the Twigg Troupe is the best, but it's easily top five."

"Out of how many?" I asked. This whole renaissance fair lifestyle was baffling.

"I would say there are about fifteen big troupes and another ten or twenty smaller troupes," Greg answered.

"Huh."

"Does it make you want to put on a corset?" Landon asked. "If so, I'm more than willing to take you to the renaissance fair."

I shot him a dirty look. "Does it make you want to play with a sword? Wait … that came out way dirtier than I imagined."

"I think it came out just dirty enough." Landon patted my shoulder. "So what happens when you guys get a show?"

"We travel around with the equipment and tent," Tess explained. "It's a lot of driving, but it's not too bad. When we get to areas that are warm, we often camp. When we're in colder climates like here, we get hotel rooms. Arthur and Adele are pretty cheap when they want to be."

"So you go to a town and you all have to pretend to be related," Landon prodded. "I'm not sure why they needed the subterfuge."

"You'll have to ask Arthur about that, because the rest of us don't understand either. But we were told to mind our own business," Tess said. "When you sign a contract, it's generally for about six months. They can fire us, but we can't quit while we're under contract."

"That doesn't exactly seem fair," I noted.

"Arthur and Adele never cared about fair. That's not the way they roll."

"How do they roll?" Landon asked, his interest piqued. "Do they mistreat you guys?"

"I guess it would depend on how you define 'mistreat,'" Greg replied. "It doesn't matter now. We're contractually obligated to do this job. That Mrs. Little woman made it quite clear that if we tried to leave she would sue Arthur. He wasn't happy, but he agreed to do the job, and since we can't get out of our contracts we're forced to perform, even though no one wants to do it."

"Were you close with Adele?" I asked Tess.

Tess snorted, catching me off guard. "No one was close to Adele," she said. "She didn't want anyone to be close to her. She made this big speech when I auditioned, going on and on about how she always wanted kids and would treat me like I was really part of her family.

"Then, the first day on the job, she can't remember my name and she wouldn't stop yelling at me when I asked questions," she continued. "She belittled me, called me stupid and then threatened to force me to cut my hair if I didn't stop flipping it over my shoulder."

"Why would she possibly care about that?" I asked.

"She said that when a woman flips her hair over her shoulder it's a sign that she's a tramp," Tess answered. "She said that none of the Twiggs are tramps, and if I did something that made people think I was a tramp she would fire me and make sure I never got another job in a renaissance troupe."

"Which explains why you guys were sneaking off to kiss in the woods," Landon surmised, exchanging a quick glance with me. "I'm not sure what to make of this."

"It doesn't matter what you make of it," Tess said. "We're all going to lose our jobs anyway. Adele was the one who did all the hiring, and Arthur is a total mess now that she's dead. The only thing he's said to us since he found out is that we have to do the job and that we'll talk about everything else when we get back to Florida. He didn't sound very hopeful."

"He's going through a trauma," Landon offered. "You might not have liked Adele, but she was his wife. He loved her."

"They fought all of the time," Greg countered. "I'm not sure he really did love her. He spent most of his time trying to get away from her."

"That's not how he described their relationship to me," Landon said.

"Yeah, but he also pretends I'm his son and Tess is his niece even though that's not true," Greg pointed out.

"Yeah. I'm starting to see that." Landon heaved out a sigh. "Now that the truth is out, I don't suppose you want to change your story about who might've wanted to harm Adele, do you?"

"Sure," Tess said without hesitation. "Everyone who ever met that woman wanted to do her harm. She was the least liked woman in the troupe. Heck, she might've been the least liked woman on the planet."

"No, Mrs. Little still has her beat there," I muttered.

Landon slid me a sidelong look, running his tongue over his teeth as he debated his next move. "Okay, you guys are free to go. Don't tell anyone that you've told me the truth. If I find out you lied, I'll come looking for you again, and it won't be pretty."

"Does that mean you won't tell Arthur you caught us?" Greg asked hopefully.

"Now that I know you're not really related, I don't care what you're doing," Landon replied. "Just ... keep it to yourselves."

"And if you're going to make out, don't draw so much attention to yourselves when heading into the woods," I added.

"Good tip," Tess said dryly, rolling her eyes as she turned to leave with Greg. She gave him a firm cuff as they headed out. "You just can't control your hormones, can you?"

"What can I say?" Greg said dryly. "I love being talked down to. It turns me on."

"I'll turn you on."

I chewed my bottom lip as I watched them go, waiting until I was sure they were gone before speaking again. "What do you think?"

"I think that Greg and his cousin Tess just gave us some very interesting information," Landon replied. "Instead of Adele being some sort of wonderful saint, which is how Arthur painted her, she was actually the opposite."

"Which means a lot of people had motive to kill her," I noted.

"Yeah, and all those people were traveling with her," Landon said.

"I'm guessing that renaissance troupes have easy access to witch books."

"I don't think they're technically called 'witch books,' but I get what you mean," I said. "They sell a lot of souvenirs and stuff. I'm betting at least one of those books deals with witchcraft in olden times, which would explain where they found the symbols and Theban alphabet."

"It would also explain why she was strangled," Landon said. "Strangling is an intimate crime. Only someone who knew Adele well would want to do that to her."

"Do you ever want to strangle me?"

"Rarely. Aunt Tillie is another story."

"Ah, I get what you're saying. It's not 'intimate' like you and I are intimate. It's 'intimate' in that whoever did it probably knew Adele well."

"Exactly." Landon nodded. "The thing is, that renaissance troupe is huge. We have an extremely large suspect pool."

"And that probably rules out Scarlet Darksbane," I noted.

"Probably."

"Crap." I tugged a hand through my hair. "I know she's guilty of something. If she's not guilty of this, I'll have to keep looking."

"You do whatever you feel is necessary," Landon said. "Just … don't go crazy."

"I never go crazy."

Landon made a face. "Never?"

"Almost never," I conceded.

"You go crazy at least once a month," Landon corrected. "Most of the time I find it mildly entertaining. Because I have to focus on the renaissance troupe – and that's a whole lot of people – I don't have the proper time to dedicate to this month's freak-out."

"I promise not to freak out to the point where I end up in jail," I offered.

"Are you only saying that because Terry would never arrest you?"

That was a loaded question. "Of course not."

"You're lying."

"I promise not to get arrested," I said, fighting to keep the snark out of my tone. "What more do you want?"

"Just a kiss." Landon kissed me quickly. "Oh, and you're buying me lunch because I know you're lying."

Oh, well, at least he understood my limits. "BLT?"

"You know it."

"Let's go." I slipped my hand into his. "I could use some soup and a sandwich myself."

We were almost out of the trees before Landon spoke again.

"How relieved were you that they weren't really cousins?"

"You have no idea."

"Me, too. I thought for sure I was going to have nightmares."

"Now your dreams are safe except for Aunt Tillie."

"And that recurring one I have where I wake up in a land without bacon," Landon added. "That one is truly terrifying."

"You're a freak sometimes. You know that, right?"

"I'm fine with it."

Oddly enough, I was, too.

EIGHTEEN

"So they're not really related?"

Chief Terry was flabbergasted when we related the story over lunch.

"Apparently none of them are legitimately related by blood," Landon replied. "It's all an act they put on."

"Well, that changes things."

Landon quirked an eyebrow. "You think?"

The entire scenario bothered me. I couldn't wrap my head around it, although I wasn't entirely sure why I was so rocked by the revelation. I was missing something … but couldn't grasp what. "Can't they get in trouble for lying to you?"

Landon flicked his eyes to me. "What do you mean?"

"They didn't tell you the truth when you first interviewed them," I replied. "Shouldn't they have to tell you the truth no matter what?"

"In theory," Landon confirmed. "An argument could be made that we didn't ask the right questions."

"Why would you think to ask if they were faking being related?"

"Good point. Still, it seems like we should've realized they weren't related. None of them look alike."

"I still think they're responsible for this screw-up," I grumbled, pushing my leftover fries around my plate. "I wonder if there's any information online."

"If you want to help, you can start there," Landon said, his eyes drifting toward the front door, his tone distracted. "In fact, I think that would be a good task for you."

Following his gaze, I found Scarlet Darksbane looking smug as she waved before sitting at a booth with Mrs. Little across the diner. She was so full of herself I wanted to slam my foot into her behind and listen to her cry while all the air seeped out of her oversized back tire.

Whoa. I think I channeled Aunt Tillie there for a little bit. Things were definitely starting to get to me.

"What was I saying again?" Landon asked, his eyes floating back to me.

"I believe you were saying that you're sleeping on the couch tonight," I prodded. I was only half joking. "As for handling the online search, I'd be more than happy to do that. I know you guys are going to have your hands full re-interviewing all of the fake Twiggs."

Landon's grin was cheeky. "Why am I sleeping on the couch?"

"You know why."

"Oh, are you jealous?" Landon poked my side, clearly enjoying himself.

"I don't know if 'jealous' is the word I'd use," I replied, opting for honesty. "I know you wouldn't cheat on me or anything."

"Of course I wouldn't cheat on you."

"It's still like a punch in the gut when you look at her the way you do." I dug in my purse for money to leave a tip and stood. "I'll be at the newspaper office if you need me. I might run over to Hypnotic later if I get bored or Brian is hanging around. It's uncomfortable to share space with him right now."

Chief Terry's eyes flashed. He was the key figure in making sure I would get The Whistler. After being removed from my position a few weeks ago because I was a suspect in a murder investigation (it's a long story), Brian tried to maneuver me out. It backfired when Chief Terry rallied the business owners against him. Brian had no choice.

He either had to sell the newspaper to me or go broke. That's essentially how I became a business owner.

"Has he been bothering you?"

I immediately regretted bringing it up. "No. I barely see him. We don't speak when we're in the building together. It's uncomfortable."

"It's going to be more uncomfortable when I help you take over that main office," Landon said. "I don't care whether or not he's ready to relinquish it. It belongs to you."

"It certainly does," Chief Terry agreed. "I'll help you move your stuff in there, too."

"Thank you." I managed a smile. "I'm sure I'll be fine. I'll let you guys know if I find anything."

"We'll do the same," Chief Terry said.

"Bay." Landon called out to stop me.

"What?"

"You're not really going to make me sleep on the couch, are you?"

I risked a glance at Scarlet and found her staring in our direction, keen interest etched on her face. "I guess that depends," I replied after a beat. "I'll talk to you in a little bit."

"I'll be waiting by my phone for your call," Landon teased. "I might even cry because I miss you so much."

"You're just saying things like that to irritate me," I groused.

"And you're both managing to irritate me," Chief Terry said. "So ... knock it off."

"You guys are a tough crowd," Landon said.

"Or maybe you're just really irritating when you want to be." I paused by the front door. "Have you ever considered that you're one big irritation?"

"Sometimes I strive for it." Landon's smile was small but heartwarming. "I'll call you in a bit. Try to stay out of trouble."

"Even I can't do the impossible."

BRIAN WAS THANKFULLY not in the office when I entered. I wasn't joking when I told Landon and Chief Terry that things were rough between us. Brian looked at it as if I stole something from him, hijacked the legacy his grandfather left him. I looked at it as if I was saving The Whistler, because Brian would've surely run it into the ground eventually.

In truth, my motivations weren't nearly as altruistic. I wanted the newspaper. I wanted to run it my way. I didn't need a big profit. I simply needed enough to live on. I wasn't keen on the idea of leveraging it into a marketing machine. I just wanted to create the best product I could realistically put out.

Viola floated in my office when I entered. She seemed eager to see me, which was alarming because she's full-on agitation when she gets going.

"Where have you been?"

"Living the dream," I replied dryly. "Why do you care?"

"Because that idiot in the front office has been here and he's packing up," Viola replied. "Are you guys closing the newspaper?"

I knit my eyebrows as I realized Viola had no idea about the change in ownership. "No. I'm buying the newspaper from Brian. After the first of the year, The Whistler will be mine."

Whatever she was expecting, that wasn't it. Viola – who doesn't breathe, mind you – visibly deflated. "Oh, so he's not trying to screw you over?" She sounded disappointed.

"Not last time I checked," I said. "He tried to screw me over a few weeks ago. That's how I ended up with the newspaper."

"So ... you beat him?"

"I guess you could look at it that way." I looked at it that way all the time. I simply didn't admit it because it made me look petty.

"Well, that's good. I certainly like you better than him." From Viola, that was high praise.

"So what's the problem?"

"I wanted to mess with him," Viola answered simply. "I've decided I'm going to start haunting people. I thought he should be my first test subject."

I pursed my lips, confused. "You're going to start haunting people?"

Viola bobbed her head. "I'm looking forward to it. I think it's a little late in my life to pick up a career, but this could be a really fun hobby, so ... why not?"

Hmm. It's never what you expect with her. The previous ghost that haunted The Whistler never changed. Even in death she remained a sometimes-terrible person. Viola didn't mean to be terrible. She often was, but not on purpose. She was wild, though, and altogether funny at times. This was not one of those times.

"How are you going to haunt people?" I asked. "I'm the only one who can see you. Well, Aunt Tillie can, but you and Aunt Tillie don't get along. Clove and Thistle can occasionally hear you, but only if they're around me when you start talking. No one else in town is likely to notice you when you're acting up. Er, I mean embracing your new hobby."

Viola ignored my verbal flub. "That will change when I learn how to move items," she countered. "That's my new goal. I'm going to learn to affect my physical surroundings."

"And do you think you'll be able to do it?"

"I do." Viola didn't suffer from self-doubt. I liked that about her.

"Okay, well ... go nuts."

"Oh, I'm totally going to get nutty," Viola agreed. "Do you care if I haunt Brian on his way out of the building?"

Actually, that sounded mildly funny if she could pull it off. "I think that sounds like a plan."

"Great. I can't wait. I'm going to start practicing now."

VIOLA REALIZED FAIRLY quickly that I wasn't interested in watching her practice, so she left to do it elsewhere. I suggested Aunt Tillie might be interested and, because she was an instigator, Viola jumped at the prospect. That left me two hours on my own to research the fascinating Twigg family. What I found was interesting, to say the least.

Brian was pulling into the parking lot when I left. I offered him a lame wave and he looked uncertain when he climbed out of the vehi-

AMANDA M. LEE

cle. I had no interest in talking to him, so I immediately volunteered that I was done in the office for the day and was heading to Hypnotic. He seemed relieved.

Clove and Thistle sat on the couch flipping through catalogs when I entered Hypnotic. The store was empty, which made it easy to relate what I'd found.

"I have so much to tell you guys," I announced, slipping out of my coat.

"Me, too," Thistle said. "I stole a sample of whatever Aunt Tillie is keeping in her flask – she has a big bottle she's trying to hide in her greenhouse and I snuck in after breakfast – and I'm going to have it analyzed."

The statement knocked me off course. "You're going to have it analyzed?"

"You bet." Thistle bobbed her head. "I think that woman is a modern-day bootlegger, and I'm totally going to nail her."

Oh, well, good. That didn't have "disaster" written all over it or anything. "How are you going to analyze it? Are you going to pay to send it to a lab or something?"

"Of course not," Thistle scoffed. "I'm going to drink it. I can tell the components of something when I drink it."

"Plus she ordered a chemistry set from Amazon," Clove added. "It seems they really do have everything there."

"I think we learned that when Aunt Tillie kept showing up with leggings that should've been outlawed," I said. "Well, if you want to give yourself another hangover I don't see the point in stopping you. Have at it."

"Oh, that hangover was just a fluke." Thistle was determined. "I'm going to figure out what that crazy old lady is up to if it kills me."

Given Aunt Tillie's stamina, I thought that was a definite possibility. "So ... I just ran into Brian." I decided to change the subject because there was no way Thistle was going to beat Aunt Tillie on this one, but telling her that would start a fight and I was in no mood for a fight. At least with Thistle, I mean. I was in the mood for a fight with

166

other people. Scarlet Darksbane sprang to mind, but that's a discussion for later.

"How was he?" Clove understood my discomfort and was sympathetic. "Is he still treating you like crap?"

"He doesn't treat me like anything. We're uncomfortable around each other, and that's not going to change. The good news is, he's leaving town after he sells, so I won't have to see him. At this point, I just want it to be over."

"It won't be long before he's gone, and we have Christmas in front of us," Thistle noted. "That will be a big distraction. You guys don't print Christmas week, so that's less time you have to spend around him. Marcus and I plan to spend Christmas at the new house so you and Landon can have the guesthouse to yourselves."

"Really?" I was surprised. "Will the new house be ready?"

"Not completely, but enough so we can enjoy it," Thistle replied. "I figured we'd all spend Christmas Eve together and then break apart for Christmas Day."

"I like that idea, but I don't think our mothers and Aunt Tillie will."

"They'll live," Thistle said. "You were going to tell us something else when you came in. What is it?"

"Right." I recovered from talk of Christmas – we still had weeks to worry about breaking the news to the family – and focused on the intriguing Twigg family. "So, none of the Twiggs are really related. They're all hired actors. I guess Arthur and Adele are related – they're married – but everyone else is hired help, and I found a ton of stuff on the internet about them."

"Wait … they're not related?" Thistle made a face. "I thought their whole shtick was that they were a family of performers."

"Yeah, well, that's a gimmick." I got comfortable in the chair at the edge. I told them about Tess and Greg, what happened when Landon and I followed them into the woods, and how things shook out after. When I was done, Thistle was beside herself.

"You know what? I don't care if you're faking being related, are related by blood or are related by marriage. It's still gross when you make out with your cousin, whether it's fake incest or not."

"It's not incest," Clove argued. "They're actors. It's no different from Peter Krause and Lauren Graham falling in love on the set of *Parenthood*. They played siblings on the show, but lived together in real life."

Hmm. She had a point. "It's still gross," I said after a beat. "The Twiggs are performing in person. That was a show. In person, even when randomly talking to people after they're done performing, they don't drop the family act."

"Bay is right," Thistle said. "That's all kinds of weird."

"That's not all," I said. "Apparently Adele Twigg was mean and mistreated most of the cast. It's hard to find work in renaissance troupes, so people stayed despite her attitude, but she fired a bunch of them over the years. They even created a message board to compare notes and complain about her."

"Ah, the internet," Thistle intoned. "The gift that keeps on giving. What did we do before we had a place to publicly complain about politics and former employers?"

"I don't remember. In this case, I'm glad the message board exists. It sounds like Adele was a real tyrant."

"Which could explain why she died the way she did," Clove said. "Someone went to a lot of trouble to kill her and then point the finger at someone else."

"Exactly." I shuffled the stack of papers I'd printed at the newspaper office. "So, take Laurie Walker, for instance. She was the oldest daughter, Laurie Twigg, for three years. She said that Adele was such a micromanager that she told everyone how they had to keep their hair and what kind of clothes they could wear when they weren't performing."

"That seems a bit much," Thistle said. "You said she was with the group for three years. Why was she fired?"

"Because she got pregnant," I replied. "She was dating someone – thankfully not another fake Twigg, because I'm not okay with all of that – and she got pregnant. Apparently she didn't want to marry the guy in real life and there was no way the character of Laurie Twigg could be a single mother, so Adele fired her."

"Is that even legal?" Clove asked. "I thought there were laws about firing people for pregnancy."

"There are, but apparently there's something in the contracts about not being able to perform their duties, and a pregnancy directly infringed on Laurie's ability to play the character of the oldest Twigg daughter," I replied. "They didn't even give her severance pay."

"I'm starting to think that Adele Twigg had a lot of enemies," Thistle said. "Odds are that it was a member of her own troupe that killed her."

"I know." I remained a bit disappointed that Scarlet Darksbane probably wasn't responsible. I wanted to run her out of town as soon as possible. "There are hundreds of complaints on that message board. I printed them to show to Landon and Chief Terry."

"So how do we narrow it down?" Clove asked.

"We?" Thistle arched a confrontational eyebrow. "Since when do you want to be involved in one of our little adventures?"

"Since whoever killed Adele Twigg did it in a way to make the rest of us look like evil witches," Clove replied. "I don't like it."

She wasn't the only one. "I'm not completely ruling out Scarlet Darksbane. It simply looks more likely that she's not to blame for this. She could be to blame for a bushel of other things, though."

"Not that we're hoping for that, right?" Thistle's eyes flitted with mirth. "By the way, I found a computer program we can feed those photos so that they can be scanned into a database. It should tell us what language she wrote that journal in."

And just like that I was off the Twigg hunt and on the Scarlet persecution train. "So what are we waiting for?"

Thistle snorted. "You were a bit too eager with your reaction there. It makes you look petty."

"I'm fine with that."

"Strangely enough, so am I." Thistle rolled to her feet. "I'll get my laptop. We might as well do something constructive this afternoon."

NINETEEN

"Anything yet?"

I watched Thistle upload the photos and hit the "search" button, and then proceeded to wait for what felt like forever. Thistle didn't look nearly as bothered as I felt about the duration of the search.

"Chill out, drama queen," Thistle ordered, resting her feet on the coffee table. "It said it might take some time. "You're being a pain."

"I can't help it. She bothers me like Mrs. Little bothers Aunt Tillie."

"Does that mean you're going to start leaving yellow snow at the end of her driveway during winter?" Clove asked.

That was an interesting thought. "I'm not ruling anything out. Speaking of that, do we know where she's staying?"

"As a matter of fact, we do." The look on Thistle's face caused me to pull up short. Her expression was a cross between amusement and anger.

"Why do I think this is going to be bad?"

"Because you're smarter than you look," Thistle replied. "I asked around. Toni Franco sells real estate. She says Scarlet is looking to rent the old Manchester house. She can't get in for at least three weeks, though, which means she's staying at one of the inns until then."

I knew where she was going before she even finished. "The Dragonfly?"

"You've got it."

"Son of a ...!"

"Maybe she didn't know," Clove suggested. "It might not have been on purpose."

"Do you really believe that?" I challenged. "She's hanging around Mrs. Little. They're obviously up to something. Now, it might not be something supernatural – I have no idea if Scarlet is capable of wielding real magic – but they're up to no good all the same."

"Bay has a point," Thistle said. "Everything we've seen with Scarlet so far seems to point to the fact that she's here to cause us trouble. Mrs. Little wouldn't be interested in her otherwise.

"Mrs. Little has been angry with us ever since the wishing well incident," she continued. "To be fair, she was angry with us long before then. The wishing well seemed to tip things over into outright hatred. I'm guessing she wants to use Scarlet as a club to hit us over the head."

"That's why Scarlet is opening a store that I'm going to bet offers exactly the same items your store does," I said. "She's going to be trouble. I haven't ruled out the notion that she's a murderer yet. Why else would she be up and in the town square like she was when Adele's body was found?"

"Maybe her inner sleep clock is simply messed up," Clove suggested. "That's possible after a move. Maybe she couldn't sleep in a new place."

Clove was so naïve sometimes I understood why Aunt Tillie was always on her case about being a kvetch.

"That still doesn't explain why she was walking around downtown right after a body was discovered," I argued. "She also looked almost happy when I saw her watching the scene."

"Was she looking at Landon at the time?" Clove asked. "He makes a lot of women happy when they stare at him."

Now she was just trying to tick me off. "Yeah, I'm done talking to you."

Thistle snorted. "Welcome to my world. She purposely agitates me every single day. She acts all innocent and sweet, but she's really diabolical."

"And you're paranoid," Clove fired back. "You always think someone is out to get you."

"Just because I'm paranoid – by my own admission, mind you – that doesn't mean people aren't out to get me," Thistle argued. "In fact, if I were someone else, I'd always be out to get me."

"You are an absolute delight." I patted her shoulder, leaning closer when the computer dinged. "What do you have?"

"Well, it's interesting," Thistle replied, furrowing her brow as she stared at the screen. "It's Cornish."

"I'm sorry. Cornish? Like the hens?"

Thistle barked out a laugh. "I think you've been spending too much time with Landon," she said. "Your mind goes straight to food for every reference now. According to this program, it's Old Cornish. I'm Googling it right now."

"I thought the Cornish language was like English," Clove said, moving around the couch so she could join us in staring at the screen. "Shouldn't the Cornish alphabet be the same?"

"Kind of, but not really," Thistle replied. "They've got the standard vowels, for example, but they throw in a lot of 'eus' and 'oes.' There are enough similarities to make us think we should be able to understand it, but it's different enough to confuse people."

"Yeah, but now that you mention it, I see the similarities," I mused. "The journal looked old, but it was well preserved. I initially assumed that Scarlet wrote it in code, but what if someone else wrote it and it's full of spells or something?"

Thistle cocked an eyebrow as she met my gaze. "Now that right there is a really interesting theory," she said. "I remember reading in one of Aunt Tillie's books when we were younger that there's an entire branch of Cornish witchcraft."

"What do you remember about it?" I was understandably intrigued.

"I'm not sure," Thistle hedged. "I think the book is back at the inn, though, if we need to double check. If I remember correctly, there was something in there about the Pellar Current."

"I have no idea what that means."

"I do." Clove brightened. "It's about a calling of magical women, grouping them together to fight off evil-doers. That's it distilled to its simplest form, of course. We'll need to conduct more research if we want more information, but Cornish witchcraft goes back to our very roots. It's essentially what we practice in a lot of ways, but we're not Cornish as far as I know."

"It's basically fighting against people who drop curses, ill-wishes, conjurations and the like," Thistle added.

"So how is that like what we do?" I asked. "Aunt Tillie curses us left and right."

"Yeah, but they're not evil curses as much as amusing curses in her book," Thistle pointed out. "She never tries to hurt us. The only time we whip out the terrible curses is if we're in real danger."

I understood where she was going. "So this journal is basically a book of protection spells?"

"I'm going to guess yes, but we need to compare it to some of the older books at the inn," Thistle said. "We can do that before dinner tonight."

That was very interesting. "Why would Scarlet have an old Cornish witchcraft journal?"

"Maybe it's like a Book of Shadows to her," Clove suggested. "She might think she has to protect herself against us. Mrs. Little probably told her as much."

That made sense, but it didn't jibe with Scarlet's actions. "Could someone use Cornish witchcraft spells to harm others?"

"I think any spell can be co-opted for evil," Thistle answered. "Is that what you think Scarlet has been doing?"

"I'm not sure what she's been doing, but I'm pretty sure it's evil," I replied. "In fact ... ." I didn't get a chance to finish because the wind chimes over the front door jangled, alerting us to the presence of a shopper. When I lifted my head, I found Scarlet Darksbane standing in the entryway. She looked smug and happy, a combination that worried me.

"Her ears must've been burning," Clove muttered under her breath.

Thistle remained calm as she closed the laptop and placed it on the table. She hadn't spent much time with Scarlet, but it looked like that was about to change. "Welcome to Hypnotic. How can we help you?"

I was stunned by Thistle's demeanor. She was professional, an air of chilly aloofness in her tone. She sounded haughty and gave the impression she was about to put Scarlet in her place, but never let the veneer of welcome drop from her face. She was utterly terrifying. Aunt Tillie would be so proud if she could see her protégé's reaction. Personally, I didn't understand why she painted such an aggressive picture right out of the gate, but I was interested to see how things would play out.

"I just wanted to check out the competition." Scarlet's smile appeared friendlier than Thistle's, but I had no doubt it was an act.

"We're not your competition," Thistle countered. "This is a town full of kitschy stores. Everyone gets their fair share. I'm sure your store won't be any different."

"Is that your friendly way of slapping me back?"

"I don't consider myself friendly no matter what I'm doing." Thistle got to her feet, the movement slow and deliberate. If we were in a horror movie, this is where I would've started running. Thistle being Thistle, though, she would've pulled a Jason Voorhees and caught up without breaking a sweat. That's how terrifying she was.

"I heard that about you." Scarlet made a big show of circling the store, her eyes focused on the merchandise rather than us. I got the distinct impression that she wanted us to believe she was much stronger and braver than she really was. She was posturing. But to what end? "You've all got quite the reputation around town."

"I'm sure we do." Thistle didn't move to intercept Scarlet – it was as if she was waiting for the woman to come to her and didn't want to cede the relationship power – but she watched Scarlet with keen interest. "We've always been a topic of discussion in Hemlock Cove. Even before the town was rebranded, back when it was Walkerville, we were famous."

"You definitely have a reputation," Scarlet agreed, her smile firmly in place when she turned. Instead of continuing her circuitous route around the store, she walked to the chair at the edge of the rug and sat without invitation. "Your great-aunt has an even more impressive reputation. What can you tell me about her?"

"She's multi-talented," Thistle replied, returning to her spot on the couch. "She's a witch-of-all-trades, so to speak."

"Margaret Little doesn't seem to like her."

"The feeling is mutual," Thistle said, shooting me a look that said "sit down" before continuing. I did as she wanted, even though I remained nervous, and crossed my legs as I watched the show. "Mrs. Little has her own set of enemies. Our great-aunt is merely one of them."

"My understanding is that your great-aunt has quite a few enemies herself," Scarlet pressed. "Margaret made it sound as if no one in town likes her."

"That would be an example of Mrs. Little being ... well, Mrs. Little," Thistle said. "Aunt Tillie certainly has her share of enemies. She also boasts a big fan club. She draws a strong reaction, whether good or bad, whatever she does."

"I see." Scarlet linked her fingers and rested them on her knee. "I get the feeling that you don't like me very much."

Clove and I exchanged a quick look. Scarlet was direct. You had to give her that. She clearly wanted to pick a fight, though.

"We don't know you," Thistle countered. "We try to get to know someone before getting our hate on."

That was an outright lie. I disliked Scarlet on sight, and Thistle and Clove joined the hate brigade simply because they were loyal to me.

"So I must be a special case?" Scarlet positively oozed smarm. "I'm mildly curious to figure out what I've done to turn you against me. I was hoping we could be friends."

"You were hoping we could be friends?" I broke in, annoyed. "You've been hanging around a woman who enjoys working against us, and you've been flirting with my boyfriend every chance you get. How is that making friends?"

I knew I'd made a mistake when I spoke, but Scarlet's triumphant grin hammered home the initial feeling. "I'm not sure what you mean. How have I been flirting with Landon?"

"Oh, don't even bother," I muttered, crossing my arms over my chest.

"He's an FBI agent," Scarlet said. "I happen to be fascinated with law enforcement, especially when they're investigating a rather brutal murder in my new home town. I mean ... what happened to Adele Twigg was terrible."

"It was definitely terrible," I agreed. "I still don't understand what you were doing up at three in the morning when the body was discovered. Why were you out there?"

Scarlet ignored the question. "I've been unsettled since it happened," she said. "I've been trying to learn as much as I can about the attack because I'm afraid for my own safety. In fact, I was just at the police station and I had a long talk with Chief Terry and Landon. He told me to call him that, by the way. Landon. It has a nice ring to it. I tried to call him 'Agent Michaels,' but he insisted it was too formal."

Scarlet's smile made me think of the witch in *Hansel & Gretel*. She was trying to maneuver me into an oven of sorts, and it only made me dislike her more.

"He's a wonderful man," she continued. "I expressed my fear over what happened and he reassured me that he was on top of things and would be around if I needed to ask questions."

I opened my mouth to say something vicious, my baser instincts getting the better of me, but I caught a warning look from Thistle and wisely snapped my mouth shut.

"He said I could come to him whenever I had questions or was worried," she continued. "I really appreciate that, because I've been so ... worked up ... since the murder. I'm afraid to be anywhere by myself."

"That must be terrible for you," Thistle drawled. "Have you considered getting a dog to make you feel safer? With your personality, snagging a man will be difficult. Dogs like everyone."

I pressed my lips together to keep from laughing.

Scarlet narrowed her eyes, the first signs of temper showing. "I think I'll just continue touching base with Landon and Chief Terry. I mean ... unless that bothers you, Bay. I don't want to do anything that makes you feel insecure."

My temper ignited again, but I managed to mask it. "I don't feel insecure." I forced a smile. "Landon and I live together. We're committed to one another. He's good at his job, and he wants to make people feel safe. I would never hold that against him."

"Plus, Landon is so gaga over Bay that it's a little pathetic," Thistle added. "He gets all mushy and pets her constantly. It's like a bad soap opera."

"Or softcore porn movie," Clove added, shrinking back when I murdered her with a look. "What? You guys are goofy sometimes."

"Yes, well, it sounds like you've got the world at your fingertips," Scarlet managed, shifting on her seat. "See. There really is no reason for us to be enemies."

"There's no reason for us to be friends either," Thistle pointed out. "You're hanging around with a woman who constantly tries to belittle and threaten us. By extension, you are on Mrs. Little's side because you choose to be friends with her. We're not in control of your friendship fate while you're in Hemlock Cove. That's up to you."

"I see." Scarlet said. "You're basically saying that we could be friends as long as I dump Margaret, even though she's been nothing but nice to me."

"Oh, I doubt very much we could be friends regardless," Thistle supplied. "Once you joined up with Mrs. Little, even the slim chance went out the window."

"Yeah, we're not going to be friends," Clove said, folding her arms over her chest. "We don't care what you do."

Scarlet flicked her eyes to me. "Do you feel the same way?"

"Probably not," I replied. I should've stuck to Thistle's script, but I couldn't stop myself from breaking off from the plan. "I don't believe we could be friends because I recognize what you're doing. I've met a few people like you over the years. The biggest, the worst, is in prison now. I helped put her there and I'm not sorry in the least.

"You like to feel out your opponents and try to get them on their heels before attacking," I continued. "You work in an underhanded manner, mete out small emotional attacks that make them look irrational while you come out smelling like a chocolate chip cookie. That's probably worked in the past for you, but it won't work now.

"We know what you are," I said. "We know what you're doing and how you're going to operate. I found the poppet. Don't bother denying it. I know it was you. I wasn't around anyone else who could've planted it that day."

"I have no idea what you're talking about," Scarlet said stiffly. "I'm trying to be friends."

"No, you're trying to do the opposite," I countered. "You want others to believe you're trying to be friendly. You're purposely being off-putting to us. You're trying to see if I'm insecure about Landon – I'm not, by the way – and you're trying to see if you can dig up dirt about Aunt Tillie. We've dealt with people like you before. We're not afraid of you."

"And as for Aunt Tillie, you should be very afraid of her," Thistle volunteered, her lips curving. "She'll take you down without even trying – and she'll enjoy doing it. Mrs. Little brought you in for a reason. She wanted someone else to fight her battles against Aunt Tillie. You're going to find that's not an easy task and she needed backup for a reason."

"And you think your great-aunt will be able to take me down?" Scarlet looked amused, but the emotion didn't make it all the way to her eyes. In her eyes, I saw something else. I was pretty sure it was worry. "I wasn't lying when I said I wanted to be friends, but if you push things I'll have no problem making you my enemies."

"I think we should save time," Thistle said. "Instead of pretending to be friends and then having a big falling out, let's just jump to enemies right from the start."

"Is that what you really want?" There was a challenge in Scarlet's eyes.

"That's what we want," Thistle confirmed.

"So be it. You'll be sorry. I'm not like any witch you've ever come across."

"That goes double for us from your perspective," Thistle said. "You can show yourself out. I think it's time for the curtain call on this show."

"Fine."

"Great."

"Good."

Thistle inclined her chin. "That's your cue. Get out."

"And don't look back," I added, my agitation bubbling. "You won't like what you see if you do."

TWENTY

"Hey, sweetie."

Landon found me in Hypnotic. Thistle and I worked on translating the Cornish journal, but everything we managed to dissect seemed to point toward an old Book of Shadows rather than a current spell book. It was interesting but ultimately uninformative.

"Hi." I flashed a smile. "Did you get anywhere today?"

"We interviewed all of the fake Twiggs a second time," Landon replied, groaning as he sank onto the couch next to me. "We had a lot more information come out this go around. Once Arthur realized the information was out he tried to control things for a bit, but that didn't last long. Things turned into a finger-pointing mess. Your father was thrilled, by the way. I think he's really growing quite fond of me."

I pressed my lips together to keep from laughing. Landon and Dad were never going to be best friends, but they both did their best to get along for my sake. "I appreciate you trying to be friendly with Dad, even though it's not your favorite thing."

"That's not true," Landon countered. "I like him ... sometimes. I'm not thrilled with the fact that he left you as a kid, though."

"It's over and done with. We can't do anything about it, so there's no reason to dwell on it."

"No, but that doesn't mean I have to like everything he's done." Landon stretched his long legs out in front of him. "Did you find anything?"

"I did." I grabbed the stack of printouts from the online forum where people spent hours upon hours complaining about the Twiggs and handed it to him. "Some of it is kind of funny. Some of it is really sad. Some of it is borderline criminal."

"Some of what?" Landon narrowed his eyes as he read the top sheet. "What is this?"

"It's the history of the Twiggs," I replied. "They're apparently not very good bosses."

"Holy moly." Landon flipped through several pages. "All of this is complaints about how the Twiggs run their business?"

I nodded. "And then some."

"Well, that widens the suspect pool." Landon rubbed the back of his neck. "If these ex-employees hate them to this degree that means someone could've been bitter enough to follow them to this location and kill Adele."

"Or someone was already here," I suggested. "I'm not sure what to tell you on that front. You'll have to get the Twiggs to turn over employee records, and from what people are saying about Arthur on that forum, he's not much better than Adele."

"Yeah, I've been getting that feeling myself," Landon admitted. "He's kind of a douche."

"According to someone named Erica Buchanan in that mess of stuff I gave you, he's also a sexual harasser and his wife blamed the victim whenever she complained about his groping hands."

Landon's mouth dropped open. "Are you serious?"

"Sadly, yes. It turned my stomach a bit."

"I bet. I'll have to go through this stuff after dinner. I guess that means I won't have any time to spend with you."

"I'll go through it with you," I offered. "I made notes on some of it, and I know where the really interesting stuff is. It will cut down on your work time."

"Thank you." Landon gave me a quick kiss. "Did you spend your entire afternoon on this?"

I shook my head. "I did that while I was at the newspaper. Viola has decided she's going to start haunting people, by the way. She's looking at it as a new hobby."

"I thought you told me only people with 'the gift' can see and talk to ghosts."

"That's true, but she claims she's going to start teaching herself how to move items because she's intent on haunting someone."

"That sounds ... delightful." Landon smirked. "Anything else?"

"Well, I came here to tell Clove and Thistle about the faux incest going on with the Twiggs," I started.

"And we're officially horrified," Thistle announced from behind the counter, her gaze intent as she tallied inventory. "We've all decided that it doesn't matter if they're really related or not. The fake stuff is just as bad."

"I don't think it's as bad," Clove argued. "I was overruled, though."

Landon shot her a sympathetic look. "That's the story of your life, isn't it?"

Clove nodded without hesitation. "You know it."

Landon tucked a strand of hair behind my ear. "So you really have been busy, huh?"

"Pretty much," I confirmed. "That was before we identified the language in the journal and your little girlfriend came over to pay us a visit." I didn't mean to put such emphasis on the word "girlfriend" but I couldn't stop myself from being irked by Scarlet's visit. Even though I wasn't worried about losing Landon, her attitude chafed.

"You know what's in the journal?" Landon was intrigued.

"It's old Cornish," Thistle replied. "We went through a lot of it. Spells and stuff. Cornish witches were a big deal back in the day – and there's still a contingent of them around today – so once we realized what we were looking at we started figuring out the spells. None of it is particularly terrifying, but it's interesting in a purely clinical way."

"Hmm." Landon's expression was unreadable. "Does that mean she's a real witch?"

"Maybe," I answered. "She could also be a fake witch who stumbled across a real book. We're not sure which yet."

"Oh, I think she's evil," Clove said. "Her attitude when she was in here makes Thistle look friendly."

Landon snorted. "Please tell me you guys didn't gang up on her."

"Of course we didn't." I flashed what I hoped would pass for a serene smile. "Given your close personal relationship with her – she made sure to stress that to me, by the way – we'd never gang up on her."

Landon stilled, discomfort rolling over his features. "I'm sorry, but … what?"

"She said she spent some time with you and Chief Terry today," I explained. "She said you were very kind to her. She was thankful for your dedicated attention to assuaging her worries."

"Is that how she phrased it?"

"Bay is the only person who uses the word 'assuaging,'" Thistle said. "What do you think?"

"Um … ." Landon broke off, uncertain. It was as if he sensed trouble but wasn't sure which direction it was coming from.

"She was mean," Clove said. "She tried to make Bay jealous, but then Bay slapped her back and said that she wasn't worried about you cheating on her."

"Did Scarlet make it seem like I was cheating on you?" Landon's eyes locked with mine. "You know that's not true, right?"

"She didn't say anything of the sort," I said. "And, yes, I know you wouldn't cheat on me. That doesn't mean I like her attitude. She was trying to infer certain things. It's a woman thing that men don't get, so don't bother trying. I made sure she knew I wasn't jealous."

"That's good. You have no reason to be jealous."

"I'm still going to punch her the next time she opens her mouth," I added.

"Well, here's hoping you won't be around her the next few days so I don't have to arrest you for assault."

I wrinkled my nose at his adorable expression. He thought he was being cute and flirty. I had some bad news for him, though, and now seemed the time to spring it. "We're going to see her tonight."

Landon swallowed hard. "Excuse me?"

"We're going to see her tonight," I repeated.

"And why is that?"

"Because Dad invited us to dinner," I replied. "He said he's been seeing a lot of you and not enough of me. He kind of trapped me into agreeing to go out there. I didn't think it would be too bad because it would allow you to monitor the Twiggs a bit while eating."

"That's fine. I'm perfectly happy to have dinner out there," Landon said. "I don't understand what Scarlet has to do with it."

"Oh, you mean your close personal friend who thinks you walk on water and wants you to keep her safe and warm?"

"Oh, geez." Landon pinched the bridge of his nose. "I thought you said you weren't jealous."

"I'm not jealous. I just totally want to punch her in the boob."

Even though it was a serious situation, Landon cracked a smile. "Okay, well ... I don't understand what the evil temptress witch has to do with our dinner plans."

"She's staying at The Dragonfly, too."

Landon's smile dipped. "Seriously?"

I nodded. "It's going to be a really tense meal. Don't forget your antacid."

"Ah, well, I should've seen it coming," Landon lamented, leaning his head back. "Things were going too smoothly today. I should've expected a big, honking roadblock to pop up. It shouldn't be too terrible. No matter what you say, you always manage to keep your manners in check."

"She's not the only one going," Thistle interjected. "We're going, too."

Landon cringed. "Well, that changes things, doesn't it? We need to stop at the gas station for Rolaids on our way out there."

"That sounds like a wise idea."

"I'M SO GLAD YOU could come."

Dad was enthusiastic when he met us at the front door of The Dragonfly. He ushered us inside, giving me a warm hug before clapping Landon on the shoulder.

"It seems like I just saw you," Landon noted.

"Yes, but this time you have someone I'm really happy to see with you," Dad said.

"You say that now, but I'll bet you change your mind over the course of dinner."

"What?" Dad was puzzled.

"Ignore him," I said. "He's crabby from a long day of questioning."

"Yes, well, I have to say that I was surprised when I realized that our guests weren't really related by blood," Dad admitted. "It does clear up some lingering questions I've had about some of the siblings slipping into each other's rooms when they thought no one was looking."

I wrinkled my nose. "Eww!"

"Yeah." Dad nodded. "Come on. Dinner will be served in about five minutes. I was worried you guys wouldn't be on time. Clove, Thistle, Marcus and Sam are already here."

I kept my smile in place as we followed Dad to the dining room, amusement washing over me when I saw the look on Scarlet's face. She sat next to Warren, Clove's father, and stared bloody daggers at Thistle across the table.

"I see we're just in time." I moved to sit next to Thistle, something I thought would give us an advantage, but Landon grabbed my arm and directed me toward the second open seat. "What?"

"I'm sitting next to Thistle." Landon was smart enough to know what I had planned and he clearly sensed trouble.

"Why?" Dad asked.

"Because I don't see her nearly enough," Landon replied. "I'll miss her when she moves out of the guesthouse. Between all the bras and panties she leaves hanging around the bathroom and her absolutely lovely attitude first thing in the morning, it's going to be a real hardship when she goes."

"The bras and panties were kind of an overshare," Dad said.

"Try living in my world for an hour," Landon countered. He sat next to Thistle, pinning her with a warning look before unfolding his napkin and placing it in his lap. He forced a smile for the Twiggs' benefit, but they didn't look any happier to see him than Scarlet did to see us. "How is everyone this evening?"

"I'm great," Scarlet purred, her glare disappearing as she beamed at Landon. "I'm so happy you're here. Our conversation earlier made me feel so much better – safe even – and I can't wait to talk to you further."

Landon recognized Scarlet's statement for what it was: a way to agitate me. "I think you must've gotten something out of our earlier conversation that I didn't realize. Can you pinpoint exactly where it was that I insinuated we were close personal friends?" Landon wasn't one to dally, and he immediately jumped into the thick of things.

"I'm sure that's not how I phrased it," Scarlet countered.

"That's exactly how you phrased it," Clove argued.

"Yes, you're a damnable liar," Thistle added at the same time. "I think if we were trapped in a fairy tale world right now, your nose would be growing."

"Can we not bring that up?" Sam whined. He was cursed with the growing nose when we really were trapped in a fairy tale book, and his reaction made me smile.

"Am I missing something?" Dad asked, taking his spot next to me and casting a worried look around the table. Unlike at The Overlook, the folks at The Dragonfly weren't accustomed to dinner theater. If we were home right now, this dinner would've already devolved into something completely irrational and out of control. There might've even been flying desserts involved.

"No," Landon answered hurriedly.

"Yes," I countered, offering my father a wan smile. "We're having a bit of a ... thing ... with Ms. Darksbane." I saw no reason to lie. In fact, if anything, growing up with Aunt Tillie taught me that the truth can be a much better weapon than subterfuge.

"A thing?"

"Oh, this is going to suck," Landon muttered.

"Have some wine." Marcus slid an open bottle in front of him. "Trust me. It helps."

Landon took the bottle without complaint. "I'm going to get drunk, Bay, so you'll have to drive. That means you're having a dry evening."

"Whatever." I didn't care about the wine. If I wanted to get drunk I knew where Aunt Tillie stashed her new liquor concoction in the greenhouse.

"I'm still confused," Dad said. "How do you guys know Ms. Darksbane? I thought she just arrived in town."

"She did," Clove said. "She came to town and went straight to Mrs. Little to make friends."

"Oh." Realization dawned on Dad. "I see."

"You see?" Scarlet turned her full attention to him. "I don't understand what the problem is. Margaret is a perfectly nice woman. She's been wonderful to me. In fact, she's the closest thing I've had to a mother since my own died a few years ago." The look on Scarlet's face was almost heartbreaking. She was good. We were raised by Aunt Tillie, though, so we were better.

"I read something about you on the internet," Thistle said, making a face as Marcus slapped her hand when she reached for the wine. "What are you doing?"

"No wine for you," Marcus replied. "Things are going to be bad enough without adding alcohol to the mix."

"I'll remember this," Thistle warned.

"You read things about me on the internet?" Scarlet prodded. "What kinds of things? My fortune-telling skills are known far and wide. I'm something of a legend."

"You certainly are," Thistle agreed. "In fact, you're such a legend a group of people claim that you approached them, offered to take a curse off them, and when they refused you really cursed them so they'd have no choice but to pay you to remove the curse."

"Wait … are we really talking about curses?" Greg asked, confused. Up until then he'd been silent and listening to the conversation with mild interest, casting the occasional look at Tess when he thought no one was looking. Apparently they were still hiding their relationship.

"Don't you have a sister to make out with or something?" Thistle challenged.

"Cousin," I automatically answered. "He likes to make out with his cousin, not his sister."

"She's not really my cousin," Greg snapped, casting a worried look in Arthur's direction. For his part, the Twigg patriarch seemed to be losing himself in a bottle of wine, paying no attention to the conversation.

"Shut up, Greg," Tess ordered. "It looks like these chicks are going to get in a girl fight. I totally want to watch."

One of the other Twiggs, a man in his mid-twenties, enthusiastically nodded. "I totally want to watch the chick fight, too. I think it'll be hot."

"It won't," Landon said. "They're not going to pull hair. They might throw a few punches. There's also a good likelihood that dirt will somehow be involved."

The man was blasé. "I'm fine with that."

"I don't understand what you're talking about," Scarlet hedged. I didn't miss the brief flash of worry that flitted through her eyes. "I would never curse someone just so I can cure them for money."

"That's not what the internet says," Thistle argued.

"Do you believe everything you read on the internet?"

"Of course not." Thistle made a clucking sound with her tongue. "I don't believe Elvis is still alive or that Tupac is living in the Swiss Alps. I don't believe the Kurt Cobain was killed as part of some vast conspiracy for his music rights. The stuff I read about you, though, that I believe."

"Well, you've been misled." Scarlet gripped her wine glass so hard her knuckles turned white. "You don't believe that, do you, Landon?"

Landon, already halfway through his first glass of wine, slammed the rest before answering. "I think you should go back to calling me 'Agent Michaels.'"

Scarlet floundered. "All because your girlfriend is jealous?"

"My girlfriend has no reason to be jealous," Landon replied. "Besides, that's not what this is."

"And what is this?" Dad asked.

"A reckoning," Landon replied. "Ms. Darksbane poked the Winchester beehive, and now things are going to get ugly."

"How so?"

"Aunt Tillie taught your daughter and her cousins how to fight," Landon explained. "That means they know how to win."

"It's actually a little terrifying," Marcus said.

"Oh, I'm pretty sure I'm trapped in a horror movie," Landon said. "Do you have more wine?"

"I'll get it." Dad levered himself up from the table. "Will the inn be standing when I get back?" He sensed the turmoil flooding the room.

"We can always hope." I flashed a bright smile. "It's going to be a long night, though. You should probably grab a couple bottles of wine."

"And then give them to us," Landon said, gesturing toward Sam, Marcus and himself. "The women are cut off."

"I'm going to remember this," Thistle threatened.

Landon was unruffled. "I hope it's the exact opposite for me."

TWENTY-ONE

"*D*o we have more wine?"

We were only twenty minutes into dinner, the Twiggs rapt thanks to the ongoing drama building between Scarlet and us. Landon, Marcus and Sam appeared to be mainlining wine to deal with the tense situation.

"You've had enough wine, Marcus," Thistle chided, pushing the empty bottle away from him. "Drink some water. I don't think I'm capable of carrying you into the guesthouse when we get home."

"And I know I'm not capable of carrying you." I cast Landon a sidelong look. He knew how to maintain his poker face, but I could sense the anxiety settling on his shoulders.

"I don't understand the problem." Dad, ever the peacemaker, was desperate to keep things from getting out of hand. "How can you guys already be at war? Scarlet has been in town for only four days. Even you don't work that fast."

"Never underestimate us," I said.

"Or what happens when someone hops on the first broom to bitch town," Thistle added.

"But ... I don't understand." Dad was never comfortable around a girl fight. Even when I was little, before he left, he'd

190

have serious discussions with Thistle and me when we squabbled. He wasn't happy with confrontation, which is one reason he didn't make it in the Winchester family. We thrive on confrontation.

"You don't have to understand," Landon offered. "It's all-out war. Those of us with penises are going to be collateral damage. Just sit back and enjoy the battle. I suggest numbing yourself with wine if you're feeling antsy, by the way. You won't stop this from happening, so enjoy it."

"Yes, enjoy it, Uncle Jack," Thistle said, her eyes narrow and focused on Scarlet. "We've got this under control."

Teddy, Thistle's father, clasped his hands together as his busy gaze bounced between faces. "Does anyone else feel as if we're sitting on a bomb? I can't stop sweating."

"I think it's neat," Tess said. "I love watching a good chick fight. I especially like it because these two don't have a problem ganging up on the redhead. She's kind of slutty and has been flirting with all of my brothers and cousins, so I would love to see her get her face bashed in."

"I only flirted with them because I thought they were sexually repressed and needed something fun to look at," Scarlet said sweetly. "Besides, it wasn't real flirting. It was harmless flirting. There's a difference."

"Whatever." Tess didn't look convinced as she twirled her pasta on her fork. "Go get her, witches. That's the deal, right? This is a witch fight. I've never seen a witch fight."

"And you're not going to now." Dad scorched me with a warning look. "That's not going to happen, right, Bay?"

He was putting me on the spot. "I don't know," I hedged.

"I do." Dad was firm. "There will be no ... whatever it is you guys do when you fight ... under this roof. I'm laying down the law."

"Did you hear that, Bay?" Thistle's smirk was evil. "Your father is laying down the law."

"I know. I'm terrified." I smiled for Scarlet's benefit, although the expression turned into a cringe when I saw the dark look on Dad's face. "I'm sorry, but she bugs me. She's been bugging me since I met her."

"And how has she been doing that?" Warren asked. "She's been an absolute delight while staying under our roof."

Scarlet preened under the compliment. "Thank you, Warren. I enjoy talking to you, too."

"That right there," Clove snapped, extending a finger. "She's flirting with you, Dad. It's gross."

"Hey, I'm not gross." Warren was understandably offended. "And like she said, that's harmless flirting. It's almost expected in some circles."

"Well, we don't like it in our circles," Thistle said. "The only people who can flirt with our men is us."

"When do you ever flirt with me?" Marcus asked dryly. "Your idea of flirting is rolling on top of me during a storm. That's not really flirting."

Thistle absently glanced at him. "What do you mean?"

"I mean that I like a little flirting now and then." Marcus crossed his arms over his chest. "When I come home from a long day of work, I don't want the first thing I see to always be you with a martini in your hand and a demand for me to rub your feet."

Thistle balked. "I don't demand you rub my feet all of the time."

"You did it last week."

"That's because they really hurt." Thistle shot me a look that demanded help. "You make Landon rub your feet, don't you?"

I immediately started shaking my head. "No."

"Bay's feet are sensitive," Landon supplied. "She's extremely ticklish. I don't mind rubbing her feet. In fact, I kind of like it, but she's much happier with a back massage."

"Oh, that's too bad for you," Scarlet cooed. "I happen to love a good foot massage. If you ever feel the need to practice ... ." She left the invitation hanging.

"Don't make me yank your hair out of your head," I hissed.

Scarlet adopted an innocent expression. "What did I do? Did you hear her? She's so aggressive."

"Oh, I see what you're doing," Tess nodded. Whether or not she was trying to be an asset, she was clearly on our side in this fray. It was interesting – and kind of refreshing. It was like adding another Thistle to the battle. Tess boasted much of the same personality traits.

"And what am I doing?" Scarlet challenged.

"You're flirting with the men to get them on your side while purposely antagonizing the women," Tess shot out. "It's a common thing on the renaissance festival circuit. We have a lot of narcissists in this field."

"I am not a narcissist," Scarlet spat.

"No? You seem like one," Tess pressed. "You're flirting with the fathers and boyfriends of these three, and they recognize what you're doing. You play innocent with the men. You paint yourself a victim and them as your attackers. You're good at it, but that doesn't mean you'll win.

"Most men want to swoop in and save a woman when she's being attacked," Tess continued. "The long-haired FBI agent looks like the type to do things like that. But he's caught, because he clearly loves his girlfriend. You're playing the victim in an attempt to drive a wedge between them. You're good, but not good enough."

I risked a glance at Landon and found him watching Tess with keen eyes.

"Is that a woman thing?" Landon asked. "I've heard that men don't always recognize female behavior for what it is. I was told it's a woman thing that I'll never understand. You recognize it, though."

"You can't possibly believe her, Landon." Scarlet wheedled. "They're going after me. I told you that this afternoon."

"She told you that this afternoon?" Now I was really going to have to yank out her hair.

"Don't worry about it." Landon patted my knee under the table. "I think I get it now."

"Do you really, or are you just saying that?"

Landon flashed me a smile. "I get it. She was playing on my ego."

"I thought you didn't have an ego."

"We both know I'm a total egomaniac," Landon said. "That's why I get along so well with your family."

"Ah." I couldn't hide my smile. "That explains so much."

"Doesn't it?"

"Wait ... what's happening here?" Scarlet's face flushed with color. "Why are you okay with me being attacked?"

"Because I'm starting to realize that I might've missed a few things," Landon replied. "I'm pretty sure you've been acting differently with us than you have with them." Landon inclined his head in my direction. "Now, I'm not saying they're always rational. They have moments when I wonder how they've managed to survive as long as they have. They're not generally terrible people, though."

Scarlet opened her mouth to argue, something I'm certain was acidic on the tip of her tongue. Aunt Tillie picked that moment to sweep into the room. She wore Christmas-themed leggings and a combat helmet, and the look on her face was quizzical.

"Did someone say something about terrible people?" Aunt Tillie asked.

Uh-oh. I pressed my lips together and flicked a worried look in Landon's direction.

Instead of being fearful, Landon's shoulders shook with silent laughter.

"This isn't funny," I hissed.

"Oh, it's hysterical." Landon pointed at the pasta on my plate. "Bulk up on your carbs, sweetie. Things just got interesting."

That was putting it mildly.

"WHAT'S FOR DINNER?"

Aunt Tillie was all smiles as she wedged herself between Arthur Twigg and Dad, her eyes momentarily darkening as they passed over Scarlet and then lighting with mirth when locking with mine.

"Seafood alfredo," Dad said, his voice a bit shaky. He had a long history with Aunt Tillie and it wasn't all pleasant. "I ... you ... um ... hmm."

I decided to help him out. "Not that we're not glad to see you, Aunt Tillie, but what are you doing here?"

"I'm having dinner with my family," Aunt Tillie replied, not missing a beat. "I thought you would be up at The Overlook, but then I heard you were out here. I have something to share with you and I thought it was important."

We had tasked Aunt Tillie with trying to decipher what had been written in blood next to Adele Twigg's body. I'd almost forgotten that. "What did you find?"

"Later." Aunt Tillie narrowed her eyes as she focused on Scarlet "You're the new witch."

"Yeah, what's up with that?" Tess clearly had no filter. I couldn't help but like her a bit. "I thought this town was full of fake witches. Are you saying there are real witches, too?"

"Not all witches are fake," Scarlet said sagely.

"That one is." Aunt Tillie pointed at Scarlet for emphasis. "She's a big, fat fake, and I'm going to make her cry like a little girl before everything is said and done." She directed her gaze to Dad. "Are you going to get me a plate? I'm starving. Where are your manners?"

Dad hopped to his feet, his face flushed. "Of course." He was clearly caught between his discomfort around Aunt Tillie and his need to be a good host. The night wasn't going as he'd planned, so he was doing his best to maintain a false sense of bravado despite the surreal nature of the conversation.

Dad slid a large plate in front of Aunt Tillie and watched with wide eyes as she dished pasta onto it. The mound of pasta was so high it almost touched the bottom of Aunt Tillie's chin.

"This looks good," Aunt Tillie enthused. "They're having pork loin at The Overlook, and as much as I love a good loin, this looks even better. Don't tell Marnie, Winnie and Twila I said that."

"Of course not." Dad looked to me for help. "I ... what were we talking about?"

"How Scarlet is evil and messing with us," I replied, grinning when Dad's forehead wrinkled. "Don't worry about it. Scarlet was never going to be a repeat customer anyway. She's waiting for the old

Manchester house to open so she can rent it. Your sterling reputation is still in place."

"How do you know which house I'm renting?" Scarlet asked, wrinkling her nose. "I'm pretty sure I didn't tell anyone but Mrs. Little about that."

"And Margaret has a huge mouth, so I'm sure she's been spreading your business around to anyone who will listen," Aunt Tillie said, sliding two sea scallops from her plate onto mine and skewering shrimp from my plate.

"What are you doing?"

"You know I don't like … whatever that is," Aunt Tillie replied. "I'm trading it for something I do like."

"Those are scallops and you like them fine when we grill them during the summer," I argued. "You called them sea chicken this past summer."

"Ooh, I remember those." Landon perked up. "Can we grill those again this summer?"

"Sure."

"Can we get our own grill and occasionally cook for just the two of us at the guesthouse?"

The question caught me off guard. "Sure, but … I'm not a good cook like my mother."

"It's grilling," Landon said. "Anybody can grill."

Aunt Tillie snorted. "Yes, that's the male motto, isn't it? Not everyone can grill, sport."

"Since when do you call me 'sport?'" Landon challenged.

"Since I'm hungry and too weak to think up something derogatory to call you," Aunt Tillie replied, unruffled. "I need to keep up my strength to insult the new witch. You get a pass for the night."

"Oh, we should throw a party." Landon slipped one of his shrimp onto my plate. "I know you like the shrimp and the scallops."

"Oh, it's cute that you're sharing." I grinned.

"Ugh, I think I might puke," Dad muttered. "You guys are so sickly sweet sometimes."

"They get off on it," Aunt Tillie said. "The key is to ignore them. If you comment on how gross it is, it only gives them power. If you ignore it, they stop being annoying."

"Is that true?" Dad was intrigued.

"I only tell the truth."

Dad turned to me. "Is that true?"

I couldn't help but smile at Aunt Tillie's dark expression. "Not really. We're pretty schmaltzy all of the time right now."

"It's because they're moving in together," Aunt Tillie said. "They're in the full bloom of romance. It will probably dissipate after they spend two weeks living together and they realize it's not all kisses and hugs. I'm guessing once the sex haze clears there will be plenty of bickering."

"Don't say things like 'sex haze,'" Dad ordered.

"Stop being a prude, Jack," Aunt Tillie warned. "It's ridiculous coming from the guy who spent the first two weeks after his honeymoon going commando."

Dad's mouth dropped open as my cheeks burned.

"Don't tell me things like that," I ordered. "You're going to traumatize me for life."

"Now you know how I feel," Dad shot back. "That phase didn't last long, so ... chill out."

"Yeah, Bay, chill out." Landon poked through my pasta until he came up with an oyster. "I'm going to eat this because it's supposed to be an aphrodisiac. I expect you to reward me later."

I ignored him. "Let's stop talking about gross stuff," I ordered. "Let's go back to bugging Scarlet."

"Let's definitely do that," Thistle agreed. "Although ... you said you found something, Aunt Tillie. Did you manage to spell anything from the letters found at the murder scene?"

Arthur perked up, showing interest in the conversation for the first time since we'd sat down. "Adele's murder scene?"

"I'm sure that's the only murder scene they're working in a town this size," Tess said.

"I'm not sure I should share it here," Aunt Tillie said. "I only came to torture the new witch. I used the stuff I found as an excuse."

"Go ahead and share it," Landon said. "Everyone is going to know regardless."

"Okay, well, I messed with the alphabet letters and finally came up with a word," Aunt Tillie said, digging in her pocket and returning with a sheet of paper. She'd obviously gone through multiple attempts to spell a word, crossing out those she didn't like and ultimately settling on one she did. "As far as I can tell, there's only one word that can be spelled with what you found there."

Landon snagged the sheet of paper and stared at it. "What word is this supposed to be?"

"Well, you're not going to like it, but it spells witch," Aunt Tillie said, shoveling a huge forkful of pasta into her mouth and chewing as she spoke the next bit. "I think someone is trying to point a finger."

"At witches?" Tess asked, her gaze sliding to me. "Does that mean a witch killed Adele?"

I focused on the memory of Scarlet's face when I saw her at the scene. "That's a possibility," I said. "Of course, it's also possible someone merely wants us to believe it was a witch."

"To what end?" an anguished Arthur begged. "My wife is dead. What are you doing to find her killer?"

"We're working on it," Landon replied, his hand absently moving to the back of my neck as he watched Scarlet shift on her chair with fresh interest. "We're getting new information every day. It's only a matter of time before we solve it."

"And then the murderer is going down," Thistle added, glaring at Scarlet. "That person should be very afraid."

"Definitely," Aunt Tillie agreed, white sauce congealing at the corners of her mouth. "This is good. Is there any wine?"

"Landon drank it all," Dad replied.

"That's okay." Aunt Tillie dug in her pocket and returned with her flask. "Anyone want a belt?"

"Absolutely not," I answered instantly.

"I might have one," Thistle said, smirking when I shot her a look. "What? We have hours of this left. I'm going to need something to relax me."

She had a point. "Yeah. I need a shot of that, too."

Landon's smile was full of mayhem. "Just one big drunk family, huh?"

Hey, there are worse things to be.

TWENTY-TWO

*A*fter dinner, Dad hid the leftover wine – and gave Aunt Tillie the evil eye when she pulled out her seemingly bottomless flask – before plying us with multiple mugs of coffee. Scarlet made her escape before dessert, but not before scalding me with a dark look that promised retribution, and we were completely sober before we left.

Landon was quiet for the ride home, his mind clearly busy. I waited until we pulled into the driveway to question him.

"What do you think?"

Landon slid his gaze to me. "I think you're pretty."

I made a face. "Not that."

Landon grinned. "I don't know what to think right now. What do you think?"

"I think that someone wanted to make it seem as if Adele Twigg was murdered by locals rather than members of her own troupe," I replied, leaning back in my seat. Landon showed no signs of killing the engine. "I think that this town's history makes the people an easy target for some things."

"I think you're right."

"You do?"

Landon nodded. "Someone grabbed a book and used it to find symbols they didn't understand. I think picking the letters for 'witch' was a bit much, but it's not as if the murderer had a lot of time.

"Taken by themselves, the symbols can look creepy for those who don't understand," he continued. "I admit that was my initial reaction. Luckily, I happen to have a very smart witch friend who explains things to me."

I smirked. "Is that what I am? Your witch friend?"

"You're my very special witch friend," Landon conceded. "My favorite witch in all the land, in fact."

"That was smooth."

"I do my best." Landon fell quiet as he grabbed my hand and flipped it over, tracing his fingers over my palm as he considered how best to proceed. He seemed caught, as if he wanted to say something but wasn't sure it was the right thing to do. I decided to help him along.

"If you want to say something about the way we acted with Scarlet ... well ... I'm expecting it."

"I do, but I'm not sure how to phrase it without sounding like a shmuck."

"I've seen you act like a schmuck before. Lay it on me."

Landon smiled. "I'm sorry."

I stilled, surprised. "For what? You didn't create a very uncomfortable dinner environment. That's all on me."

"Technically that's on you, Thistle, Clove and Aunt Tillie," Landon corrected. "I'm not angry about that. I understand why you did it. I also understand that I was perhaps blind to the other things that were going on."

"Like what?"

"Like the fact that Scarlet acted differently around Terry and me. I know you might think it's simple of me, but I guess I wanted to believe her ... so I did."

"I don't think it's simple of you. I think it's simply who you are."

"And who is that?"

"Someone who wants to help."

"Yeah? I guess. I don't want to be naïve, though."

It was a simple statement, but it touched me. "You know, when I first met you I thought you were a jerk."

Landon snorted. "You were supposed to think I was a jerk. I was undercover with bad guys. I certainly didn't want you to like me and put yourself in danger."

"I get that. The thing is, even though you wanted to act all tough and dark, I could tell you had a good heart. Sure, I thought it was weird that you followed me into a corn maze in the middle of the night, and I thought there was a very real chance you were a pervert – which turned out to be true – but I recognized you for what you were right away."

"And what am I?"

"You're a good man who wants to believe the best of people."

"Ah, you make me feel all mushy when you say things like that." Landon gripped my hand. "People are sick of how mushy we are."

"They'll live."

"They will indeed." Landon ran his tongue over his lips. "I'm still sorry, Bay. I thought you were being unreasonable. I didn't see what she was doing. I should have. I was a little suspicious when she showed up out of nowhere at the police station today, but I pushed it out of my head. That was a mistake."

"I don't know. She's up to something, but I doubt very much she's responsible for a murder."

"I think you're probably right," Landon said. "She learned a hard lesson tonight when she took on four Winchesters ... and lost."

"She's not done yet," I said. "She's nowhere near done. Mrs. Little brought her to town to mess with us. She's not done messing with us. She might've thought it would be easy, but now she realizes that it'll take more effort. I think she's going to put in the effort."

"So what are you going to do?"

"Take her down before she gets a chance."

Landon's lips curved. "Well, I look forward to watching you do it."

I slid him a sidelong look. "That's it? I thought for sure you'd warn me about going to war when you're investigating a murder."

"I considered it," Landon admitted. "The thing is, I'd much rather you go to war with a fake witch I know you can beat than a killer who might try to take you out if you get too close. Usually you're in the middle of these things. Focusing on Scarlet means you're not quite as interested in the murder."

I balked. "That's not true. I want to solve the murder."

"I know you do, but it's not your job," Landon said. "I'm fine with you focusing on Scarlet. I know things can spiral out of control when you girls get going – especially since Aunt Tillie seems so keen to be involved in the process – but I'm not worried about Scarlet killing you. She's an enemy, but I know you can take her.

"The person who killed Adele Twigg clearly has a lot of rage fueling him or her," he continued. "I never want you in danger. So, if you're focused on Scarlet and general mischief, that means you're probably safe. I like it when you're safe, Bay."

"That doesn't happen often, does it?"

"No, but that's why I'm fine with you focusing on Scarlet. She makes a nice foil when a terrible enemy is running around this town."

"Oh, that was almost poetic," I teased. "You should be a writer."

"I'll stick to being an FBI agent." Landon leaned closer and gave me a kiss. "Now, do you want me to rub your feet or something else when we get inside?"

I laughed at his lame joke and hopped out of the vehicle. "Maybe you should do both," I suggested. "In fact … ." I lost my train of thought when an ethereal figure popped into view on the front walkway.

"What is it?" Landon asked, looking through Adele Twigg's ghost without seeing her. "Is something wrong?"

"We need to talk," Adele said, her expression grim.

"You know how you wanted me out of this case and focused on Scarlet?" I asked ruefully.

Landon nodded.

"I don't think you're going to get your wish."

Landon followed my gaze. "What do you see?" He instinctively put out his hand, as if to keep me back or protect me from something or someone that might come barreling out of the darkness.

"It's Adele Twigg."

"Oh." Landon slowly lowered his hand, uncertain. "She can't hurt you, right?"

"She's not a poltergeist." He'd learned a lot since we started dating, even witnessing a truly terrifying spirit that was out for blood. He knew he couldn't protect me from everything, but that didn't stop him from trying.

"It's okay." I wrapped my fingers around his wrist and forced him to lower his arm. "I'm perfectly okay."

"Right." Landon straightened. "Try to get her to come inside so you don't catch a cold while talking to her." He moved toward the front door. "I'll make some hot chocolate."

"We'll be right along," I promised.

"Okay. You have five minutes before I go all alpha and come looking for you."

"Thanks for the warning."

TALKING ADELE INTO ENTERING the guesthouse wasn't easy. She went on and on about how people in town said we were real witches and she didn't want to get hexed. I finally had to remind her that she was already dead, so there was no way I could kill her a second time.

She wasn't happy, but she capitulated.

Landon had a mug of hot chocolate ready for me when I entered, and he lifted the blanket he sat under on the couch so I could get comfortable. He offered up an easy smile, but let me handle most of the questioning.

"I take it you've come to the realization that you're dead, huh?"

Adele's expression was sour. "No one likes a know-it-all."

"I have it on good authority that Landon loves it when I think I know it all," I countered.

"He looks like a deviant," Adele stared at Landon. "He's probably a sex fiend."

"He's an FBI agent."

"That doesn't mean he's not a sex fiend."

She had a point. "Well … he's not a sex fiend."

Landon snorted. "Don't lie to her. I'm totally a sex fiend, Mrs. Twigg. That doesn't mean I don't want to solve your murder."

Adele widened her eyes. "Can he see me?"

I shook my head. "No. He doesn't have the gift. I'll repeat what you tell me. Have you remembered anything about the night you died?"

"No. It's all a blur." Adele went back to scowling. "I remember being at the meeting. I remember you were there. You sat with a big man and whispered constantly. It was rude."

I did my best to rein in my temper. "I'm sorry you thought I was rude. As for the man I was sitting with, that's Terry Davenport. He's the chief of police."

"I thought he was your boyfriend until I saw this one." Adele pointed a derisive finger at Landon. "This one seems to fit your personality more."

I had no idea if that was a compliment or dig, so I let it go. "What happened after the meeting? Did you leave with someone?"

"I …." Adele's features twisted as she tried to remember. "I don't know. Everything goes dark. I remember the meeting breaking up. I remember Margaret suggesting we get coffee together. That's all I remember."

I stilled. "Margaret? You mean Mrs. Little?"

Adele nodded.

"You were supposed to get coffee with her?" I cast a look to Landon. "Did you talk to Mrs. Little?"

"I try to refrain from talking to that woman as much as possible, but I'll make a note of it for tomorrow," Landon replied. "Did they actually have coffee?"

I shrugged. "She can't remember."

"Okay. I'll ask about it tomorrow."

I sipped my hot chocolate before turning back to Adele. "We know

about the scam you guys had going. We know those aren't your kids –
and nieces and nephews – and whatever else you claimed they were."

"It's not a scam," Adele corrected. "It's an act."

"Yes, well, it bordered on a scam in some respects," I argued. "You
wanted people to believe you were one big family – I guess happiness
fit in there even though your actors were miserable – and it was
important for you to keep up appearances."

"That's because people associate renaissance fairs with family fun,"
Adele's tone was dark. "We weren't trying to scam people. We were
simply trying to deliver what they wanted."

"Fair enough." There was no sense arguing with her. It would get
me nowhere. "You have a lot of enemies. We've seen the comments
online. We know about the people you fired."

"Those people were not holding up their end of the bargain," Adele
snapped. "The contract terms were fair and non-negotiable. They
knew what they were getting into when they joined up."

"And the woman you fired for getting pregnant?"

"We want a wholesome environment."

"The guy I read about who was fired for hitting on a woman in the
crowd?"

"That's not allowed."

"The guy fired for dating one of his fake sisters?"

"Fornication is not allowed."

She was a real piece of work. "What about the people with your
troupe right now?" I asked, changing course. "You've made a lot of
enemies in the past. It's only fair to assume that you have a fair
number now. How many members of the current troupe hate you?"

"I think you're overusing the word 'hate,'" she replied. "My
workers didn't hate me. They respected me. They loved me. There
might've been a bit of fear in there, but it wasn't something I reveled
in. It was, however, necessary."

Yeah. A huge piece of work. "People hated you, Adele," I countered.
I couldn't sugarcoat it for her. If she expected to remember, she
couldn't delude herself. "Most of the people in your troupe who we've

questioned since your death haven't exactly expressed regret about the way you went."

"They're merely putting on an act," Adele sniffed. "They're professionals, after all. They can't fall apart – even though I'm sure they want to."

Yeah, she was clearly delusional. "You haven't really answered the question," I prodded. "Did you have specific problems with anyone in your group?"

"I was the boss. I had problems with all of them at one time or another. We were a family, though. It's normal to fight with family. You always make up later."

"Not always," I argued. "Someone remained angry enough to kill you."

"Well, it wasn't a member of my group." Adele was adamant. "It was someone from this town. This ... stupid, stupid town!"

"You were strangled, Adele. That's usually reserved for someone who wants to kill up close and personal. Most strangers don't want to do that unless you're dealing with a serial killer, which I doubt you were because you're the lone victim."

"It wasn't one of my troupe members."

"Fine." I held up my hands. "Just for curiosity's sake, though, if it was someone from your troupe, who would you blame?"

"I just told you ... ."

"I know. It's a hypothetical question."

"Fine." Adele mimed dragging a hand through her hair, her frustration palpable. "It could've been any one of the girls. They all had issues with me because I wouldn't let them wear skimpy corsets and threatened to fire them if they hooked up with any of the men."

"Did you threaten the men for the same reasons?"

"No. The women are the ones who tempted the men. The men didn't do anything. They can't control their hormones."

"That is an antiquated thought process," I said. "Still, you're basically saying the women hated you more than the men."

"Pretty much," Adele conceded.

"Ask her about her husband," Landon interjected. He'd been listening to my end of the conversation with keen interest.

"What about Arthur?" Adele asked, making a face. "He didn't do this."

"How can you be sure of that?" I countered. "You don't remember what happened. Were you and Arthur happily married?"

Adele barked out a harsh laugh, taking me by surprise. "Arthur and I married for convenience … and a few tax breaks. I wouldn't use the word 'love' where our relationship is concerned."

I tried to reconcile Adele's dark words with the man I saw at dinner. He spoke only a few times – granted, he didn't have many openings because we monopolized the entire conversation – but I assumed he was lost in grief, and at least two bottles of wine I watched him down.

"You and Arthur didn't have a good relationship?" I asked after a brief pause.

"We had no relationship other than business," Adele replied. "We ran the business together and otherwise went our separate ways. He has a girlfriend, for crying out loud."

"A girlfriend?"

Landon leaned forward, intrigued. "Did she just say Arthur had a girlfriend?"

I nodded.

"Who?"

"Who is Arthur's girlfriend?" I asked, almost dreading the answer.

"That little harlot Tess Anderson," Adele replied, not missing a beat. "They've been sleeping together for almost a year, but she thought I didn't know. Well, I knew. That's why I never let her move up the food chain and take a lead role in the show."

My stomach twisted at the look of outright hatred on Adele's face even as doubt crept in. "Tess is in a relationship with Greg."

"Greg?" Adele furrowed her brow. "That's not right. She's dating Arthur. She's been trying to talk him into divorcing me and taking her on as a new partner."

"How do you know that?"

"I eavesdrop whenever I get the chance," Adele replied. "It's not hard. We're on top of one another all the time."

"But … we saw her in the woods with Greg."

"She might be playing with Greg's emotions, but she's glommed onto Arthur for the money," Adele countered. "She probably thinks she has a clear shot at the lead spot now. That just figures."

I shifted my eyes to Landon, conflicted. "Well … I think I have more suspects for you."

"I can't wait to hear about it."

"You might think differently when I'm done."

"Lay it on me."

I did just that. When I was finished, Landon was horrified.

"She's sleeping with her fake uncle and her fake cousin? I'm going to be sick."

"I told you."

Landon rubbed the back of his neck. "Adele was right, by the way. Nobody likes a know-it-all."

"Except you, right?"

"Meh. I happen to love one. You're still a pain in the butt." He rested his cheek against my head. "This whole thing keeps getting more and more twisted."

"Tell me something I don't know."

"I just said you were a know-it-all."

"If you're not careful this know-it-all will make sure Mom yanks bacon from the breakfast menu for the foreseeable future," I warned.

"Have I mentioned how much I love know-it-alls?"

"That's what I thought."

TWENTY-THREE

J slept hard, my head resting on Landon's shoulder as I curled into him. He woke me with a kiss and a wink – and a little morning fun – before we showered and headed to the inn for breakfast.

Aunt Tillie sat on the couch in front of the television, her attention focused on a book resting on her knees as she kibitzed at the television.

"No one cares about that stupid story," Aunt Tillie muttered, not bothering to glance in our direction. "Give me some real news. Real news is not some moron in New York turning one-hundred years old."

"I see you're feeling chipper this morning," Landon said, grinning as he moved to the side of the couch. "I worried you might be hungover after last night, but you look pretty together."

"Of course I'm together," Aunt Tillie scoffed. "I'm always together."

"I wouldn't go that far, but … okay." Landon shifted his eyes to the book on Aunt Tillie's lap. "What's that?"

"It's a history book," Aunt Tillie replied. "I'm researching Cornish witchcraft."

"Did you find anything?" I asked.

"Nothing that will help us in our war against Scarlet Darksbane. But it's interesting. They tend to believe the same tenets we do."

"That's what Thistle said. I kind of forgot about all of that with everything that happened over dinner last night."

"I thought dinner was delightful." Aunt Tillie's smile was a mix between serene and snarky. "It's one of my favorite interludes ever."

"Do you keep a list?" Landon asked.

"No."

"Then how do you know it was one of your favorites?"

"The same way you keep track of your favorite Bay memories," Aunt Tillie replied. "Sometimes you just know."

"I guess you do." Landon offered me an easy grin before shuffling toward the door. "I'm sure you have things to discuss with Aunt Tillie. Whatever you're planning for the day, try to remember that I might not be able to get to you right away if you're arrested."

"Chief Terry won't arrest me." I was almost positive that was true. "He'll simply pretend he doesn't hear the complaints when Mrs. Little and Scarlet lodge them."

"You have a point. Don't be too long."

I watched Landon disappear through the door, waiting until it was just the two of us to sit next to Aunt Tillie. "What are you really looking for in that book?"

Aunt Tillie adopted an innocent expression. "I just told you."

"And I know when you're lying."

"How?"

"I grew up with you. If I remember correctly, you once schooled us on how to lie."

Aunt Tillie broke out in a wide smile. "I forgot about that. Thistle was a natural. Clove piled it on too thick. You, though, you had days when you were really good at it and others when you were really bad."

"And what does that tell you?"

"That you're an inherently honest person with faults who can lie when necessary," Aunt Tillie replied. "That's the best way to be."

"Good to know." I tapped the open page of the book. "Tell me what you've found."

"It's not much," Aunt Tillie cautioned. "I'm just reacquainting myself with some of the tenets."

"It says here that Cornish witchcraft is also referred to as traditional witchcraft," I noted. "What does that mean?"

"You were raised in a witch house where we had our own rules, but you'll find traditional witchcraft isn't all that different from what we espoused," Aunt Tillie explained. "It's essentially a pre-modern form of the craft."

"Meaning?"

"Meaning that Cornish witches like old traditions and eschew modern trappings," Aunt Tillie supplied. "They also can be broken down into the traditions they believe in, like Feri, Cochrane's Craft and Sabbatic craft."

"None of those things mean anything to me."

"That's because you only embraced the spells and never the history. Feri is distinct from Wicca. There's a strong emphasis placed on sexual mysticism."

I raised an eyebrow, amused. "Don't mention that to Landon. He'll want to convert."

"He does have a perverted streak," Aunt Tillie agreed. "Cochrane's Craft focuses on the horned god and mother goddess. There are also some groups that embrace polytheism. We've never much gone for that."

"You told me when I was a kid that the only good horned god was a dead horned god."

"I was trying to teach you a lesson about horny gods," Aunt Tillie corrected. "I found out you were a bit too young at the time to absorb the lesson and your mother wasn't happy when you repeated it to her."

"Ah. I kind of remember that."

"Yeah, it was always in one ear and out the other with you when you were a kid," Aunt Tillie said. "The other group is the Sabbatic craft group. They're more like us. They embrace Sabbaths and ritual gatherings, although the ones they held back in the day are nothing compared to what we practice now."

"Okay, but what does all this mean?"

"I don't know yet," Aunt Tillie admitted. "I'm not sure what to make of it. I don't think it's a coincidence that Scarlet Darksbane has a Cornish spell book. There must be a reason behind it."

"Maybe she's really a witch."

"Maybe, but the woman I saw at that table last night was not one who boasted real power," Aunt Tillie said. "She's a charlatan as far as I can tell. All of her power comes from manipulating others and making them believe she has magic."

"That's different from what we do," I mused. "We don't want anyone to know we have legitimate power. We spend all of our time hiding it."

"Speak for yourself," Aunt Tillie countered. "I don't care who knows that I have power."

I almost believed that. Memories of her warning us not to show off when we were in high school pushed to the forefront and ruined the illusion. "I think part of you believes that. You didn't always think that way."

"No. I told you those things to protect you. I didn't care about protecting myself."

"And now?"

"And now you don't need protection," Aunt Tillie said. "You can take care of yourself. You've proved it time and again. Thistle and Clove, too. You grew into a strong woman – and I may change my mind the next time you annoy me – but you're a decent witch, too."

My heart warmed at the simple statement. "Wow. I think that's the nicest thing you've ever said to me."

"Don't let it go to your head," Aunt Tillie chided. "You're not as strong as you could be. It's because you don't apply yourself. When I'm gone, there will be no one left to teach the old ways. Your mother and aunts never embraced it. I have higher hopes for you and your cousins."

"You'll never leave us. You're too mean to die."

"Everyone dies, Bay. I'm no exception. I've got decades before that happens, though. Don't worry. I'll still be around when your kids need someone to teach them about magic ... and mischief."

I hoped that was true.

"But I can't figure out what's going on with this Scarlet woman," she continued. "We don't know her real name, so it's impossible to trace her lineage. Landon is busy with the murder – and that should take precedence – but we need to figure out exactly who she used to be."

"Maybe we don't need Landon to do it," I suggested. "Maybe we only need to find someone who knew her."

"And how do we do that?"

"That message board. There were a ton of people who knew her in different places. We can contact them."

Aunt Tillie brightened. "See. Right there!" She waved a finger in my face. "That's a good idea. You're smarter than you look."

"Don't ruin our moment," I warned, getting to my feet. "We'll talk after breakfast. I'm sure we can find a place to look."

Aunt Tillie smiled as she followed me. "This day is certainly looking up."

The fact that she thought so was utterly frightening.

CHIEF TERRY WALKED into the dining room as Aunt Tillie and I stepped through the swinging door. His smile was warm and friendly when he gave me a half-hug before sitting.

"You look like you're up to no good. Whatever it is, I don't want to know about it."

Thistle lifted her head at the end of the table, meeting my gaze. "Have you been plotting with Aunt Tillie without me?" Her tone was accusatory. "You know that's the only time I like to spend with her. How could you cut me out?"

"It was spur of the moment," I said. "I'm sorry. Don't worry, you're definitely part of our plan."

Thistle wasn't appeased. "I might not want to join you now."

"Oh, you'll want to join us," I countered. "Trust me."

"What about me?" Clove asked, her expression mistrustful. "Are you going to leave me out of this adventure?"

"Of course not."

"We need someone to drive," Aunt Tillie added. "You're a decent driver."

Clove was annoyed. "You only want me because I can drive?"

Aunt Tillie tilted her head to the side, considering. "You're also good when we need to manipulate people with tears. That might come in handy today."

"Whatever." Clove rolled her eyes. "We all know I'm only going because I don't like being left out."

"So why are you complaining?" Aunt Tillie challenged.

"Because that's what I do."

"Fair enough."

I filled my plate with scrambled eggs, hash browns, sausage links and toast, and glanced around the table. It was only family and friends this morning, which I found suspect. "Where are the renaissance people?"

"They had a work meeting this morning," Mom replied. "Apparently they have to be in town early because the new festival opens tonight."

That had totally slipped my mind. "Mrs. Little is serious about making sure this thing goes down, huh?"

"She is," Mom confirmed. "She's also apparently giving Scarlet Darksbane a huge tent in the middle of everything. She wants to make sure that Scarlet is introduced to the town properly."

"Where did you hear that?"

"Shelly Watkins told me," Mom replied. "We were discussing items to provide for the bake sale and she mentioned it."

"There's a bake sale, too?" Landon was intrigued. "What are you making?"

Mom shot him a fond smile. "Blackberry pie and pumpkin pie."

"Yum." Landon darted his eyes to me. "We're definitely going to the bake sale."

"That's fine." I shifted on my chair. "What are you doing today?"

"What we've been doing," Landon replied. "We're going to question and watch the workers. They're still our best shot at figuring out who murdered Adele. With the added information you gave me last night, we have a particular place to look today."

"What information is that?" Chief Terry asked.

I related my conversation with Adele's spirit. The renaissance workers were out, so there was no need to hide it. "So, basically she claimed she was well-loved even though she treated her employees like crap, but then accused Tess of sleeping with her husband."

"From what you just said, it sounds like Adele didn't love her husband," Chief Terry noted. "It was a marriage of convenience, not love."

"Yeah, but I've been giving that some additional thought," I said. "She said that he had a wandering eye. I get the feeling it wandered with more people than Tess. Maybe they did marry for love at the beginning – or at least love on her part – and opted to stay together even though he cheated on her. I have no proof that's the case, because Adele isn't exactly honest when she tells me things, but it's a weird feeling I've got.

"That's my guess. I could be wrong. Adele doesn't exactly have a rock-solid view of herself. She paints herself as this benevolent leader and misunderstood soul, someone who really tried to do good by everyone she encountered but failed because of their weaknesses, not her own."

"That's interesting," Landon said. "I watched you when you spoke with her last night. You seemed frustrated with her attitude."

"Oh, I was definitely frustrated with her attitude," I agreed. "She meanders all over the place during a conversation. I think it was important to her to be loved, but she misconstrued fear with love. She wanted her underlings to love her, maybe even revere her. When they didn't, she settled for fear. I think she was a tyrant of sorts."

"Which means it could be any worker – past or present – who targeted her for death," Chief Terry said. "I'm guessing the killer didn't plan it."

"I've been thinking that, too," Landon said. "I think she ticked someone off, he or she killed her, then panicked and painted the symbols. The killer thought he could get away with it because he was in a witch town. It was probably a solid rationalization at the time."

"The added problem we have now is that we're on a timetable," Chief Terry said. "Thanks to Margaret Little, these people are stuck in town until Sunday. That's only three days. After that, they'll be leaving and taking our entire suspect pool with them."

"And once they leave they'll have the freedom to run," Landon added. "We don't have a lot of time, and we have far too many suspects."

"You have Tess and Arthur," I pointed out. "From what Adele said last night, they seem like the most logical choices."

"And they'll be the people we question first," Chief Terry said. "If they don't crack, we're simply going to have to watch them to see what we can discover. Maybe Greg will be willing to squeal – or at least tell us something we don't already know – if we ask him about Tess's extracurricular activities with Arthur."

"I look for Arthur to clam up if we question him about Tess," Landon said. "He's not the type to admit to anything. He'll probably deny it."

"Then maybe we should question them separately," Chief Terry suggested. "They'll both be in the town square, so we can each take one of them. We can at least force them to nail down alibis and then compare them."

"You think they killed her together?" I asked, horrified.

"I have no idea," Chief Terry replied. "There's absolutely no way of knowing right now."

"At least we have a plan." Landon bit into a slice of bacon and turned to me. "What are you going to do today? I know you have something planned with Aunt Tillie, but it would be helpful if I knew what. I don't want to worry about you ticking off a potential murderer."

"We won't be dealing with the Twiggs today," I said. "I figure that's your job."

"I'm happy that you're staying out of it. What are you going to do?"

"We're tracking down some of the people Scarlet scammed and talking to them so we can find out more about her," I replied. "We'll be busy with our own adventure."

Landon opened his mouth, his mind clearly busy. For a moment I thought he would try to dissuade me from my course of action. Instead, he merely nodded. "Have fun. Don't get into too much trouble."

"Would I get into trouble?"

"Absolutely. Even if you wouldn't, you're taking Aunt Tillie with you."

"That's because I'm a master interrogator," Aunt Tillie said. "Trust me. We'll know everything there is to know about Scarlet Darksbane by the end of the day. I'll crack those scammed women like rotten nuts."

"And I can't wait to hear your report," Landon said, waiting until Aunt Tillie focused on her breakfast to lower his voice. "Don't get arrested or terrorize a bunch of people, Bay. Try to be low key when you question these people. They're probably not going to be open to witches, especially after what Scarlet did to them."

"It will be fine," I said. "We know what we're doing. It will be smooth sailing."

"That will be a nice change of pace."

TWENTY-FOUR

"Are we there yet?"

Thistle sat in the backseat of Clove's car with me, her eyes lit with mischief as she stared at Aunt Tillie in the passenger seat. We were almost two hours into our trip and we were starting to get antsy.

"We'll be there in ten minutes." Clove focused on the road. The traffic in Grand Rapids was busier than we were used to. "You have the address for where we're meeting this woman, right?"

"It's at a magic store, believe it or not," Thistle said. "I'm dying to hear this story. I'm starting to wonder if this is how Scarlet operates. She tries to hang around with other purported magic purveyors, she messes with them and then she takes off when she's about to get hammered."

I cast her a sidelong look. "How did you come to that conclusion?" I asked. "All we know so far is that we're meeting a woman named Silver Fox – and that name definitely has to be made up – and that she owns a magic shop. We don't know anything else."

"I'm extrapolating," Thistle explained, making a face. "I'm allowed to do things like that."

"Why not wait until we have actual facts so you don't have to extrapolate?"

"Why don't you bite me?"

"Why don't you eat dirt?"

"Why don't you … ?"

"Shut up," Aunt Tillie barked. The visor was lowered so she could spy on us in the mirror, and the glare she sent us was right from her road trip playbook from when we were kids. She hated road trips in general, but the ones that included us almost always ended with screams and threatened curses.

"Yeah, shut up, Bay." Thistle smirked as Aunt Tillie narrowed her eyes. "You're upsetting our great-aunt. She doesn't like horseplay in the car."

"I don't like the sound of your voice, mouth," Aunt Tillie corrected. "You're giving me a headache."

"That could be because you insist on wearing a combat helmet in the car," I pointed out. "You've accidentally knocked your head against the window so many times you probably have a concussion."

"The helmet protects me from head injuries."

"I've met you. You've clearly had a head injury in your time. I don't think it's working correctly."

Thistle beamed. "Nice one."

"Don't make me crawl back there and wire your mouths shut," Aunt Tillie threatened. "I'll do it, too. I might even enjoy doing it. You won't enjoy it."

"That was a totally lame threat," I said. "It's not possible for you to wire our mouths shut. It's not like you carry wire around in your purse."

Aunt Tillie shot me a haughty look. "Would you like to test that theory?"

Uh-oh. "Not particularly," I replied, licking my lips. "I like my mouth the way it is."

"That's what I thought." Aunt Tillie crossed her arms over her chest and faced forward, keeping the visor down so she could watch Thistle and me should we get out of hand a second time. She really was a road trip kvetch. Now probably wasn't the time to point that out, though.

"Just out of curiosity, what's the plan here?" Clove asked, using her turn signal to exit the freeway. "How are we going to use whatever information we find on Scarlet Darksbane to get her out of town?"

"Is that our ultimate goal?" I asked, confused.

"Definitely." Thistle bobbed her head. "I want that store space for a studio. We need to get rid of Scarlet if we want that to happen."

"Isn't that personal gain? I mean … we're supposed to believe in karma and stuff."

"Karma is totally real," Aunt Tillie said. "It's also totally overrated. Don't worry about karma. We create our own karma."

I narrowed my eyes. "That's not how it's supposed to work. I mean … well, it is. If we do something bad, then something bad is supposed to happen to us. I don't think that we can simply wish for the karma we want."

"Oh, geez." Aunt Tillie rolled her eyes. "Here we go. The whining has already started. I thought you guys would hold off from doing that until the trip home. Some things never change."

"Oh, stuff it," Thistle fired back. "We're having a simple conversation about karma. I agree with Bay. I don't think you can manufacture karma."

"That shows what you know," Aunt Tillie countered. "I manufacture karma all the time. Why do you think I always beat Margaret and she's left to do things like bring in ringer witches to mess with us?"

"Some might argue that since we're the ones taking a road trip to deal with that witch we're dealing with karma," I pointed out.

"No one with any brains," Aunt Tillie shot back. "Now, we're almost to the store. When we get there, I want you to let me do the talking."

"Why would we want that?" Thistle protested. "Whenever we let you do the talking we end up with a case of bad karma shoved up our butts."

"Oh, well, that is a lovely visual," Aunt Tillie drawled. "I can't believe you actually managed to snag Marcus with that mouth. He's a wonderful boy and you're … evil."

"Everything I am is because of you," Thistle teased. "Oh, and Marcus happens to love my mouth. He can't enough of it."

Aunt Tillie shot Thistle a dirty look. "Has anyone ever told you that you're a filthy harlot?"

"Only people without penises."

"That might tell you something, Thistle. Now, stop talking to me. I can't listen to your voice for one more second. You're on my last nerve."

Thistle flicked her eyes to me, triumphant. "Pay up. "I told you I could unhinge her by the time we landed in Grand Rapids. I won."

"I don't know if that counts," I argued. "She didn't threaten to curse you or try to crawl in the backseat and throw you from the car."

"It totally counts," Thistle snapped. "You have to pay up."

"That did it." Aunt Tillie unbuckled her seatbelt and moved to crawl into the backseat with us. "I've had it. You're going to wish you'd never met me before this is all said and done."

"We're already there," Thistle said, leaning forward to slap her hand against Aunt Tillie's forehead and keep her in the front. "This definitely counts, Bay."

I couldn't argue with that. "Fine. Lunch is on me."

"You're on my list," Aunt Tillie hissed, slapping at Thistle's hand. "You're so on my list."

Thistle clearly wasn't bothered by the threat. "Yeah, yeah, yeah."

SILVER FOX STOOD IN an ankle-length skirt, her arms folded over her chest and Manic Panic-colored hair flowing over her shoulders. We were right on time – despite a scuffle between Aunt Tillie and Thistle in the parking lot – and Silver was clearly ready for us.

"We're the Winchesters," I announced, forcing a smile. "We spoke on the phone."

Silver returned the smile. "Yes. I can't say I wasn't surprised to hear from you. I've had time to reflect since your call, and I realize that it shouldn't have surprised me."

"I'm Bay." I extended my hand. "This is Thistle and Clove. They're my cousins."

"And you?" Silver smiled as she met Aunt Tillie's gaze.

"I'm their chaperone," Aunt Tillie replied. "I'm supposed to be the one doing the talking, but they've never had respect for their elders."

"I believe that's the curse of a grandmother," Silver said. "They clearly love you, though, whatever they've done to anger you. I can read it in their auras."

Aunt Tillie wrinkled her nose as she glanced at me. "She's full of crap. I can see your aura and you're already wondering where we can go for lunch. You're food-obsessed thanks to your boyfriend. It's totally changed your aura."

Silver drew her eyebrows together as she looked me up and down. "You do have a bit of bacon shine in here."

"Oh, whatever." That was a load of crap, and I wasn't just saying that because Aunt Tillie tried to teach me to see auras when I was a kid and I totally failed. I was pretty sure they were bunk. Mostly. Well, maybe. Okay, I believe in auras and hate that I can't see them. Sue me.

"We drove a long way to talk to you. We have some questions about Scarlet Darksbane."

"And hopefully I have the answers you're looking for," Silver said. She flipped the sign on the door, informing customers that she was on a lunch break and would be back in an hour. "Come into the back. I have tea and we can get comfortable."

"I would be a lot more comfortable with bourbon," Aunt Tillie announced as she followed. "It's been a long trip, and I forgot how much I hate road tripping with these morons."

"You talk big, but you love them, too," Silver countered.

"Not today I don't."

"Even today." Silver's smile was soft as she gestured toward a sofa, loveseat and chairs. "This is my parlor. We can discuss things here without fear of being overheard."

"Are you worried about that?" I asked, sitting in the chair and smiling when Silver delivered a cup of tea. I wasn't much of a tea drinker, but I didn't want to be rude. That, of course, was Aunt Tillie's job.

"Tea tastes like crap without bourbon," Aunt Tillie announced. "I can't drink tea if it doesn't have a kick."

Silver snorted, and retrieved a pint bottle of Jim Beam from the tea caddy in the corner. "I would hate for you to drink crappy tea."

"Cool." Aunt Tillie smiled as she grabbed the bottle. "I can tell I'm going to like you already."

"And I think the same of you." Silver sat in the chair next to me and glanced between faces before continuing. "I can't believe the infamous Winchesters from Hemlock Cove are in my store. I never thought I'd see the day."

"We're infamous?" Thistle asked dubiously as she sipped her tea. She snapped her fingers to get Aunt Tillie's attention so she would pass the bourbon. "How have you heard about us?"

"The Sabbath circles aren't very big," Silver replied. "They feel big at times, but they're actually quite small. Your Sabbath celebrations are whispered about with fevered excitement. Everyone wants an invitation, although it's been at least three years since you've opened your rituals to outsiders."

I tilted my head as I racked my brain. "Has it been that long?"

"We've been busy," Clove volunteered. "A lot has happened. We don't mean to cut people out. It's just … we don't have a lot of choice in the matter at times. We've always got something going on."

"Yes, we hear about the murders and mayhem, too." Silver's lips quirked. "You're kind of like the royal family of magic in Michigan. Did you know that?"

"I always did fancy myself in a tiara," Aunt Tillie said.

Silver stared at the combat helmet for a long beat. "Perhaps you've fashioned your own tiara."

"I like that idea," Aunt Tillie said. "Not to cut you off when you're being all worshipful and stuff, but we're on a bit of a timetable."

"Aunt Tillie." Clove's voice was low and full of warning.

Aunt Tillie ignored her. "We need to know about Scarlet Darksbane."

"What do you want to know?"

"Well, for starters, what's the deal with her name?" Aunt Tillie asked. "It's an absolutely stupid name – Silver Fox isn't any better, just for the record – and I'm curious as to why you're picking fake names rather than sticking with the ones you were born with."

"There's power in a name," Silver noted. "You know that. Power can be used for good or evil, so many of us opt to create a new name to protect that power."

"If you need a fake name to protect your power you don't have much of it to begin with," Aunt Tillie said.

"Fair enough. But not everyone is born with power. You were, which is why you're famous. The rest of us are left to create power, and it's never as strong as those who are born with it."

"Does that mean Scarlet wasn't born with power?" I asked. "We've been laboring under the assumption that she's not a real witch. Is that true?"

Silver shrugged. "I guess that depends on what you consider a real witch," she said. "Is a child any less real if you adopt her rather than give birth?"

"I think you're taking offense at what I said when none was intended," I said. "The thing is, we don't have a lot of time, and Scarlet is clearly up to something. I don't want to offend you, but we need answers."

Silver heaved a sigh. "Perhaps I'm being too sensitive. It wouldn't be the first time. As for Scarlet, she's ... not even a made witch. She's a scam artist. You should be very careful around her."

"We're not afraid of her," Thistle said. "We need to know about her past. What can you tell us?"

Silver blinked several times in rapid succession and then let her shoulders deflate as she leaned back in her chair. "She was born Mary Kinney in Columbus, Ohio. She moved with her mother to Grand Rapids when she was in third grade. I know, because we were in the same elementary school.

"We were friends and spent a lot of time together up until junior year of high school. That's when her mother went to jail for retail fraud and Mary was sent back to Ohio to live with her grandmother," she continued. "I didn't see her for a long time."

"I thought retail fraud was shoplifting," Clove said. "Who goes to jail for that?"

"People who are caught several times and refuse to stop stealing," Silver replied. "I didn't think about Mary much while she was gone. We were friends while she was here, but it was more out of habit than anything else, if that makes sense."

"You didn't like her," Thistle surmised. "Even back then, you sensed there was something wrong with her, didn't you?"

"Sensed there was something wrong with her?" Silver cocked her head. "I think that's giving me too much credit. I knew she was a user, but when you're that age ... well ... you're not always the best judge of character.

"I didn't hear from Mary after she left, and I didn't miss her over the years," she continued. "Then, out of the blue, she showed up more than ten years after I last saw her. I was working in another store at the time, learning the trade and researching the craft. I was a novice, but Mary came storming back into my world and claimed to be an expert. She had a different name and an interesting new persona. I was intrigued."

I glommed on to the obvious word. "Claimed?"

"I didn't realize at the time what she was," Silver cautioned. "She asked me to be a part of her coven, and I was eager to accept. I wanted to meet others like me, and Scarlet seemed to have the inside track.

"The first few months were informative and entertaining," she continued. "Then I started to hear whispers. Scarlet would tell coven members that she could read a dark aura about them, that they were cursed and doomed for terrible things. She would offer to remove the curse, but attach financial strings to doing so. That went against the rules of the coven, but she did it anyway."

"Were you suspicious?" Thistle asked.

"Yes, but I wasn't comfortable enough to challenge her at the time.

Mind you, this was five years ago and I was still coming in to my own."

"Continue," I prodded.

"Things went on like that for a few months," Silver said. "Scarlet kept talking about the evil curses and people whispered behind her back because they thought she was crazy. Then they started to have a bad run of luck out of nowhere and the whispers shifted. It happened to more and more members until, suddenly, people started to believe what Scarlet said. I'm still not sure how it happened."

"So they paid her to remove the curses," Aunt Tillie surmised. "When did you realize she was putting the curses on everyone in the first place?"

"I think I always suspected, but it took the other coven members longer to realize it. When they did, retribution was swift."

"What happened?" I asked.

"She was drummed out of the coven, and then it was suggested – rather aggressively – that she should leave town," Silver replied. "Scarlet was never one to lose, so she threatened to find strong witches with which to fight us. Everyone disregarded her, but ... here you are."

"That doesn't sound like she's completely a fraud," Thistle noted. "She clearly found a book at some point and used it to curse others. That has to be the Cornish journal we found."

"Cornish?" Silver arched an eyebrow. "Is it red with dated writing?"

I nodded. "We found it in her safe."

"What were you doing in her safe?"

"Breaking in." I saw no reason to lie. "I also found a poppet in my sock. It wasn't strong, but she copied the design from somewhere. What do you know about the book that she's carrying?"

"Just that another coven member found it at an estate sale and it went missing about the time Scarlet was drummed out of the group," Silver explained. "That's very interesting."

"I think that depends on how you look at it," Aunt Tillie said. "We've been watching her because we're convinced she's a fraud. She's allied herself with one of our enemies. We've also had a murder and initially we wondered if Scarlet was involved. Do you think she would be involved with a murder?"

Silver was taken aback by the question. "No!"

"Are you saying that because you were friends with her for a long time?"

"No. I'm saying that because she's too lazy and worried about self-preservation to commit a murder," Silver replied. "That's simply not how she operates."

I was coming to that conclusion myself. "Can you tell us anything about her that we might consider important before we take her down?"

"Simply to watch your back," Silver replied. "Scarlet has a reputation for either sleeping her way to the top or manipulating others out of the top position. I'd guess she doesn't understand how strong you really are. To her, magic was always a game. She doesn't boast real magic, so she probably thinks no one does. That will be your advantage."

"We don't need an advantage over her," Aunt Tillie countered. "She's merely a gnat ... and gnats get swatted."

"Don't underestimate her," Silver warned. "She will lash out if backed into a corner."

"Yeah? Well, we punch rather than slap," Aunt Tillie said. "That woman will be sorry she ever came to my town. I promise you that."

Thistle reached over and snagged the bottle of bourbon from the table before Aunt Tillie could add more to her cup. "You've had enough. You're talking like a supervillain."

Aunt Tillie balked. "I'd make an excellent supervillain. I could do it professionally."

"That's what we're all afraid of."

We really were, but this time something told me that Aunt Tillie's penchant for power games was going to play to our advantage. I looked forward to it.

TWENTY-FIVE

*C*Ue ate an early lunch in Grand Rapids – the city offered far more choices than Hemlock Cove – and then headed home. The discussion for the ride focused on Scarlet. While Silver didn't offer any big surprises, other than Scarlet's real name, everything we learned was confirmation of what we already suspected.

"I found some stuff when I Googled Mary Kinney in Ohio," Thistle announced when we were about ten miles from Hemlock Cove. She'd been busy on her phone for the past hour. "I can't guarantee that all of this is her, but I did find a few mug shots that definitely belonged to her. She's not a real redhead."

"I don't think any of us believed that hair color was real," I said. "The boobs aren't real either."

"Definitely not," Thistle agreed. "She was arrested for the first time when she was eighteen and she was flat as a board then. I'm guessing some of her scam money went into physical enhancements. I think her nose is different, too, although it's hard to tell with these tiny photos."

"She probably realized that she could manipulate men with her looks," Clove supplied. "She's been falling all over herself when it comes to Landon and Chief Terry. She wants to lock them up early, because they're law enforcement."

"What was she arrested for?" I asked.

"Shoplifting was the first," Thistle replied. "It sounds like she learned that little gem from her mother."

"I hate thieves," Aunt Tillie complained. "They're total dregs. We should lock them up forever."

"I think there are different levels of theft," I argued.

"You're only saying that because you guys have been making plans to raid my greenhouse," Aunt Tillie countered. "You're dying to know what's in my new blend."

Thistle lifted her eyes, suspicious. "Who told you that?"

"I know things."

"Whatever. As for Scarlet, she was arrested at least six times under her real name that I can find. Ohio has a great mug shot site. I wish we had it for Michigan thugs and criminals. I don't think she was arrested under her current name in Ohio."

"That doesn't mean she wasn't arrested under it in other states," I pointed out.

"You need to force Landon to run her," Aunt Tillie ordered. "We want all of the information before we take her down and make her cry."

"Landon is busy with a rather brutal murder," I reminded her. "I think he has his hands full."

"Yeah, what's up with that?" Aunt Tillie turned so she could meet my gaze. "Why aren't you neck-deep in that investigation? You're generally all up in his business."

I shrugged, unsure how to answer. "I'm trying to focus on my own business and leave him to his."

"Why?"

"Because."

Aunt Tillie wasn't going to accept that as an answer. "Because why?"

"Because ... because we're living together now," I replied.

"I don't see what that has to do with anything. Besides, you're not technically living together until he lets go of the old apartment."

"All he has left to do there is clean," I said. "It's almost completely empty. He's selling a few pieces of furniture and then he's done. He spends every night here. This is his home now."

"Despite where he laid his head three nights a week, this has been his home for the last six months," Aunt Tillie pointed out. "I think you're worried about something else."

"And what would that be?"

"I can't always see what's in your very busy head, Bay," Aunt Tillie replied. "You need to tell me what's bothering you and we'll go from there."

That sounded reasonable. I grew up with Aunt Tillie, so I knew she had something else up her witchy sleeve. "It's just ... I'm worried that living together and working together will cause fights. I'm not in the mood for fights. Well, actually, I don't hate it when we fight because making up is a lot of fun."

"You're such a pig," Aunt Tillie complained.

I ignored her. "The thing is, I don't know that fighting right now is good because he's fighting with Thistle almost every day. I don't want to push him from little fights with Thistle to big fights with me."

"Why?"

"I don't think big fights are good. I like the little ones."

"Yeah, but do you think that's going to force him to leave or something?" Aunt Tillie asked, her eyes keen.

"No. I know he won't leave again. We've been over it a hundred times, and he doesn't like it when I worry. I know he won't leave."

"So what are you worried about?"

"That he might ... regret ... moving here," I answered without hesitation. "Maybe he'll come to realize that those three days away were good for him because he could relax without all of the drama. I don't know if you guys have noticed, but we have a lot of drama."

Instead of being sympathetic, Aunt Tillie let loose a derisive snort. "Sometimes you're more of a kvetch than Clove. It's beyond annoying."

"I heard that," Clove whined.

"I meant for you to hear it," Aunt Tillie shot back. "Bay, you need to suck it up. You're interested in the investigative part of what Landon does. He's actually happy to have you around, although he's letting you take a step back this go around because he doesn't want to pressure you."

"I also think he's worried that Bay is going to let her obsession with Scarlet cloud her judgment on the investigation," Thistle added. "He's fine sitting back and watching what she does with Scarlet because he figures it won't be nearly as dangerous as tangling with whoever killed Adele Twigg. And, let's face it, Adele's killer won't hesitate to go after one of us if it becomes necessary."

They had a point. I would never admit it, but they had a point. "Let's just focus on Scarlet," I suggested. "Once we take her down, if the murder isn't solved I'll volunteer my time. I've been trying to help with the murder a little. I'm the one who talked to Adele's ghost, after all."

"Only because she sought you out," Aunt Tillie said. "I find it interesting that she did that when she seems to dislike the whole witch vibe of Hemlock Cove. I wonder if she knows who killed her and is torn because she isn't sure she wants that person to pay."

That was an odd thought. "What do you mean?"

"She built something with that troupe," Aunt Tillie explained. "Whether or not we understand it, that group was important to her. Maybe she knows that the group will be ruined if she tells the truth."

Hmm. "Under that scenario, the mostly likely culprit is Arthur," I noted. "I think she honestly loved him, even though he didn't love her the way she wanted."

"You're assuming the killer was alone," Aunt Tillie pointed out. "Have you ever considered it might have been a team?"

I nodded without hesitation. "Ever since I heard that Arthur and Tess were dating I've started to wonder if they did it together. Maybe Tess wanted to be in charge and Arthur offered her the chance to if they got rid of Adele."

"It does sound like Adele was a righteous pain in the posterior,"

Clove said. "Maybe she simply became too much for them to put up with."

"Yeah. It's sad, but I think that's definitely a possibility. We'll know more when we get back to town. Landon and Chief Terry were going to question Arthur and Tess first thing this morning. Hopefully they came up with something."

"While you talk to them, I'm going to start brainstorming a plan for Scarlet," Aunt Tillie said. "I think the sooner we can move her out of town the better."

Her words caused me to wince. "You're not going to do anything crazy, are you?"

"Would I do that?" Aunt Tillie was full of faux innocence and light.

"Absolutely."

"Then I guess you'll have to wait and see, won't you?"

Yeah. That wasn't frightening at all.

LANDON STOOD AT THE edge of the festival grounds when I approached. I left Thistle and Clove to rein in whatever terrible plan Aunt Tillie was about to unleash on the unsuspecting Hemlock Cove denizens and crept up behind him, giving him a fervent hug before he recognized my presence.

"Hey, be careful," Landon warned. "My girlfriend might show up any second. I don't want her to find out about you."

I narrowed my eyes. "Ha, ha."

Landon chuckled. "Okay. I'm willing to be schmaltzy, but you have to make it quick."

"Oh, Carlos, I've never loved you more," I teased.

"I love you more than the sun and moon combined, Esmerelda. Just don't tell my girlfriend. She's not the understanding sort."

Landon turned to face me, giving me a full-on hug before releasing me. "I wasn't sure when you'd get back. Did you get anywhere?"

"We did." I nodded. "Most of what we got was confirmation of Scarlet's nature, but we got a few things to use against her when it comes time for battle."

"You have no idea how much it turns me on when you say things like that." Landon tucked a strand of hair behind my ear. "Do you think you could wear a Wonder Woman outfit next time you do?"

"I'll consider it." If he had a Wonder Woman fetish I was more than happy to play along. "How about you? Did you talk to Arthur and Tess?"

"We did." Landon's smile slipped. "Terry took Arthur and I took Tess. We figured she might be more likely to open up to someone closer to her own age."

"And?"

"And she denies having an affair with Arthur. Adele occasionally accused her of that but she denied it," Landon replied. "She told a very long story about Adele being paranoid regarding Arthur and firing several former performers because she was convinced he was having affairs. According to Tess, they never happened. Or at least she doesn't think they ever happened. One of the women Adele accused of having an affair was reportedly a lesbian."

"Huh." I wasn't sure what to make of that. "Do you think she's telling the truth?"

"I have no idea. She's hard to read, so it wasn't obvious if she was lying."

"What about Arthur?"

"He had a different reaction," Landon replied. "He completely exploded at Terry and accused him of manufacturing stories to sully his wife's good reputation. He thinks we're desperate to pin the murder on him because we don't want to put the effort in to solve the case."

"That's not true."

"We're trying, but not getting anywhere," Landon said. "The whole thing is a mess. I'm not sure where we're going next. Tell me what you found."

I related my afternoon to him – leaving nothing out, because I knew he liked it when Aunt Tillie melted down – and when I was done, his expression was hard to read. "What do you think?"

"I think you already have the answers you were looking for,"

Landon answered. "You suspected she was a grifter. It sounds like you were right. Heck, it sounds like she stole that book she has from someone else and has no real power of her own. That makes me feel better about whatever you guys have planned for taking her down."

"Just because she wasn't born a witch doesn't mean she's powerless. We shouldn't underestimate her."

"I'm glad you're being cautious, but she doesn't particularly worry me." Landon shifted his eyes to the tent in the middle of the festival hoopla. Scarlet stood next to Mrs. Little, their heads bent together, and they occasionally darted smug looks in our direction. "Aunt Tillie will eat that woman for lunch. Mrs. Little brought her in to use as a weapon, but she doesn't care that Scarlet will ultimately be the sacrificial lamb."

"That's funny because her real name is Mary." I giggled at my own joke, earning a cocked eyebrow from Landon. "What? It's cold. I find stupid things funny when I'm cold. Mary had little lambs. Sue me."

"Oh, well, come here." Landon wrapped his arms around me and rested his cheek on my forehead. "I'm not saying you should be reckless when facing off with Scarlet. I'm really not. She won't be a match for you guys. I'm not worried about what's going to happen with her."

As if on cue, Scarlet picked that moment to head in our direction. I watched her approach with a glare. "What are you worried about?"

"The fact that we have a killer in our midst and we're running out of time," Landon answered without hesitation. "I know what Adele told you – and it seemed like a good lead at the time – but now I'm starting to wonder if Adele made up the story."

"Yeah, I wouldn't put it past her," I admitted. "She's ... off. I'm starting to wonder if she knows who killed her but is keeping it to herself because she knows the troupe will disband if the truth comes out."

Landon pursed his lips. "I wondered that myself after talking to Tess. I don't know anyone who would protect a murderer to keep a renaissance troupe running, but everything I've learned about Adele seems to suggest she would do just that."

"So what are you going to do?"

"Watch and listen," Landon said. "I expect you to do the same even though you'll be focused on someone else." He forced a smile as Scarlet approached. "And here she is now."

"Here she is now?" Scarlet echoed, faking a big grin for Landon's benefit. "Were you talking about me, Landon? I don't think that's wise given the way your girlfriend feels about me. She'll get jealous and unruly if you're not careful." She wagged a playful finger. "You don't want to make her jealous, do you?"

"It's Agent Michaels," Landon reminded her, causing me to bite the inside of my cheek to keep from laughing when Scarlet's smile dipped. "As for being jealous, Bay has nothing to be jealous about. As far as I'm concerned, she's the only woman in the world."

"That's laying it on a bit thick," I said.

"I'm fine with that."

"Speaking of women, I met one today that I'm betting you would've found quite attractive." I had no idea why I decided to take the approach I did, but I was interested to see how Scarlet would react. "Her name was Silver Fox. She's a witch in Grand Rapids."

And there it was. Scarlet's eyes narrowed as she clenched her hands into fists at her sides.

"Silver Fox?" Landon snorted. "What is it with these names? I thought Thistle was the strangest witch name I ever heard."

"Oh, no." I shook my head, never moving my gaze from Scarlet's face. "There are a lot of nutballs out there."

Landon recognized what I was doing and played along accordingly. "It sounds like you had a nice afternoon in Grand Rapids."

"It was very illuminating."

"Yes, well … ." Scarlet licked her lips. "I have to run to my store. We're doing a big display in the main tent. I hope you're not too jealous that I'm the featured witch at this weekend's festival."

"Oh, no." I let loose a grim smile. "I'm looking forward to you being the center of attention tonight."

As far as threats go, it was mild. Scarlet understood the meaning behind my words, though. "Yes, well, I'm sure I'll see you around tonight. I really need to run to my store."

"Have fun." I raised my hand in a mocking wave. "I'm sure I'll see you around, too."

"That was mean," Landon said when she was out of earshot. "But it was funny."

"Yeah. Speaking of funny, I need to get back to Hypnotic. Aunt Tillie is plotting, and I'm afraid she's going to come up with something huge and garish when it comes to taking down Scarlet."

"That would definitely be her way," Landon agreed. "Will you join me for a fun festival dinner tonight before the action starts?"

"I will gladly join you for a festival dinner. You know how I feel about hot dogs."

"Yes, the same way I feel about bacon."

I smacked a quick kiss against his lips. "I'll see you in a little bit."

"Try to be good," Landon called out. "If you can't be good, be careful."

"I'm always careful."

"Be ten times more careful than that."

TWENTY-SIX

*L*andon was still at the police station when I finished plotting with Aunt Tillie, Thistle and Clove, so I made my way to the festival grounds to kill time before the show opened. In less than an hour, Mrs. Little's newest endeavor would be open to the public. For now, it simply looked a little sad.

"Is it just me, or is this kind of a pathetic festival?"

I jolted at the voice, sliding a sidelong look in Tess's direction and ordering myself to keep from squealing out of fright. I didn't sense her approach, didn't so much as see her shadow. She could've attacked without me even realizing it. Sure, she wasn't very big, but she was a suspect in a brutal murder, and Landon wouldn't be happy if he found out I'd let my guard down.

"We've had better festivals." I found my voice and was happy it sounded normal. "I'm not sure what Mrs. Little envisioned with this one, but it's not up to Hemlock Cove's normal standards."

"And what are Hemlock Cove's normal standards?"

I slipped my hands into my pockets and shrugged. We didn't have snow yet – something I was thankful for, because Aunt Tillie was an absolute nightmare when she decided it was time to start plowing – but a definite chill flitted through the air. I could feel winter barreling down. "We have a festival every month. Sometimes we have two festivals. The beginning of December has always been festival-free. I don't think Mrs. Little gave this one enough thought."

"Why not just have a Christmas festival?"

"We do. The entire Christmas week is a festival, though we don't get a lot of tourists that week. They start coming again after the first of the year because we have so many ski resorts in this area. The Christmas festival is mostly for the residents."

"I bet you guys go all out." Tess almost looked wistful.

"We do," I confirmed. "Christmas is a big deal for a lot of people. I prefer Halloween, but my mother and aunts absolutely love Christmas."

"Even your crazy great-aunt?"

I smiled. Tess was one of the few Twiggs to enjoy Aunt Tillie's performance during dinner at The Dragonfly. "She loves Christmas the most. I'm not sure why. She has a sentimental streak she doesn't like to show to anyone. It comes out around Christmas every year."

"That sounds nice." Tess rubbed her forehead as she sat on one of the nearby picnic tables. She seemed lost, a bit irritated and altogether weary.

"You've gone through a lot in the last few days," I noted, taking a seat next to her. I was close, but not so close that she could lash out and hurt me if she decided to attack. I felt odd for suspecting her – she seemed small and vulnerable – but someone killed Adele in a terrible way and Tess was as good a suspect as anyone. "I'm sure you would've preferred being able to skip this festival and head straight home."

"I don't technically have a home," Tess clarified. "I'm on the road for most of the year."

"You mentioned that before." I racked my brain. "You guys drive with the tents and supplies and everything, right?"

Tess nodded.

"How did that work for Adele and Arthur again?"

If Tess was suspicious of the question, she didn't show it. "They have a house down south. They flew home while we did most of the traveling and set-up. Then they'd fly in for the performances and right out again. They said they had to do it that way because they had a lot of business to conduct during the down time."

In a weird way, that made sense. "Their house is in Florida, right?"

"Yes."

"Where does your family live?" I asked, changing course. "You'll probably visit them during Christmas, won't you?"

"We have a job in California the week before Christmas," Tess replied. "We get a week off for Christmas. I grew up in New Jersey, but ... I'll probably go home with Greg to visit his family."

"That sounds nice." I faked as much enthusiasm as possible. "Have you met Greg's family?"

"He has a sister, three nieces and nephews, and a drunken mother who barely remembers his name," Tess replied. "Still, it's better than what I have."

Surprisingly, my heart went out to her. "I never gave it much thought before, but the renaissance festival circuit is probably filled with loners. People who are close with family members don't generally take off for fifty-one weeks out of the year."

"I think that's true," Tess said. "My mother got locked up for being a junkie whore when I was fourteen."

I cringed at the term. "I'm sure she wasn't that bad."

Tess was blasé. "No. She was literally a junkie who sold her body for drugs. She had me when she was fifteen. She shouldn't have kept me. I know a lot of people think otherwise, that biology is the most important thing, but they're wrong.

"I was glad when she was taken away," she continued. "I had to go to a group home because my grandmother didn't want to take me. I would've got in the way of her bingo nights, you see. It was still better than living with my mother.

"When you're in a home like that you spend all your time dreaming about something better because you're convinced that it can't get much worse," she said. "My something better was traveling. I didn't care where I ended up as long as I was always on the go. When I learned about renaissance festivals, I thought they sounded great. I liked the idea of dressing up and being someone else."

"How old were you when you joined?"

"My first troupe? I guess I was eighteen, although just barely," Tess replied. "This is my third renaissance troupe, and even though Adele was a real pain, I've enjoyed myself."

"What will you do if this troupe closes up shop?" I watched Tess's profile for signs of distress and the way the muscle in her jaw clenched told me I hit her exactly where it hurt.

"The troupe won't close," Tess scoffed. "I know I said I thought so the other night, but I was just talking to fill the silence. I don't really believe it. Adele is gone, but Arthur is still here. He'll keep running things. Adele won't be around to terrorize us any longer, but things will continue largely the same."

I decided to play a hunch. "That's not what I hear." I kept my eyes on the festival, but was aware of Tess's movements out of the corner of my eye. "Someone said that Arthur is considering closing the troupe because it's impossible to run without Adele."

"No. That's not true."

"I swear that's what I heard. Apparently Adele did a lot more work than everyone realized, and now it's more likely that the business will be broken up."

Tess reached out, her fingers digging into my arm as she grabbed hold. Her face was whiter than any ghost I'd ever seen and her eyes filled with fury. "Who told you that?"

I was caught, but I didn't want her to know it. "I don't know. I heard a few people talking. I was around some of the festival organizers earlier and they were chatting about it." The lie was just vague enough to be believable.

"Well, it's not true," Tess hissed. "The troupe will be fine. Someone else will step in and run things the way they're supposed to be run. I have no doubt about that."

"Okay, well … ."

"It's not true." Tess gritted her teeth as she dug her fingers further into my skin.

"Ow!" I jerked my arm away and rubbed it, frowning at the flash of glee rolling across Tess's face.

"What's going on here?" Landon asked from behind me. I didn't turn to look at him, afraid if I did that Tess would attack.

"Tess and I were just talking about the future of the Twigg group," I supplied, keeping a firm hold on my arm. "I happened to mention I heard there was talk of the troupe shutting down now that Adele is dead, but Tess doesn't seem to think that will happen."

Landon moved up to the side of the table, his eyes busy as they bounced between our faces. "I heard that, too."

"You heard what?" Tess snapped, her tone dark.

"I heard that this particular festival circuit is going to cease operations now that Adele is gone," Landon replied, not missing a beat. "Several people told me that while we were conducting interviews."

"Which people?" Tess was furious.

"I forget," Landon replied smoothly. "You all start to look the same after a few questions. I can go back over my notes tomorrow if you're really interested."

"Why not tonight?"

"Because I'm off duty and about to have dinner with my girl-friend." Landon slipped his arm around my waist and helped me from the table. "You're welcome to join us. Isn't that right, Bay?"

That was the last thing I wanted, but I instinctively nodded. I knew Tess wouldn't join. "Sure. That sounds nice."

"Thanks for the offer, but we have an opening act to put on tonight and I have a few things to take care of." Tess wiped off the seat of her pants as she stood. "Thanks for the information. I hope you stop by later to see the show."

"We'll definitely do that." Landon's demeanor was calm, but I sensed the turmoil raging beneath his serene façade. "I've never seen a renaissance festival before, so I'm looking forward to the show."

"Yeah, well, you're in for quite the treat." Tess turned toward the main tent. "I have to get going. Enjoy your night."

"You, too," Landon murmured, watching her go. He waited until he was sure she was out of earshot to speak again. "What was that?"

"A very unhappy girl."

"Do you want to be more specific?"

I shrugged, uncertain. "I'll tell you over dinner." I rubbed my arm again. "I'm starving and want to fill myself full of junk. They have hot dogs, elephant ears, ice cream, funnel cakes, doughnuts and falafel."

Landon snorted. "You'll make yourself sick if you eat all that."

"Is that a challenge?"

"Sure. I love a good eating competition."

I knew he'd say that. "Then let's do it."

"WHY DID YOU LET me eat so much?"

I ruefully rubbed my stomach as I stared down at my mostly clean plate an hour later. There was a good possibility I might throw up … or explode. I ate way too much junk, which meant I was going to run on a sugar high for the next hour and then crash.

"Me?" Landon's eyebrows winged up. "Since when am I in charge of what you eat?"

"You should've stopped me. Now I feel sick."

"Oh, poor baby." Landon planted a kiss on my cheek. "Just let it digest for a few minutes. You'll be okay." He took a moment to scan the crowd. When he turned his attention back to me, he was clearly disappointed. "This festival bites."

I didn't bother to hide my smile. "Make sure Mrs. Little knows your opinion. I think she got a little too full of herself. She thought she could launch this thing without a plan, but it didn't turn out very well, did it?"

Landon shook his head. "I've gotten used to some of the whacked-out stuff you have in this town. I even liked that festival you had in early November where everyone dressed up like pilgrims and played scenes from *The Crucible*. But this one is pathetic. They don't even have a kissing booth. How can you have a festival without a kissing booth?"

"Don't worry." I absently patted his hand. "We have one for the

Christmas festival. There's mistletoe everywhere. You'll be able to kiss chicks to your heart's content."

"I only want to kiss you."

"You can do that whenever you want." I offered up a soft smile when he leaned closer, but I held up my finger to stop him from planting his lips on mine. "Just not right now, because I might puke."

"You sure know how to suck the romance out of a moment, sweetie."

"Yes, I'm thinking of having business cards made up that say exactly that." I rested my head on Landon's shoulder as I rubbed my stomach. "Did you see where Tess went?"

"No, but I'm eager to watch her during the big show," Landon replied. "You knew exactly how to set her off. She's not happy."

"It was just a feeling I got," I admitted. "She thinks of the festival as her home, even though it's constantly moving."

"Do you think she killed Adele?" Landon was serious when he caught my gaze. "She's small, but if she had help she probably could've handled the body. It either has to be a lone man or a team. I'm leaning toward team."

"I learned a long time ago that betting against your instincts is probably a bad idea. Still, we don't know Tess is guilty. She could simply be upset because she convinced herself that things would be fine after Adele's death and I just threw her entire world view into a tailspin."

"We don't have any evidence that it's her," Landon agreed. "But her reaction was not normal. I definitely want to watch her. In fact, I placed a call to your father this afternoon because I want him to watch her and Arthur for me."

I stilled, surprised. "You called my dad for a favor?"

"I did."

"What did he say?"

"I explained what I wanted and he said that he would be sure to watch them for me," Landon replied. "He was friendly and open to the suggestion."

"Hmm. Maybe he's starting to like you."

"I wouldn't get too excited," Landon cautioned. "I don't think we're going to start fishing together any time soon, but things are warming a bit."

I smiled. "I can't picture you fishing."

"Hey, I live in the country now," Landon reminded me. "I need a hobby that's normal in the country."

"You could grow corn."

"No."

"You could golf."

Landon made a face. "Hitting a ball with a stick has never been my favorite activity. Just for the record, I feel the same way about baseball and tennis."

"Good to know. You could … hike."

Landon rolled his eyes. "There's nothing fun about wandering around in the woods. Trust me. I've spent enough time wandering around with you in the woods to know that bad things happen out there. I'm thinking that fishing is the way to go."

"You know you have to clean the fish after you catch them, right? They smell. They're also slimy."

Landon tilted his head to the side. "How do you feel about getting a hammock? We could make joint weekend naps in a hammock our new hobby."

I giggled. "I like that idea."

"Me, too."

We lapsed into silence, comfortable enjoying each other's company without forcing conversation. I was just about to suggest moving inside the tent so we could get a good seat for the evening show when Mrs. Little appeared at the edge of the table.

"Oh, now what?" I didn't mean to sound whiny, but the words were out of my mouth before I thought better of uttering them.

"I hate to interrupt your public fornication, but I'm looking for Scarlet."

"Fornication?" Landon furrowed his forehead. "I think you've been without male companionship so long that you've forgotten what that entails. We were just sitting here."

"Making out."

"We weren't making out," Landon argued. "Bay had her head on my shoulder and I had my cheek on her head. If you want us to make out, I'm up for it, but Bay might puke, so it might turn into a weird fetish show. Are you ready for that?"

"I'm good," Mrs. Little said dryly. "I'm looking for Scarlet. She was supposed to meet me at my store so we could talk about her big debut. She's not in her store and I called The Dragonfly and they say she hasn't been back there in hours."

That was interesting. "Maybe she decided she didn't want to be the focal point of your show," I suggested.

"And why would she do that?" Mrs. Little challenged. "She's going to be everyone's favorite witch when I'm done with her."

I had serious doubts about that. "I haven't seen her since this afternoon."

"I haven't either," Landon said. "I'm sure she'll show up."

"She'd better." Mrs. Little's tone was dark. "If she goes missing I know exactly who to blame and I'll call in the Coast Guard to arrest you."

"The Coast Guard handles maritime issues," Landon pointed out.

"Fine. Then I'll call in the National Guard. How do you like that?"

Landon shrugged, unbothered. "At least you've given it some thought."

"If you see her, tell her I'm looking for her." Mrs. Little stalked off without a backward glance.

"What do you make of that?" I asked as I watched her waddle back to her store.

"Either Scarlet ran because she knew you found out the truth or she's hiding because she's worried Aunt Tillie will spread the truth to everyone tonight."

"Which do you think?"

"I have no idea."

"Hmm. I'm actually feeling better."

"That's good."

"Do you want to get some ice cream?"

"You and I spend way too much time scheduling our lives around food. Have you noticed that?"

"Is that a no?"

"Heck no. I want some hot fudge."

That sounded exactly how I wanted to spend the next twenty minutes.

TWENTY-SEVEN

"*W*ell?" Landon kept me close as we left the main tent shortly after ten. Chief Terry stood by the opening. They'd texted one another throughout the show, Landon telling Chief Terry to be on the lookout for Scarlet, but other than that he'd been focused on the performances. I was interested, too, of course. Landon was almost obsessive while watching.

"She's not at her store and her vehicle isn't parked anywhere near the downtown area," Chief Terry replied. "I have no idea where she went."

"Did you call my father?" I asked. "She's staying at The Dragonfly, so it only makes sense that she might be holed up there."

Chief Terry shuffled from one foot to the other, uncomfortable. "I thought maybe you could do that."

"Why?"

"I just thought – he's your father." Chief Terry averted his gaze and exhaled heavily.

"Okay." I reached for my phone, momentarily glancing at Landon before hitting the button to call my father. He picked up on the second ring.

"This is a nice surprise." Dad sounded happy. "You don't usually call on Friday nights. Is Landon working or something?"

"Landon is with me," I replied. "It's not technically a social call." I felt guilty. I'd been much better about spending time with my father lately, but I was still easily sidetracked where he was concerned. "Landon said he called earlier, but ... ." I wasn't sure how far I should push things.

"This is about Scarlet Darksbane, right?" All the warmth left Dad's voice.

"It is," I confirmed. "Is she there?"

"No."

"Has she been there?"

"Ever?" Dad sounded agitated, and I couldn't blame him. I was asking him to spy on one of his guests.

"I know this is outside of your comfort level," I offered. "But it's important. She was supposed to be down here for a big introduction Mrs. Little had planned. She didn't show up, and she's not at her shop."

"Well, she's not here," Dad said. "I haven't seen her since breakfast."

Even though I knew it would irritate him, I pushed. He was our only source of information. "Did she say anything to you?"

"Like what?"

"Like ... what her plans were for the day or anything."

"Are you asking if she confided in me that she was going to war with my daughter?" Dad asked. "If so, she didn't. She was pleasant and chatty. That's the way she is. She asks a lot of questions and then pretends she cares about the answers."

"Why do you say it like that?"

"Like what?"

"You said she pretends to care about the answers," I prodded. "How do you know she doesn't really care?"

"It's obvious by the way she acts," Dad replied. "She gushes over men and talks down to women. I'm pretty sure you've already noticed."

"I have," I confirmed. "If you see her, can you do me a favor and text me? I just want to know if she shows up."

"I will but I'm going to bed soon," Dad replied. "We have to get up early because the festival starts tomorrow. If she comes in after … well … it's not as if we have a curfew or anything."

"I understand. Just … if you see her before you go to bed I'd appreciate a text. I'm sorry if this puts you in a tough position, but we have a lot going on these days."

"We all have a lot going on these days, Bay. It was nice to talk to you. I'll text if I see her." His tone was cold and caused my heart to pinch.

"How about we have lunch tomorrow," I suggested in an effort to tamp down my worry. "I'll be at the festival all day. It might be nice to hang out together for a bit."

Dad's tone softened. "That sounds nice. I'll see you tomorrow."

"Yeah." I disconnected and stared at the phone. "He said he hasn't seen her and he's annoyed that I only bothered to call because I wanted something. I need to be better about that."

"He's the one who abandoned you for years," Chief Terry argued. "He should be happy that you bother to give him any time at all."

I fixed him with an amused look. "You know I still love you, right? You'll always be my favorite."

Chief Terry looked embarrassed. "I wasn't fishing for a compliment."

"You don't have to. I always think about you in complimentary terms."

Chief Terry's lips curved. "Thank you. I feel the same way."

"Oh, geez." Landon rubbed his forehead. "If anyone else acted that way with my girlfriend I'd totally punch him."

"That's because you're a Neanderthal," I said. "You like to pound your chest and use words like 'mate' when you refer to me."

"I have never used the word 'mate' when referring to you."

"You've thought it."

"I'm pretty sure you're exaggerating," Landon said. "It doesn't matter. Scarlet Darksbane either got distracted or is in the wind."

"I wonder why," Chief Terry mused. "She must be worried that you found out something important when you visited Grand Rapids. Landon told me that you made sure she knew that you spoke to her old friend Silver. What's up with the odd names, by the way?"

"It's the way of posers," I explained. "They don't have the magic, so they cover with distracting names. It's a common practice. Although, to be fair, Silver claimed she could see auras."

"Do you believe her?"

I shrugged. "Seeing auras isn't something only witches can do. It's a fairly common gift."

"Well, for now there's nothing we can do about it," Chief Terry said. "Let's regroup and discuss things over breakfast. Hopefully we'll know more then. As of now, we know Tess is acting weird and Scarlet Darksbane isn't around. Neither necessarily means anything – certainly not proof of murder."

"We have only two days to figure out what's going on here," Landon added. "Once that troupe leaves – and we have no way to make them stay – we'll lose our suspect pool."

"Then we'll have to start early." Chief Terry patted the top of my head, his big hand warm, and smiled. "I'll see you for breakfast. Thank you for calling your father."

"I know why you didn't want to do it, and I don't blame you," I offered. "It's a weird situation. You'll always be my favorite, though. I meant it when I said it."

Chief Terry beamed as Landon snorted and wrapped his arm around my waist.

"I'm your favorite," Landon corrected. "He can be your second favorite, but I demand top billing."

"Oh, geez! You're so much work," I teased.

"And don't you forget it."

EVEN THOUGH IT WASN'T all that late I was exhausted when we got back to the guesthouse. Thistle and Marcus were already tucked away in her bedroom, so I was happy to brush my teeth, change into pajamas and crawl into bed.

Landon was beneath the covers when I closed the bedroom door. He smiled and lifted them as I shut off the light and shuffled across the room. My feet were cold when I pressed them against his.

"Holy crap, Bay," Landon complained. "Your feet are like ice! Why aren't you wearing socks?"

I shrugged. "Maybe I like to feel my skin against yours. Have you ever considered that?"

"Only during summer," Landon replied, sliding his arm under me and arranging us so my head rested on his shoulder and we could share body heat. "Just think, when summer rolls around again we'll have this place all to ourselves."

"Yeah." That sounded nice. "What do you think we'll be doing?"

"I think we'll be grilling. And I'm totally getting that hammock we talked about so we can make napping outdoors our new hobby."

I giggled. "That's my type of hobby."

"I'll be handling more cases in this immediate area, which means I'll be driving to a few neighboring towns and cities, but I'll never be too far away. You'll be the owner of the newspaper, so you'll have different duties, too."

"Yeah." I rubbed my cheek against his T-shirt. "What do you think really happened to Scarlet?"

The question caused Landon to shift so he could stare into my eyes. The room was dark, but the moon was bright enough that it offered some illumination. "I don't know. Are you worried about her?"

"Worried?" That wasn't the word I would use. "I'm suspicious. She wasn't happy when she found out we'd talked to Silver. She couldn't hide it. She might've panicked and run, but that doesn't seem to match the woman we've come to know over the past few days."

"Maybe she initially thought you guys would just roll over or something. If she did, she made a big mistake. For all we know, Mrs. Little could have lied about how formidable you guys are."

"Maybe." That didn't sound likely. "Aunt Tillie had a big plan to embarrass her in public, tell everyone in attendance what she did while in Grand Rapids, and then curse her to be stuck with the 'Everything is Awesome' song from *The Lego Movie* in her head for the next thirty days while smelling like three-day-old tuna fish left out in the sun."

Landon chuckled, his chest shaking with mirth. "You have to give her credit. She always picks inventive ways to curse people."

"Yes, she's gifted that way," I agreed, sliding my hand beneath Landon's shirt and resting my fingers on his muscled chest. "Do you think she'll come back and attack us from behind? Do you think she's out there plotting?"

"She might, but I doubt you have anything to fear. You figured out she put that poppet on you within thirty minutes. If that's the best she can do ... ."

"She has that book," I reminded him. "She could move on us. She might not even realize what she's doing when she lets the curses fly."

"She's not a real witch," Landon said, his hand absently moving up and down my spine. "She's a fake witch. I'll put my money on a real witch every time – especially when that real witch is you."

"I think you're only saying that because you're sweet on me."

"I am definitely sweet on you." Landon gave me a soft kiss, his eyes pressed shut. "You need to sleep, sweetie. We're going to have a big day tomorrow between watching potential murderers and hunting down a rogue witch. You need your rest."

"I know." I nestled closer. "I love you."

Landon tightened his grip on me. "I love you, too. We'll figure it out. I think we're close. We're only missing a small piece of the puzzle. When we uncover that, we'll uncover everything."

I could only hope he was right.

I WOKE IN THE exact same position I fell asleep in, Landon's warm body pressed to mine. I felt comfortable, safe and content.

Then I heard someone chewing. I'm not talking quiet chewing. This was big, loud and sloppy.

I rolled to my back and looked to the end of the bed, frowning when I found Aunt Tillie munching on a candy bar while watching us sleep.

"What are you doing?"

"You two sleep all twined up together," Aunt Tillie noted, dodging the question. "I don't understand how you breathe."

"We just do." I rubbed the sleep from my eyes. "What are you doing here?"

"I need to talk strategy, but you people refuse to wake up at an acceptable time. Why is that? Are you lazy by nature or is it a couple thing? Just for the record, Thistle and Marcus are already up and out. They were leaving when I came in. Thistle said we have to be at Hypnotic to make another plan before the festival starts."

"Since when do you follow Thistle's orders?"

"Since I happen to agree with them." Aunt Tillie shifted and poked her finger into Landon's knee. "He sleeps like the dead."

"He's tired." I slapped her hand away. "Don't get him going. He deserves sleep. He needs it."

"Oh, you're such a whiner." Aunt Tillie made a disgusted face. "Besides, he's awake. He just doesn't want me to know it because he thinks it will make me go away."

As if on cue, Landon opened one eye and glared. "What will make you go away?"

"Nothing right now," Aunt Tillie replied. "I need to talk to Bay."

"Do you have to do it in our bedroom?"

"It's not your bedroom yet," Aunt Tillie replied. "It's not your bedroom until you get rid of the apartment."

"Soon," Landon muttered. "It will happen soon. I just have to clean it. I'm spending every night here, so it's technically my room. You should get out."

"I'm good." Aunt Tillie wasn't one to back down, and this morning wouldn't be any different. "So, I called The Dragonfly and talked to your father."

"Oh, geez." I slapped my hand to my forehead. "Why would you do that?"

"Because I was curious about whether Scarlet returned to her room," Aunt Tillie replied. "I've got big plans for her, and I can't unleash them if she's not around to beg for mercy."

"You're the only person I know who wants someone to beg for mercy," Landon noted. "What do you think about that?"

"I think it's funny that you have more hair on your face than on your chest when you wake up in the morning," Aunt Tillie replied, not missing a beat. She poked her finger into Landon's bare chest for emphasis. "Do you shave or wax?"

Landon wrinkled his nose. "Why do you even care?"

Aunt Tillie shrugged. "I'm curious. Back in my day, men didn't try to make themselves look like women. There were no naked chests. When you started sleeping with someone you often woke up wondering if you'd done it with Bigfoot the night before."

"Oh, my ... why do you have to say things like that?" I was understandably frustrated. "Now I'll have nightmares. I've seen photographs of Uncle Calvin. He wasn't that hairy."

"How do you know I was talking about your uncle?"

"Because the idea of you sleeping with anyone else will surely make my head explode."

"Mine, too." Landon offered up a lazy grin as he shoved his hair back from his face. "Go back to the part of the conversation where you mentioned calling The Dragonfly. What did Jack say?"

"He said that Scarlet hadn't returned before he went to bed last night. I told him to check her room – which he totally whined about, by the way – and he said it didn't look as if anyone had slept in the bed."

Landon propped himself up a bit, his fingers busy as they brushed over my arm. "Was her stuff still there?"

"Hey, you ask good questions," Aunt Tillie teased. "I made sure to ask that one, too. I did it before you, so ... ." She blew out a wet raspberry, causing Landon to make an exaggerated face as he wiped his cheek. "All her stuff was still there, at least as far as Jack could tell. He was irritated and kept reminding me that he asked me never to call or visit."

"He should know better than that," I pointed out. "You never do what you're told."

"That's why I always win." Aunt Tillie pronounced. "I told him that he was unnaturally crabby and then asked him if he was going through Malopause. He didn't think it was funny. He never did have a very good sense of humor."

"I'm almost afraid to ask, but what is Malopause?" Landon asked.

"Male Menopause."

"Yup. I should've seen that coming." Landon laid back and stared at the ceiling. "So Scarlet Darksbane is missing. All of her stuff is still at The Dragonfly and she hasn't been seen – at least as far as we know – since last night."

Aunt Tillie bobbed her head. "Pretty much."

"What do you think it means?" I asked.

Landon shrugged. "She could be hiding."

"Or?"

"Or she could've left and not bothered to pick up her stuff."

That didn't seem likely. "Maybe we should break in to her store again and see if the journal is gone."

"I'd rather not risk breaking into a business on a Saturday, which just happens to coincide with a busy festival in downtown Hemlock Cove," Landon said. "We'll keep our eyes open for her, but she's not our biggest concern."

"Unless she was taken by a killer or is the killer," Aunt Tillie pointed out.

Landon rubbed his cheek as he debated the point. "I think both of those are unlikely. Why would a killer take her? She has no ties to anything. Also, why would she be the killer? As far as we can tell, she's a grifter but there's nothing violent in her past. Why would she kill Adele Twigg?"

Aunt Tillie shrugged. "Maybe her plan was to frame us from the beginning."

"To what end?"

"I don't know, but you're definitely being a killjoy," Aunt Tillie said. "I still think something funky is going on here."

"I agree something funky is going on," Landon said. "But we won't know more until we touch base with Terry, so there's no reason to freak out."

Aunt Tillie snorted. "Sometimes I think you get this family and other times I think you don't. If we didn't freak out we'd have absolutely nothing to do with half of our time."

Landon grinned. "I'm sorry. I forgot. Feel free to freak out."

"Thank you." Aunt Tillie primly got to her feet. "By the way, Winnie made pancakes that actually have bacon bits in them this morning. She's going to surprise you."

Landon perked up. "Why did you bury the lead?" He tossed off the covers and hopped out of bed. "Get moving, Bay. Your mother is experimenting with bacon. I think it's my lucky day and I don't want to miss a moment of it."

I offered up a rueful smile. "I guess we're done cuddling for this morning, huh?"

"We can cuddle any time. Bacon pancakes are a first."

He had a point. "Does that mean you'll be a flirty fool all day?"

"You have no idea."

I returned his smile. "Maybe it's my lucky day, too."

"There's no maybe about it. You're going to get lucky so many times."

He probably didn't mean it as it sounded, but I'd take it all the same. "Let's go. We have a missing witch to find and a murderer to capture."

"Don't forget the bacon pancakes."

"And those. It's going to be a busy day."

TWENTY-EIGHT

*L*andon and I drove to town separately. I was already in Hypnotic, my coat halfway off, when he walked through the front door.

"Wow," Thistle shouted. "There's an added spring to your step this morning. You're practically floating." She turned an accusing look to me. "Did you do something dirty while the rest of us were up at the crack of dawn to get work done?"

"Don't look at me that way," I ordered. "He wanted nothing to do with me this morning. Mom invented a new kind of breakfast for him, so he's all about her right now."

"That came off filthy, but I don't even care after the pancakes." Landon tapped the end of my nose. "That was the single best breakfast I've ever had. If I wasn't already dating you I'd totally ask out your mother for her cooking skills alone."

I narrowed my eyes. "That is not the way to keep me happy."

"Oh, I'm sorry. Did I hurt your feelings?" Landon's voice was full of mirth. "You know you're my favorite."

"Only until you start dreaming about those bacon pancakes," I muttered, folding my arms over my chest.

"You have a point." Landon's grin was impish. "I'll still love you forever. You'll simply have to take the occasional backseat to the pancakes when your mother makes them. I'm sorry, but it is possible to love two things at once."

"So now you're saying that my competition is pancakes, huh?"

"You don't have any competition, at least where I'm concerned, but speaking of that, we checked Scarlet Darksbane's store." Landon sobered, real work forcing him to forget about the bacon pancakes and focus on something serious. "She's not in her store. As far as I can tell, most everything is exactly the same as when we were in there the other night."

"Did you kick down the door?" Clove asked, genuinely curious.

Landon shook his head. "Chief Terry has master passkeys for all of the businesses in case there's an emergency."

"Did you tell him that we were in there the other night?" I couldn't help but worry that Landon would admit we broke the law, and Chief Terry would have no choice but to arrest me.

As if reading my mind, Landon snickered. "Don't worry about that," he said, squeezing my shoulder. "I didn't mention your late-night excursion. If Scarlet is truly missing, though, I'll have to."

"Why?" I hated how whiny I sounded.

"Because we'll have to process the building and there's a very good chance that our fingerprints will be everywhere," Landon replied. "It probably won't come to that, but … ."

"Oh, well, great," I muttered, throwing my hands in the air. "I don't think I'll do well in prison. I've seen *Orange is the New Black*. Someone will make me her wife and it won't be pretty."

Landon's lips quirked. "You're so dramatic sometimes. You're not going to prison. If we need to make up a story about why we entered, we'll do it. Right now we're in a holding pattern. Scarlet isn't there and, if I had to guess, she hasn't been there since we saw her at the festival yesterday."

"So … where is she?"

Landon held his hands palms out and shrugged. "We have a couple of possibilities but we're honestly not sure right now."

"What possibilities?" Thistle asked, pouring a mug of tea as she rubbed the side of her face. She'd physically been up for hours, but mentally she was dragging. None of us were morning people, but she was positively the worst.

"Well, for starters, she could've thought that Bay had enough information to ruin things for her in Hemlock Cove so she ran," Landon replied. "Her car is missing, but she seems to have left all of her belongings behind. I don't see why she'd do that given the fact that Bay only messed with her a little bit. It's not out of the realm of possibility, though."

"Maybe she thought Bay found out something else that she did in Grand Rapids," Thistle suggested. "Maybe there was more to find and we simply didn't realize it."

"That's another possibility," Landon conceded. "Maybe Scarlet's rap sheet is more extensive than we realized. We have a call in to the police down there. Because of that possibility, I want you three to be extra careful. If you see her, don't approach her. Call or text me, tell me where she is and give her a wide berth."

"You said you didn't think she was a threat," I protested.

"That was before she pulled a disappearing act over something that should've been relatively minor," Landon argued. "A grifter would've jumped at the chance Mrs. Little gave her last night. That means something frightened her away.

"I have no idea what's going on here, but if Scarlet was frightened enough to run after what Bay said, she must be hiding something bigger," he continued. "We don't know what that is, but I'm not willing to risk any of you to find out."

"Ugh. He's so bossy," Thistle complained.

"Welcome to my world." I feigned annoyance, but flashed Landon a smile to let him know I understood. "There's another possibility you haven't mentioned."

Landon held my gaze. "And what would that be?"

"That she killed Adele Twigg," I replied. "I know you're leaning toward an intimate connection leading to the murder, but maybe Scarlet killed Mrs. Twigg as a way to point the finger at us."

"I don't understand," Landon admitted.

"Think about it," I prodded. "Mrs. Little brought Scarlet to town. She wanted Scarlet to throw us off our game. As much as I dislike Mrs. Little, I hardly think she'd be party to murder. That would reflect badly on the town, and that's the last thing she wants.

"Maybe Scarlet is unbalanced," I continued. "Maybe she misunderstood what Mrs. Little wanted. Heck, maybe she decided it didn't matter what Mrs. Little wanted and killed Mrs. Twigg.

"We already know she has access to at least one witch book," I said. "Maybe she got those symbols from another. Thistle found out that the words spelled 'witch.' Scarlet might've thought that would be enough to point the police in our direction."

"I'm not going to argue with you, because it never goes well with me, but I'm not sure I buy that Scarlet is crazy enough to kill Adele Twigg in an effort to frame you guys," Landon said. "I mean, why did she pick Adele? Was it due to convenience? There had to be other people who were more convenient.

"Plus, why strangle her?" he continued. "That's reserved for people you really hate. If she wanted to kill someone and blame you guys, why not go the easy route and stab her or smack her over the head? When you strangle someone, you're often looking them in the eye and watching the life drain from them."

He had a point. Still … . "I think something bigger is happening here. We're missing the big picture."

"Okay, but I don't think that big picture involves Scarlet being a murderer," Landon said. "I'm not ruling it out. You're right about something big going on. We have a murderer in our midst, so I want you to be careful when you're running around today."

I stared at him for a long moment. "You're not going to try to force me to promise to stay in Hypnotic or the newspaper office all day, are you?"

Landon smirked. "No. Why? Did you think I would?"

I shrugged. "I don't know. You don't have much of a sense of humor when danger is afoot."

"And that won't change," Landon said. "Still, you're an adult. You can take care of yourself."

"Since when?"

"Since I have faith you understand that you'll be hurting me if something bad happens to you," Landon replied. "You see, the thing is, I've come to the realization that you don't worry about yourself nearly as much as you do others. It seems to be a Winchester genetic trait."

"I wouldn't get too smug," Thistle said. "You have that trait, too."

"I do, which is why it took me so long to recognize the trait in Bay," Landon conceded. "She cares about others more than herself. If I expect her to be careful, I need to remind her that she'll be hurting me if she does something stupid."

I pursed my lips. "You're fighting dirty."

"Whatever it takes to keep you safe."

"Fine." I huffed. "I promise to be careful and think about your well-being first and foremost."

"You don't have to go that far." Landon leaned over and gave me a firm kiss. "Just be careful. It's important."

My cheeks warmed at the earnest expression on his face. "I'll be careful."

"Great." Landon turned his attention to Thistle and Clove. "You be careful, too. I have no idea if Scarlet Darksbane is involved in Adele Twigg's murder, but I'm starting to think there's a good chance that she's dangerous. Do not approach her when you're alone."

"You already told us that," Thistle said dryly.

"Yes, but you have a tendency to hear only what you want to hear," Landon pointed out. "You two are important, too."

"More important than bacon pancakes?" Thistle teased.

"Only Bay is better than those pancakes. You're a close third. For now, we're going to be searching the area. I'll be in touch if we find something."

"I'll meet you down at the festival at noon," I offered. "We can get lunch together before the big show begins."

"That sounds like a plan." Landon ran his hand over the back of my head. "Be good. Be safe. Don't do anything stupid."

"Would I do that?"

"Only every day of your life." Landon gave me another kiss. "If you find anything, text me right away. This situation has me on edge."

"You and me both."

LANDON WASN'T GONE FOR more than ten minutes before Aunt Tillie appeared in the doorway. She was bundled in what looked to be a faux fur trench coat and she had earmuffs on under her combat helmet.

"You look like a crazy Russian madame," Thistle announced, shaking her head. "Where did you get that coat?"

"I found it online," Aunt Tillie replied, unruffled. "I like it."

"How did you manage to find one so short?" I asked. "Is it petite?"

"It's the largest children's size."

Oh, well, that explained why it looked so ridiculous. "At least you'll be warm," I said. "Have you heard any gossip while you were out and about?"

"Scarlet is still missing, and the cops haven't made an arrest in Adele Twigg's murder," Aunt Tillie replied. "It's pretty much the status quo."

"Yeah? Landon thinks we're close to breaking the case. Hopefully we'll have more information by the end of the day."

Aunt Tillie offered up a dismissive wave. "I know you think that Landon can do no wrong and he's smarter than the average cop, but he doesn't know what's going on. Do you want to know why he doesn't know?"

"Not if you're going to say something insulting."

"He doesn't know because it doesn't make sense," Aunt Tillie said. "We're missing a piece of the puzzle."

"Actually, Landon pointed that out himself," I said. "He's out looking for it right now."

Aunt Tillie snorted. "He was at the bakery when I walked past. He had a doughnut and coffee. I know he ate his weight in bacon pancakes this morning, so the fact that he can add a doughnut to the mix says a little something about what a glutton he is."

"He's probably there questioning Mrs. Gunderson," I protested.

"He doesn't need a doughnut to do that," Aunt Tillie countered. "You'd better rein in his eating habits if you want him to live a long life. He's worse than a teenage boy with a credit card and access to a pizza shop."

She had a point. "Just … leave him alone," I ordered. "This case has everyone worked up."

"Are you worked up?" Aunt Tillie met my gaze. "Are you worried about what's going to happen?"

It was a hard question to answer. "I think something is going to happen," I admitted after a beat. "I have no idea what, but I'm antsy."

Instead of making fun of me, which was her way, Aunt Tillie merely nodded. "You're probably right. Whatever it is, it's going to seem simple when we finally find it. We'll wonder why we didn't see it before."

"So what do we do?" Clove asked. "Landon doesn't think that Scarlet's disappearance has anything to do with Adele Twigg's murder. It seems a really random coincidence to us, but what if he's right? What if we're dealing with two completely separate things?"

"I guess that's possible, but I don't buy it," Aunt Tillie said, serious. "Hemlock Cove is tiny. What are the odds we have two entirely unconnected crimes happening at the same time?"

"I don't know, but I guess we'll find out." I rolled my neck. "Do you still plan to out Scarlet if she shows up at the festival?"

"Absolutely." Aunt Tillie brightened considerably. "I'm going to out Margaret for being an itchy jockstrap at the same time."

I made a face. "You can't call her that. People will think you're a bully."

"You let me worry about being a bully," Aunt Tillie chided. "You need to worry about … whatever it is you're worrying about. I'm guessing that part of your day will consist of interviewing people about the festival."

"You've got that right," I agreed. "I need to go grab a notebook and a camera from the office."

"Why don't you do that while we talk strategy," Aunt Tillie

suggested. "We'll want to take down Margaret at the same time we eviscerate Scarlet."

"If Scarlet even shows up," I countered. "She could be out of the state for all we know."

"She could be," Aunt Tillie agreed, "but I don't think so. I think she's planning something. She pulled back last night because she realized we had dirt on her. She'll try to find a way around that before resurfacing."

"How do you know?"

"I'm omnipotent."

Thistle snorted. "Only in your imagination, you old bat."

"Hey!" Aunt Tillie extended a warning finger. "Just because we're up to our necks in other enemies doesn't mean I won't smite you. You're officially on my list."

"Yeah, yeah, yeah." Thistle didn't look remotely worried. "You should get the stuff you need, Bay. We'll all go to the festival in another two hours. It's probably best if we stick together."

"You're right." I grabbed my coat from the back of the couch. "I shouldn't be more than fifteen minutes or so. When I get back, we'll talk strategy."

"We'll be talking strategy while you're gone," Aunt Tillie corrected. "You can catch up when you get back."

I knew exactly what she was doing. She wanted to drown out the voice of reason – me! – before I had a chance to launch a good argument. That's why she wanted me out of the building while she moved on Clove and Thistle. Unfortunately, I really did need to run to the office.

"Fine." I blew out a sigh. "Don't settle on anything until I get back. I won't let you outvote me if I don't like what you have planned."

"This is a democracy, young lady," Aunt Tillie reminded me. "We'll vote how we vote."

"Whatever."

I WAS RELUCTANT TO LEAVE Hypnotic because I knew Aunt

Tillie would manipulate Clove and Thistle to get what she wanted. It was better to get my errand over with now rather than later, though.

The town was bustling as I moved through the downtown area, raising my hand to wave at friendly faces and taking a moment to admire the way Landon looked as he stood next to Chief Terry at the edge of the festival grounds. He didn't look in my direction, his gaze intent on the big tent at the center of the hoopla. He was agitated. I could practically feel it. Much like me, he knew we were running out of time, and he didn't like it in the least.

I used my key to unlock the office door, pulling up short when I caught sight of scuff marks on the wooden floor by the entryway. Someone had been inside, and from the looks of the small boot treads it was a woman.

I raised my eyes, confused, and locked gazes with Scarlet Darksbane. She sat behind the front desk, her eyes wide, and rested her hands on the top of the wooden surface.

"It took you long enough. Do you have any idea how long I've been waiting for you?"

Well ... crap!

TWENTY-NINE

*S*carlet wasn't the one talking. In fact, now that I looked at her more closely, she appeared shaky and terrified. The voice came from behind me, and I turned to find Tess standing close to the door with a gun in her hand.

Well ... this was even worse than I initially envisioned.

"How's it going?" As far as greetings go, it wasn't my best offering. I was so flummoxed I couldn't think of anything else to say.

"How's it going?" Tess was amused. "You don't seem surprised to see us. Why is that?"

I flicked a quick look to Scarlet, but she was so ashen and uneasy that she didn't look in my direction. She was too busy focusing on the gun.

"I had a feeling you were involved," I answered. "Once we found out you were sleeping with Arthur things made more sense. Plus, well, your reaction to what we said yesterday was downright weird. It was obvious you had a hand in Adele's death."

That was an outright lie, but I figured it would be better to play a hunch than admit we were still scrambling for information.

"How did you find out I was sleeping with Arthur?"

I licked my lips, unsure how to respond. "Well ... ."

"Did Arthur tell you?" Tess barreled forward, not waiting for me to answer. "It would be just like him. He's such an idiot. He actually thinks we have a future. Can you believe that?"

I couldn't believe a lot about this situation. "Arthur didn't tell me." I decided to tell the truth. Either Tess would think I was crazy or be afraid. Both outcomes had certain advantages. "Adele told me about the affair."

"Adele?" Tess's eyebrows winged up. "Adele told you about the affair after knowing you for twenty minutes? How is that even possible?"

She didn't understand. Not yet, at least. "I didn't really talk to Adele that night at the meeting," I countered. "She told me after."

"After? After what? She was dead later that night."

"By your hand, right?" I licked my lips. "You needed help. I'm guessing Arthur wasn't your help. That leaves Greg."

"Yes, it's been a busy couple of days," Tess confirmed. "Greg and I planned to take out Adele from the beginning. We've been together for years, and after spending two months with the Twiggs we realized how we could fix things to our advantage. We grew up together, and the troupe offered us the life we'd always dreamed about."

That explained part of it. The rest remained murky. I needed to figure it out, keep Tess talking, and buy time until Aunt Tillie and Thistle realized I'd been gone too long. They would alert Landon and he'd come looking for me. That's what I hoped for, but to get there I needed to keep Tess focused on the conversation.

"So you and Greg joined the troupe together but agreed that you should seduce Arthur on your own," I said as I tried to muddle through the information. "You wanted Arthur to fall in love with you because you thought he might divorce Adele and hand over the reins to the troupe. Once that was handled, you could've kept your relationship with Greg going behind Arthur's back."

"Something like that, but you almost ruined everything by bringing it up at dinner the other night," Tess said. "Luckily Arthur was too drunk to notice. That wasn't exactly the plan, though. Ultimately it didn't matter. When we first started we thought Adele and

Arthur had a real relationship. After a few weeks of watching them it became clear that Adele wanted a real relationship, but Arthur wasn't keen on that because he had a wandering eye."

That honestly didn't surprise me. "He liked younger women, right?"

"Exactly." Tess made a face as she scuffed her foot against the floor and then sat in the wooden chair next to the nearby wall. I couldn't escape through the door given her location, but I could run down the hallway. It led to Brian's office, and the windows inside were big enough to escape through. It probably wasn't my best plan, but it was a backup should I need it. My biggest problem was that Landon would be wide open should he choose to walk through the front door. Tess could shoot him before he even had a chance to draw his weapon. I couldn't risk that. I had to get her away from the door.

"How long did it take you to seduce Arthur?" I asked.

"Not long. He was still upset from losing his last girlfriend. She got pregnant and Adele fired her. I'm not sure Adele realized the baby was Arthur's, but she was definitely suspicious that Laurie Walker and Arthur were getting it on."

"How do you know that?"

"Celeste told me. She's another troupe member. She's Greg's fake sister and my fake cousin. She loves spreading gossip. We figured that out when we met her, so we cozied up to her right away."

"Why did you decide to kill Adele in Hemlock Cove?" I asked. "You had to pick this location for a reason."

"Yes and no," Tess replied. "Adele was on my last nerve. I knew she was aware of my relationship with Arthur. She thought it was real, and I think she was worried that I would steal Arthur away and he would marry me."

"Wasn't that the ultimate plan?"

"Yes, but in Adele's head my feelings for Arthur were real," Tess explained. "She thought I was in love with him. She recognized that I wanted to take over control of the troupe, but she honestly thought I loved that old fool."

"She was blind to Arthur's faults," I surmised. "They married as a business arrangement, but she fell in love with him over the years. She thought he'd eventually feel the same about her, but she didn't realize he was only attracted to younger women."

"Yeah, he's a real piece of work," Tess agreed. "He's terrible in bed, but he expects you to fake it and pretend he's great. Apparently that's how it worked for him with all the women he dated before me. I hate faking it, but his ego couldn't take it if I didn't. Even with the Viagra he's flat-out terrible."

I definitely didn't need that much information. "You still haven't told me why you picked Hemlock Cove."

"I didn't," Tess clarified. "I've been working Arthur for a long time, and he refused to divorce Adele. I thought it would be easy once I slept with him a few times, but he was more rational than I realized."

"He knew that he would be out a lot of money if he divorced Adele, right?"

Tess nodded. "He could've survived the storm and we could've built the troupe back up together," she said. "Greg and I had a long-term plan. Arthur was going to divorce Adele and marry me. I was going to get pregnant to trap him. The kid would really belong to Greg. Then poor Arthur would die in his sleep and leave everything to me. It wasn't something that was going to happen overnight, but we could make it a reality in a few years. It was exactly the sort of life we dreamed about for ourselves."

"But Arthur wouldn't get with the program," I deduced. "You couldn't marry him and lay claim to the troupe while he was still married to Adele."

"And he refused to divorce her." Tess's expression was sour. "He said that she was the brains behind the operation – which was ridiculous, because she was a horrible person. He wouldn't divorce her. He said he would arrange for us to always be together, but we could never marry. He thought that would be enough for me."

"That's because he didn't recognize the fact that you were only interested in him because of the money," I said. "He thought you really loved him. Eventually, he would've gotten over the love when you grew older."

"Yeah. He kept saying that love was enough and we would be happy even though he was married to Adele."

"So you had no choice but to kill Adele." In a weird way, it made sense. Tess was determined to bring her plan to fruition. When Arthur wouldn't follow the path she laid out for him, Tess decided to force the issue. "Did you fight with Adele before it happened?"

"Yes," Tess confirmed. "The plan was to kill Adele right after Christmas. We were going to make it look like a suicide. But Adele had other plans. She saw Arthur and me in his truck after the meeting. She knew what we were doing.

"I wasn't ready to put our plan in motion, so I tried to evade her. But she caught up with me on the other side of the library," she continued. "She accused me of having an affair with Arthur. I denied it at first because … well, because I wasn't ready. Then she started calling me names – slut. Whore. Homewrecker. She wouldn't shut up."

"And you lost it," I said. "You didn't like being called names and you were already planning to kill her … ."

"It was easier than I thought," Tess admitted, taking on a far-off expression. "I thought it would be hard. In fact, I was going to make Greg do it. But it was easy. And she deserved it. Even at the end, when she realized what was happening and there was no way to stop it, Adele kept calling me names and trying to hurt me. I guess I showed her, huh?"

The simple statement was enough to cause my stomach to twist. "I guess so," I gritted out. "Where did you get the idea for the witch symbols?"

"Adele showed me a book she bought before we came to Hemlock Cove," Tess replied. "She told me the history of the town. She wanted ideas for introducing a witch bit into our act. It wouldn't be anything major, but she was excited at the prospect."

"That's where you found the symbols," I said. "That's where you found the Theban alphabet and you used it to write the word 'witch.'"

Tess smirked. "I'm impressed. I wasn't sure the cops would figure that out."

"The cops didn't figure it out. We did."

"Because you're witches?" Tess was back to looking amused. "I thought all the witch stuff in this town was for show. Isn't that the reason Margaret Little brought in this chick?" She jerked her thumb in Scarlet's direction. I'd almost forgotten the other woman was there. She was so quiet, working so hard to make herself small that she almost became invisible during Tess's confession. "I thought they wanted to pretend they had stronger witches coming in and that's why they brought the new face to town."

I pressed the heel of my hand to my forehead as I tried to work out the final bit of the mystery. "You tried to make it look like witches because you thought they'd focus on someone in town. But Chief Terry and Landon kept questioning you guys, and you didn't like it."

"It's not just that," Tess said. "Arthur was starting to get suspicious. He didn't come right out and say it, but I saw the way he looked at me. He refuses to spend time with me now because he thinks everyone is watching. That doesn't work for the new plan."

The new plan? "You were going to get pregnant right away," I surmised. "You needed to have sex with Arthur to make sure the timing worked out."

"I'm already pregnant," Tess corrected. "But you're right about the timing. I need Arthur to get with the program. I'm afraid he won't do it if he believes I'm responsible for Adele's death. Plus, well, I think he's suspicious about Greg and me now thanks to you people. He never even asked about my relationship with Greg before. I told him we grew up together and were best friends. Arthur was fine with that until you started poking around and caught us."

"So you're pregnant and need Arthur to believe he's the father so he'll marry you." I slid a sidelong gaze to Scarlet, things finally coming in to focus. "You knew Scarlet was the newbie and the rest of us were likely to close ranks and have alibis. You needed someone who didn't have an alibi for the time Adele was killed."

"I also needed a witch to explain all of the symbols," Tess confirmed. "That had to be Scarlet. I've seen the way you've been watching her. Your boyfriend was focused on us, but you've been focused on her."

"Not because I think she's a murderer," I protested. That was mostly true. I could never fully shake the idea that Scarlet was to blame, but that didn't mean I suspected her of being the real culprit.

"No, but your suspicions were enough that your boyfriend would turn on Scarlet if he believed she killed you." Tess's smile was enigmatic. "Why else do you think we're here?"

I was dumbfounded. "You kidnapped Scarlet last night."

"They knocked me out," Scarlet volunteered, speaking for the first time. "I was about to leave my shop for the festival when they came in. I didn't realize what they were doing until … well, until it was too late. When I woke up, I was tied up in a van. They left me there overnight. It was terrible."

I tried to muster some sympathy for her – I was sure it was a trying ordeal, after all – but I couldn't come up with more than a passing moment. "We know what you are … and what you've done. You're done in this town. It was actually smart for Tess to focus on you."

"That's what I thought." Tess was smug. "I was worried that you weren't going to come to the office today. I knew you worked here, but separating you from your cousins and boyfriend isn't easy. You're almost never alone."

"It worked out for you this time," I noted. "You've got all the pieces in place. I'm here. You can kill me. Then you can kill Scarlet and make it look like we both struggled and killed each other. That's the plan, right?"

"Yup."

My stomach rolled. She had it all figured out, which meant there was nothing I could do to force her to back down. I needed to stretch the conversation a bit longer if I wanted to survive. "What about Greg? Where is he?"

"He's at the festival watching your boyfriend," Tess replied. "He wanted to be here, but we needed to make sure that the FBI agent was kept far away. Greg will make sure he stays there while I finish things up."

"You can't kill us," Scarlet whined. "I haven't done anything. This is all a mistake. Kill her. She's the one you want."

"I need both of you." Tess was calm. "The FBI agent and chief won't believe that Bay killed Adele. They will believe you killed Bay, though. They'll also believe you killed Adele. That allows us to walk free and clear.

"It's nothing personal," she continued. "I just need both of you to make this happen. I won't say I'm sorry – because I'm not – but this is the way it has to be."

I opened my mouth to say something, but a hint of movement in the hallway caught my attention – Viola was watching the scene unfold with impassioned eyes.

"Tillie is coming," Viola announced. I was the only one who could see or hear her, so it didn't matter how loud she was. "I saw what was happening and got her. I didn't know she was at Hypnotic, but I thought there was a chance Thistle and Clove could hear me. I lucked out."

I pressed my lips together and nodded.

"She's ticked off, by the way," Viola added. "I wouldn't want to be this one when Tillie gets a hold of her." She floated to Tess and made a face. "I've been working on moving things like I told you, but I'm not there yet. I can't knock the gun out of her hand."

"It's okay," I murmured, forgetting for a moment that Tess would find my reaction odd.

"Who are you talking to?" Tess asked, glancing around.

"The newspaper has a ghost," I replied, opting for honesty. "Her name is Viola. She was just telling me something interesting."

"A ghost, huh?" Tess snorted. "I have to give it to you guys. You go all out with this witch stuff."

"We do," I agreed, rubbing my sweating palms against my jeans. "That's how I found out about you and Arthur. Adele's ghost is still hanging around. She told me."

"She told you about Arthur and me, but not that I killed her?" Tess was understandably dubious. "It doesn't sound like she's much of a ghost."

"Yes, well, you're not much of a human being," I said, lifting my eyes to the ceiling when the light flickered. "I think you're about to learn a little something about real witches, though."

"Oh, yeah?" Tess followed my gaze. "What's that?"

"Real witches are something to be feared. Some of them are even wicked," I answered, instinctively covering my face as the lightbulb exploded. "And here comes the wickedest witch of them all. Scarlet, get down and cover your head!"

"What's going on?" Scarlet shrieked.

I didn't get a chance to answer because the front door blew open, revealing Aunt Tillie, her combat helmet firmly in place and her coat billowing in the wind she summoned.

"Here she comes," I shouted, dropping to my knees as Tess flew to a standing position. "You're in a heckuva lot of trouble now."

THIRTY

"What the ... ?"

Tess's face went slack as Aunt Tillie strode into the room. Most women in their eighties wouldn't seem imposing. Aunt Tillie was the exact opposite. She was a vision of fury and rage.

"Drop the gun," Aunt Tillie ordered.

"Gun?" Tess looked confused.

"What's happening?" Scarlet screeched.

"Shut up," I ordered, wiping small bits of glass from my face as I focused on Aunt Tillie. "It was Tess and Greg all along."

"I figured that out when Viola came to visit." Aunt Tillie didn't look away from Tess. "She's as scattered as ever, and I still hate talking to her. Occasionally, though, she has good information."

"Did you get Landon?"

"Clove is getting him."

"He needs to know about Greg," I argued. "He'll run when he realizes that we've got Tess."

"Don't worry about that. Clove has all the pertinent information. I'm pretty sure Landon and Terry are taking down Greg right now."

Despite the surreal nature of the situation, Tess managed to collect herself and raise the gun. This time she pointed it at Aunt Tillie. "I don't know what you think you're doing, old lady, but I am not in the mood to play games."

"Who are you calling old?" Aunt Tillie challenged. "I'm middle-aged."

"Only if we lived in an alien world where people live to be two-hundred," Tess snapped.

"That would totally be cool." Aunt Tillie's smile was evil. "I would want to be the queen of the aliens, of course, but I'm up for it. They would look upon me as a benevolent ruler and build statues to worship me."

Tess was flustered. "I ... what does that have to do with anything?"

"You brought up aliens," I pointed out, shuffling closer to Tess. If I could grab the hand that held the gun I could take control of the situation. Tess could still hurt Aunt Tillie if she fired. The odds of her being able to get all three of us were slim, but I wouldn't risk Aunt Tillie. Sure, she's a pain in the posterior, but she's still family.

"What are you doing?" Tess jolted back at my approach, whipping the gun in my direction.

Aunt Tillie didn't give her a chance to fire, lashing out with a muttered curse and causing the gun to fly out of Tess's hand. It skittered across the floor, sliding underneath the chair Tess had sat in moments before.

"What was that?" Tess's voice quavered. She was finally starting to understand exactly what she was up against.

"That was witchcraft," Aunt Tillie replied. "Some of it is real. The redheaded wonder hiding under the desk doesn't have real magic, but others do."

"And you're one of the others?"

"You could say that." Aunt Tillie's lips curved. "Now, I believe you're out of options, girlie. You can put your hands out and wait or I'll knock you out. Which do you prefer?"

Tess was caught. She had to know it. The expression on her face told me she wasn't quite ready to give up, though. She remained desperate to get away.

"Screw you!" Tess grabbed Aunt Tillie by the shoulders and shoved

AMANDA M. LEE

her to the side, making a break for the open door.

I caught Aunt Tillie before she hit the floor. She's powerful, but even she isn't immune to a broken hip.

Tess was down the stairs and running along the sidewalk before Aunt Tillie regrouped and followed. Much like a killer in a horror movie, Aunt Tillie didn't bother increasing her pace. Instead she narrowed her eyes and whispered, magic lashing out and racing down the pathway. The bolt – which I'm sure only Aunt Tillie and I could see – caught Tess at her feet and caused her to pitch forward. The renaissance worker landed face first on the pavement, her shoulders rising once before falling a second time.

"Is she dead?" Scarlet asked, her head popping up from behind the desk.

"No," Aunt Tillie answered. "She only wishes she was."

I hurried down the steps, intent on making sure Tess wasn't a threat, but Landon reached the fallen woman first. He glanced down at her, then up at me, and merely shook his head.

"Do I even want to know?"

"Probably not." I let loose with a shaky breath. "Holy crap! We solved it."

Landon cocked an eyebrow. "We did. You're still in big trouble. You know that, right?"

"I didn't do anything," I protested. "They were waiting in the office for me. How could I know that?"

"I have no idea." Landon grabbed the cuffs at his waist and lowered them to Tess's wrists. "But I'm worked up enough that I feel you need to be in trouble. I can't explain it, but ... you're grounded."

I rolled my eyes. "Whatever."

"You're definitely grounded," Landon muttered. "As soon as she's cuffed, you're also getting a big hug. You scared the crap out of me."

"Isn't that normal for your relationship at this point?" Aunt Tillie challenged. She hadn't so much as broken a sweat.

"That doesn't mean I like it."

"Oh, suck it up, Fed. Everyone is fine and we solved the case. There's nothing to complain about."

278

Landon opened his mouth to argue and then snapped it shut.

"And that's how you handle mouthy men, Bay," Aunt Tillie said, grinning as Landon scowled. "I'll start giving lessons if you feel you need them."

I didn't bother to hide my smile as Landon's gaze lanced into me. "I think I'm good."

"Suit yourself."

TWO HOURS LATER I HAD a fresh kebab and rice to eat while Landon and Chief Terry compared notes. Both Greg and Tess were in custody – the latter making a stop at the hospital first – and the case was essentially closed.

"Greg admitted to everything once I had him in custody," Chief Terry explained. "He blamed everything on Tess and said he was in fear of his life."

"Do you believe him?" I asked, holding up my fork so Landon could take a bite as he settled next to me.

"Not even a little," Chief Terry replied. "They were clearly in it together."

"What about Arthur?" Thistle asked, sitting next to Chief Terry with a mountain of food before her. The festival was a complete bust thanks to the arrests, and the vendors were practically giving the food away instead of throwing it out.

"He claims he had no idea that Tess was responsible for Adele's death," Chief Terry replied. "He didn't deny the affair, but said that he genuinely respected Adele. He also claimed that he had no idea that Tess wasn't really in love with him."

"If he didn't see it, it's because he didn't want to," I said. "My understanding is that Arthur had a wandering eye and would pretty much sleep with anyone as long as they were younger."

"Yes, well, as long as those women were legal, that's not a crime," Landon said, smirking when he saw the way my eyes fired. "I, of course, love only one woman. Even when she gets older, that won't change."

"That was smooth." I gave him another bite. "But you're still in trouble."

"I guess we make quite the pair." Landon kissed the tip of my nose. "What happened to your witch friend? We questioned her, but she was a total mess. She kept talking about exploding lights and magic."

"Aunt Tillie puts on quite the show when she wants to."

"Where is Aunt Tillie?"

I pointed toward the main tent, where Aunt Tillie was having a good time with the renaissance troupe props that hadn't been reclaimed. "She thinks she's going to have a sword fight and be named queen of an alien realm."

"Well, she saved you, so whatever makes her happy." Landon slipped his arm around my waist. "How do you feel? No matter what you said, I know you thought Scarlet had a part in this."

"And it turns out I was wrong," I conceded. "She's merely a scam artist, not a murderer."

"I think she's learned a bit from this one," Chief Terry noted. "I heard she informed Margaret that she's leaving town. She demanded back the money she paid for the building. She said the town is full of freaks, and she's not staying."

"She's leaving?" Thistle perked up. "That means that building will be available again."

"Are you really going to buy it?" I asked.

"I'm going to try," Thistle replied. "If I can get it for the same price Scarlet did I'm definitely buying it. We'll be able to expand the store and put a gallery in. I've been dreaming about that for a long time."

"Then you should definitely do it," Chief Terry said. "You've always had a creative streak. Often, when you were younger, I wished you'd focus on art rather than mischief. It seems as an adult you've hit a happy balance."

I grinned at his teasing. "So that's it, huh?" I couldn't help feeling a bit let down. "The murder is solved. The enemy witch is on her way out of town. Aunt Tillie didn't get to unleash her revenge. It feels ... anti-climactic."

"It's almost Christmas," Landon pointed out. "I'm fine with anti-climactic."

"Yeah, speaking of that ... ." I licked the kebab grease running down my hand. "I was wondering how you'd feel about spending Christmas Day alone, just the two of us."

"Instead of with your family?"

"We'll spend Christmas Eve with them," I replied. "It's Christmas, so family is important. But I think Christmas Day should be just us. We'll start some new traditions."

"Well, we are officially living together." Landon ran his hand over my back. "I think it's a plan. In fact, if we could keep things quiet through Christmas I'd consider that the best gift ever."

"Oh, don't get ahead of yourself," I warned. "Aunt Tillie loves Christmas. She'll do something decadent before it's all said and done."

"Isn't that what she did today?"

"Today was nothing. She'll do something bigger and bolder. Just wait."

"That sounds terrifying." Landon stretched. "So, do we essentially have this festival to ourselves since everything else fell apart?"

I nodded. "Even you couldn't eat all of the food we have access to."

"That sounds like a challenge."

I smirked. "I guess we'll see."

"We definitely will." Landon got to his feet. "Who wants to have a fake sword fight with Aunt Tillie in the main tent?"

Thistle groaned. "Are you serious?"

Landon nodded. "I'll be on her side. You'll be against us – unless you're afraid to take us on."

Thistle recognized the gleam in his eye. "You're on. I will crush both of you!"

"Bring it." Landon held out his hand to me. "You're on my team, right?"

There was only one answer that would make both of us happy. "Now and forever."

"Then let's do it."

Made in the USA
Monee, IL
04 March 2022

92278398R00166